Clitapalooza

Her flower blooms power

by Billie Best

Widowspeak
Publishing

Paperback ISBN 978-1-7345964-4-1
Ebook ISBN 978-1-7345964-5-8

Cover Design by Brenda Rose

Cover Art
CATTLEYA LABIATA var MEASURESIANA
Botanical illustration by Boyle, Frederick, b. 1841
No restrictions, via Wikimedia Commons
File:The_Woodlands_orchids_described_and_illus._with_stories_of_orchid_
collecting_(1901)_(14590946719).jpg

Widowspeak
Publishing

Widowspeakpublishing.com

Also by Billie Best

How I Made a Huge Mess of My Life (or Couples Therapy with a Dead Man)

I Could Be Wrong: 50+ blog posts, short reads, big laughs, wit & wisdom

Clitapalooza

Her flower blooms power

by Billie Best

Table of Contents

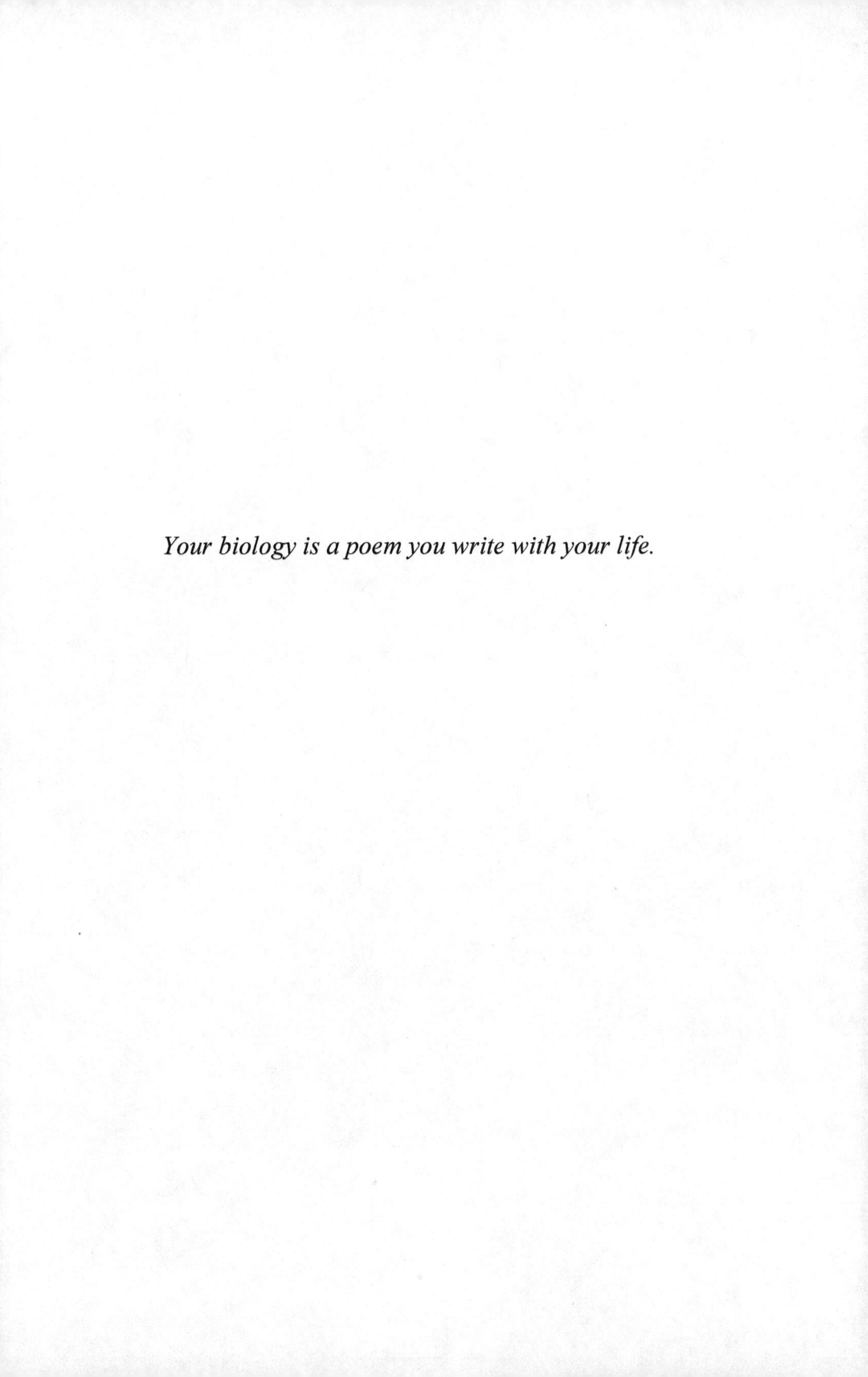

Your biology is a poem you write with your life.

Prologue

From: A.S.
To: Legal Department Admin
Subject: ClitBit patent application

Here's the summary you requested —

Following on BioMantrix success with the Pleasure Systems PS-1000 and NanoSmile oral care devices, ClitBit will be introduced to the same market through the same channels with the same business model:

- Subscription-based services embedded in a mobile device,
- Connected to a user app,
- Controlled by the BioMantrix artificial intelligence platform, and
- Supported by state-of-the-art chatbots.

As with Pleasure Systems, the ClitBit market sweet spot is women 40+ seeking "libido solutions" as partner availability declines.

ClitBit will be the first-to-market nano machine designed to enhance the 8,000 nerve endings in a woman's clitoris to provide orgasms on demand using the same interface and metrics as the PS-1000.

A nano-scale device, ClitBit is injected as simply as getting an ear pierced, GPS equipped and subject to continuous software upgrades.

As with NanoSmile, customer relationships with ClitBit users will be managed by personalized customer service avatars leveraging the real-time global database of women's biological metrics aggregated across all three product groups, Pleasure Systems, NanoSmile, and ClitBit, as well as our medical patient portals and health insurance systems.

BioMantrix is uniquely positioned to achieve first-mover-advantage with this low-cost, high-volume category killer delivered to millions of users worldwide and serviced entirely by AI.

ClitBit. It's like opioids without the constipation. (Ha, ha. But you get my point.) I look forward to our discussion at the meeting next week.

Business plan attached.

1 The Pleasure System

Inside the lovely little covered basket was a smooth red phallus with a short fat arm. *Cool bathtub toy*, Meryl thought as she held it in her hand. PS-1000 was embossed along the side. *Sounds like a game*. She didn't own a vibrator. Looking at this one she gave a sympathetic sigh. Uma had been putting all her energy into her clinic and Girl Church since her husband died. She didn't allow time for a romantic relationship. So, this thing was her fuckbuddy. *Evidently.* Meryl mused about her best friend's choice to replace a man with a plastic toy. She couldn't imagine it. Then she noticed her thumb stroking the vibrator. *Bob.* Her mind hula hooped through her husband and the phallus in a smear of melting magenta popsicles. *A dick is a dick.* She smiled and placed the phallus back in the basket on the side of Uma's bathtub.

In the kitchen Uma was making their drinks.

"I saw your new johnson in the bathroom," Meryl said.

Uma rolled her eyes and smiled. "It comes with an app on my phone. But I don't use the app much. It feels like a game. I just want the orgasm, not the score keeping."

"How is it?"

"It's like a Peloton for your twat."

"Nice."

"I got an email inviting me to be a beta tester. They were looking for influencers over 50, and I was curious. So, I signed up and they sent it to me."

"Cool," Meryl said. "Influence me."

"It's robotic. All the controls are on your phone. You can design your own ride. Put the dimensions into the app and it changes the shape and speed. Then it measures your orgasm."

"But is it satisfying?"

"I'd say so."

"Really?"

"It does whatever you're in the mood for."

"A jackhammer or a sailboat?"

"Exactly."

"Wow. Consider me influenced."

Uma laughed. "You're easy, Meryl."

"That's what Bob says."

They laughed together.

Meryl understood that she and Bob had an enviable sex life. They always had. Uma had watched it develop from their earliest days together as grad students, so she understood, too. The couple had hot lava flowing between them.

That year Meryl and Bob were planning to spend the summer at home instead of going on a long vacation because Bob was teaching a summer course. So, they splurged on new patio furniture, a two-person chaise lounge, and an outdoor fireplace. To christen the merchandise, when the stars came out, they opened a bottle of wine, smoked a joint, and reclined, curling their bodies together and kissing under the night sky. Meryl tangled her legs with his.

"I can see the moon in your eyes," he whispered, caressing her with the tip of his nose.

"How did I get to be so lucky?" she smiled and kissed him.

Sometimes their love making was like dancing. Other times it was a yoga meditation. They let their bodies lead. Even menopause hadn't disrupted their union. All through the misery of her metabolism leaping hot to cold, calm to anxious, pleasant to snappy, clear to fogged, all through the unpredictability of her body, her appetite for sex had remained. It was just how she was wired. She liked sex. Even when she was dry and needed lube to slip him into position, she was enjoying herself. She was enjoying him. She didn't just love Bob; she loved his body.

Since their twenties they had been partners in this biology. They knew each other's moves. She nibbled on his lip as he relaxed. Skin slick, tender mouths, necks, breasts, luscious private places. She slid her panties off and tossed them, unzipped his pants, and touched him. Inhaling his thighs against her cheeks, she knew just how to excite him with the most delicate flicker of her tongue, deep breathing his scent, sucking him like a lollipop until he swelled and shot into her mouth.

He took delight in doing the same for her, lowered himself across her soft belly and gently pulled at her patch with his lips. The tip of his tongue flicked up and down and around her wanting, teased and sipped her, unwrapped the petals of her rose until she gasped and moaned. This was their tango. Ecstasy fanned in a wide wake of comfort and profound inner peace, a psychic bond that held their symmetry. For forty years they shared this extraordinary experience together, perfectly in synch, completely satisfied.

Then Meryl blew it up.

At 60, Meryl's brain experienced a quake that shifted all her thinking in unexpected ways. One day she looked in the mirror and instead of seeing success, she saw failure. She wasn't a tenured university professor; she was a hen laying eggs in artificial light. A captive of her value to the system. Her life was the same day after day. Egg after egg. And for the longest time that felt like success.

Just keep going straight and level, stable and predictable, that was the goal. Had always been the goal. Each day she had cloned herself from the day before until all her days blended one into the next in a long stretch of wallpaper repeating itself into infinity like a mathematical formula.

For her entire adult life, teaching math in a classroom had been her destiny, her work, her pride. Suddenly all that repetition felt like a lack of imagination. She had lost her originality and she wanted to feel unique again. So, she dive-bombed her career.

Meryl and Bob had been professors at the University since they got their degrees. Their social lives revolved around campus life. They were popular with their students. They were financially secure. Tenured. Her CDs rolled over automatically, and their mortgage was paid. She had achieved her dreams and now her life made her want to pull her hair out. She had to quit her job.

To smooth her departure, she gave Bob one short, crisp sentence that told the whole story. "Meryl is leaving the University to write a book." It was a lie. But it was the alibi she needed to make him comfortable with her decision. She intended to rewild herself.

Rewilding was an idea she learned from land conservation, but as soon as she heard it, she felt like it applied to her. Her life was as developed as a suburban shopping mall, and she wanted it to feel like a wildflower meadow. The needs of her students, her commitments to her colleagues and her obligations to the University overpopulated her brain. Their lives, their problems, their goals, were invasive species that crowded her out of her own interests until there was no room left to think new thoughts.

Being a professor had become too formulaic, too repetitious, too plastic. She needed to reclaim herself, to conserve her resources before she became invisible and disappeared. It was a radical feeling that instigated a radical response. As though from hypnosis, one day she woke up an extremist, craving uncertainty, yearning for risk, and idealizing randomness. She just wanted to go wild.

The main thing was no obligations, no rules, no goal. She was going to be spontaneous. Unpredictable! Then serendipitously, Uma invited her to a garden club lecture on pollinators, followed by a butterfly safari and a tour of a butterfly house at a local nursery. That day Meryl heard a giant sucking sound in her head as butterflies flew in to take over her brain and occupy the mental space where her career had once been. It was a done deal.

Meryl quit the University to rewild herself. At her home, the dilapidated greenhouse attached to the back of their colonial farmstead became her new butterfly house. Her empty calendar filled with butterflies, and she thought she would rewild herself by their example.

~ : ~

Confident in the sturdiness of her marriage, and driven to achieve immediate results, Meryl made this major life decision without a thoughtful discussion with her life partner, Bob. She assumed she could just cajole him through her choice even if he disagreed. But as she settled into playing with her new butterfly habitat in her resurrected greenhouse, he turned chilly.

"When are you going to forgive me?" she asked innocently as she came into the kitchen holding her dirty hands out in front of her.

"I'm not sure." Bob frowned as he rinsed his coffee mug at the sink.

"I'm dividing roots while the plants are dormant," she answered his unasked question.

"How's the writing coming?" He put his mug in the dish drainer.

"Please don't ask me that again." She ran water over her hands and studiously scrubbed her fingernails with the vegetable brush.

"I've never seen your hands so dirty."

His eyebrows hunched together like blackbirds crowding on a wire. She knew that look, his unruly hair, thick but thinning black, streaked but not as grey as hers, stark and stern. At the sink, they were standing so close their hips and shoulders touched. It was the end of December, and the house was cold and drafty. Drawn to his body heat, she took a dishtowel and dried her hands, looked him up and down, gave a demure smile, and pressed herself into his chest to change the subject. But just as her lips were about to land on his, he pulled his head back out of reach.

"Why? Just tell me why? Why have you done this?" he asked. "You're too smart for this."

"I can feel the dirt in my brain," she said. "Something about putting my hands in damp soil gives me a rush like a glass of wine on an empty stomach."

"It's psychosomatic," he said matter-of-factly.

"No, it's not. It's real. My feelings are real."

"Maybe. Or maybe you're living in a fantasy, trying to make meaning from nothing."

"Maybe I am." Her pitch ascended. "Maybe there's nothing out there. But I have to find it for myself."

He laughed. "Really?" His blackbirds fluttered in a brief murmuration, then bunched again in a deep squint. "You're not making any sense."

"Stop looking at me like that. I'm going through a big transition here. Where's your compassion?"

"This big transition as you call it was completely unnecessary." He waved his hand in the air. Blackbirds scattered. "You could have taken a sabbatical."

"I need to get off the grid and experience real life. Plants and animals."

"Isn't that why we live here and not in town?"

"Time. I want time."

"At what price?"

"Please don't hate me."

"I don't hate you, Babe. I just think you're wasting your time."

"I need to waste my time!" she yelled.

He took a step back from her. Eyes wide, blackbirds spooked. Confused.

"I need to know what that means," she said earnestly. "It's my time."

He rolled his eyes and gave up. Face sagged, went back to his armchair, continued to read his pile of student essays, signaling end of discussion.

Meryl watched him walk away from her, folded the dishtowel, and considered hopping in the shower, putting on a tight t-shirt and kneeling in front of him with her hands on his thighs. But she didn't. She wasn't giving in. Instead, she went back to her greenhouse and sat at her potting bench to stare at a chrysalis.

A couple days later, she tried again. It was his habit to be at home in his chair reading papers written by his students, marking them with his favorite pen, drinking coffee with the countenance of Buddha in jeans and an Oxford shirt. She came up behind him, ran her fingers through his hair and kissed the top of his head. In the past this might have been a signal for him to set his work aside and go for a roll in bed with her. But instead, he set his papers aside, slipped out from under her lips and walked his coffee mug to the kitchen.

That stung.

"Since I was a teenager, I've measured myself against the calendar," she said righteously. "As though the mere passage of time is an obligation to accomplish something." She paused for effect and got nothing. "I'm all done with that."

"So, I see," he said quietly.

"I'm not selling my time for a paycheck anymore. I'm claiming it for myself."

"Time is money, my dear," he sighed.

"No, it's not!" she yelled.

He looked at her over the top of his reading glasses, eyebrows gathered in judgement like wraiths on the Supreme Court. She had always been her own person, done her own thing, gone off on her own path, didn't need his permission. Never asked. When they first met, he found her independence charming, impressive even. She was an entirely whole woman. Her self-confidence freed him to be himself. She had the ability to hold her own point of view, one very different from his, without being disparaging. They got along well because they lived in separate minds and had separate experiences. He had always appreciated their separateness. Until now. Now he felt excluded.

~ : ~

Back in her greenhouse, Meryl left her body and rose above herself in an amorphous mist. Her mental map was changing. She could feel a difference in her thoughts as she floated away from the rigors of academia into the vast sea of self-discovery. She had always believed in math. Measure, calculate, manage, repeat. Unassailable logic. It didn't matter what industry, what problem, what goal, it was math that delivered the answer. Numbers. Then on that butterfly safari last summer with Uma, she saw a chrysalis for the first time and realized some things were beyond math. There was magic out there, magic she had missed, magic that didn't need math. The life force. Pre-math, pre-history, pre-Meryl. Timeless. That was her epiphany and she wanted to explore it.

She wanted to find her way back to who she was before time mattered. Before she was overdeveloped by the structure of her education and her career. Before the dawn of her ambition. Before she disappeared into adulting. The specter of old age haunted her.

She had seen what aging did to others, and she wasn't going to just wait for it to happen to her. But what else to do with herself? What was the plan for the next third of her life? She needed a new purpose. A higher purpose. A soul purpose. Her power, her interests, her ingenuity were seeds sprouting inside her. Nurturing them compelled a new way of living.

She became a student at the University when she was a teenager. She met Bob when she was a grad student. She had been a tenured professor since she was 39. Now most of her life was behind her and she was plateaued, disillusioned by the charade, and discretely depressed. Time had taken advantage of her like that hen in her cage plopping out eggs until the day she became soup. Surprise! You're not useful anymore! Goodbye, Meryl. That was the tyranny of time, and Meryl was not going to let herself become soup.

And yet, letting go of time wasn't as simple as she had imagined. In her first few weeks at home, she tried to live by the sun, but it was early winter. Her days were short, and her nights were long. Her sense of time became slushy. She wandered around her house and looked at her possessions, the aggregation of a lifetime, and she realized she didn't feel anything for them anymore. They didn't need her. But in her butterfly house every object seemed to have meaning, and a purpose.

So she spent her daytime in the place where she knew her efforts mattered. Then, once the sun set, she read books about butterflies. And that made her sleepy. She went to bed before Bob and got up in what felt like the middle of the night. Her circadian rhythm put her and Bob on completely different schedules.

The unintended consequence of disconnecting from the University was that she was no longer on Bob's calendar. They were on separate tracks, moving at different speeds in different directions. When she popped out of bed at dawn, she missed waking up with him. They weren't getting ready to go to work together, so they weren't getting dressed and undressed together. Instead of being naked around each other, they crossed paths in the kitchen at the coffee pot. She tried to make breakfast for him, but he refused her offer, said he would grab a bagel in the cafeteria. Weeks dissolved without a tender touch, without a kiss, without an orgasm.

Shit.

Sex had always been their currency, an equal exchange, pleasure for pleasure. It was the glue that kept them tight. But now Bob felt disrespected. His work was a lifetime of achievement, 40 years of learning and teaching. English literature was the cultural lens through which he found himself. He was at the pinnacle of success in his field. That was an investment he wasn't ready to relinquish. He didn't know who he would be without it, and unlike his wife, he wasn't willing to venture beyond his hard-earned expertise.

Bob just wanted things to remain as they were, as they always had been. When Meryl quit her job, he lost something, and he wanted it back. But all she seemed to want from him was sex. Not his thoughts, not his opinions, not his insight or his knowledge. Just sex. And so, obviously, his only leverage in this marital stand-off with his wife was to withhold sex.

~ : ~

In January, Uma organized a retirement celebration for Meryl after yoga at Girl Church. It wasn't a party in the cocktails-and-cake sense, more of a rite of passage to mark her evolution from one phase of life to the next.

Sitting with her circle of friends, Meryl unwrapped the gift, and recognized the covered basket. She knew what was inside without even opening it and gave a glance to Uma. Their eyes met. Uma grinned and nodded.

"Pleasure Systems," Meryl read the logo and winked at Uma. "I wonder what this could be…Oh!" She swooned with mock surprise and held up the phallus for everyone to see. "A PS-1000. Just what I've always wanted."

Uma shared Meryl's sarcasm. "Your retirement is a milestone," she said. "I thought we should acknowledge it with a trophy symbolic of your achievement. Congratulations."

"Congratulations," the women chimed.

"You've graduated from the patriarchy," Khadija said dryly, rolling her eyes.

"It's your own pet man," Eleanor mused, sitting straight and angular as a grasshopper.

"Oh, jeez." Sue blushed. She was twice the size of Eleanor.

"Wow." Claire's big blue eyes opened wide. "Are you getting divorced?"

"No," Meryl laughed.

Meryl and Uma had been best friends since they were assigned to be roommates their freshman year in the dorm, years before Meryl met Bob. Uma, a round-faced Black woman with a kind vibe and biting insight. Meryl, a studious renegade, pale and athletic. The two found common ground in their verbosity. Talking was their thing. They talked a lot. Frequently. For years. About life and school and being a woman, hashing out their problems in marathon colloquies over coffee at the diner in sessions they called Girl Church.

Girl Church got them through college, grad school and Uma's residency at the hospital. It was their refuge, and their resource. Fueled by caffeine, at Girl Church they planned their careers, considered the advances of men, structured their marriages, and worked through menopause. Sitting in a red vinyl booth face-to-face gave them focus, they loved each other, and the decades passed. Uma opened a women's clinic. Then her husband died. Not long after, she bought the yoga studio in town and named it Girl Church. It was an extension of her medical practice.

"I love you guys," Meryl said to her friends. "Thank you."

"Your reward is a genie in a basket," Eleanor smirked, eyes twinkling.

"If my dog got that it would be gone in a minute. Snap!" Claire snapped her fingers and her boobs jiggled.

"I don't see any controls." Sue narrowed her eyes skeptically and leaned in. "How do you turn it on and off?"

"With the app, of course," Uma replied with a flourish.

"Oh, jeez." Sue frowned and leaned away with her hands on her knees. She'd been a corporate attorney. Then breast cancer disrupted her ascendance in the firm. "I wouldn't do that," she warned.

"You should name it," Khadija said mischievously, hijab framing her face.

"Are you going to hide it from Bob?" Claire stared at the vibrator as though it might be dangerous. "I don't think my husband would like it."

"She doesn't need her husband's permission to have an orgasm," Khadija snipped.

"I do," Claire said defensively. "I would feel like I was cheating on him." She blinked and watched Meryl for clues.

Khadija's face puffed up like a muffin top. Words sparked on the tip of her tongue, but she waited for someone else to speak first.

As a young married woman, Claire had had two miscarriages that left her humiliated, and grief stricken. When she finally did carry her third pregnancy to term, she required an emergency C-section. For years after that, she squirted spermicide into her vagina every day because it made her feel safe. Then menopause and a series of infections brought her to Uma's clinic. Uma encouraged her to join the yoga group where she could learn to manage her anxiety.

Khadija was not a mother, but she was a dutiful daughter, and she well understood the obligation of a woman to be a caregiver. After her father died, she and her mother emigrated from Pakistan to the United States and through her father's academic connections, she found a job as a research assistant at the University. Then her mother fell and broke her hip, and Khadija felt obligated to keep her at home instead of putting her in a rehab facility where she didn't speak the language. By the time she brought her mother to Uma's clinic, Khadija was deeply depressed, isolated, and exhausted.

As a physician treating these women Uma had witnessed her patients' difficulties with caring for themselves. Some like Claire simply didn't know enough about their bodies. Others, like Sue and Khadija, needed encouragement to tend their emotional needs. Eleanor, a generation older than all of them, came with the building.

When Uma bought the yoga studio, it had been a well-known den of hippies called Planet Aquarius, and Eleanor had been the high priestess. She was a Vietnamese orphan adopted as a baby by University professors who had long since passed. Over the years she had been a tarot card reader, a tattoo artist, a chanter, and a sage smudging forest bather. When Uma changed the name of the business to Girl Church and shifted the programs from alternative lifestyles to women's wellness, Eleanor stayed on as her best customer.

Since that time the sharing circle had had its ups and downs. Then this particular group of women self-selected to stick with each other and commit to their collective wellness. Now they were friends. They knew one another, didn't always agree, but their differences gave them strength. That was the point of the circle. Not to agree. To provide emotional support. They didn't call it group therapy. Their time together wasn't as structured as that, but it had many of the same benefits, especially after the stretch and tone workout Uma put them through before they started talking. That integration of their loosening bodies and meditation opened their minds when it came time to focus on one another in the circle. So, when Khadija and Claire got into one of their snits, the other women just let it go.

"Sail on, Meryl," Sue said, holding herself upright, elbows locked in a stiff lotus posture. "I know how I felt when I finally quit the grind. But once you settle into the idea that your time is your own, it's exhilarating."

"Work shouldn't be such a miserable experience," Eleanor admonished. "We're spiritual beings."

"It wasn't miserable," Meryl countered. "I enjoyed being a professor. But how long is a person supposed to do the same thing over and over again? I have callouses on my brain."

"You're brave," Khadija said wistfully. "Is that what your book's about?"

"I don't know." Meryl looked down at the vibrator in her lap.

"How can you write a book if you don't know what it's about?" Claire asked.

"I can't," Meryl sighed.

"I don't get it."

"The book is just a decoy," Meryl explained. "I needed an easy explanation for leaving. Everyone knows professors write books."

"So, you're not writing a book?" Khadija tilted her head at Meryl.

"Bob doesn't really buy into me quitting. But he gets writing a book. Rewilding is a little too squishy for him."

"It sounds squishy to me, too," Sue huffed. "Is that even a word?"

"You're consciously evolving," Eleanor soothed.

"We're all acting out our changing brain chemistry," Uma injected.

"I never thought I would quit teaching," Meryl admitted. "I thought I would be teaching until I was 80. But I want to explore other interests."

"Like butterflies," Uma said.

"Yes, like butterflies."

"I never thought I would quit either," Sue said. "Being a lawyer was the most important thing in my life. And then, one day it wasn't."

"You're rewilding yourself, too," Eleanor said to Sue.

"What does that mean?" Claire asked.

"It's like I've lived my whole life as a tiger in the circus," Meryl explained. "Doing tricks on command. And now I'm setting myself free in the jungle."

"Wow." Claire was impressed. "I would never do that."

"Neither would I, Claire," Uma chuckled. "But Meryl's very different from us."

Meryl laughed so heartily her hair fell out of its clip.

"In a way, you're leaving Bob behind," Khadija observed. "It must be weird for him."

Uma turned her eyes toward Meryl and bugged them out as if to say, *I told you so*.

In October, when Meryl first mentioned to Uma that she planned to quit her job, the two of them had been having coffee at the diner and Uma nearly splashed her latte. "You're doing what!?"

Meryl took a sip from her cup. "I'm rewilding myself," she repeated.

"I hope you're not going to stop washing your hair." Uma was a professional, always styled, always making a statement with her clothes. Unlike Meryl who always looked like she'd just come in from hanging laundry.

"I can't do this anymore," Meryl defended herself. "I'm quitting at the end of the year."

"Why are you telling me this now? You must have been thinking about it for a long time."

"I have. Since before we went on that butterfly safari. I know it's extreme. But I needed to make the decision for myself. And I needed to tell Bob before I told you. I didn't want him to feel like it was a conspiracy. He loves you."

"Well, thank you for that."

"So, it's a done deal. I'm out."

Uma winced. "Don't walk away from tenure. Take a sabbatical. You're entitled to that. But don't leave all your benefits on the table."

"That's what Bob said." Meryl looked out the window.

"He's right. Take some time off."

"I don't want my life to be timed. Also, I feel really guilty about the benefits. I don't need them anymore, and college is so expensive for students. It doesn't seem fair."

"Meryl, you're too young to retire. No one with tenure retires at 60. You could stay at the University until you're 70. Or 80."

"It feels like a cage to me. I need to break free."

"But why take the risk? What for? Keep the job and give your money away. Start a scholarship fund. But don't quit now."

"I've avoided risk my whole life."

"That's pretty much what adulthood is. Avoiding risk. You identify your limits and live within them. It's called stability."

"Fuck stability."

"What did Bob say when you said, fuck stability?"

"I didn't exactly say that. I told him I was writing a book."

"A book about what?"

"He didn't ask, and I didn't say."

Uma sat back against the red vinyl booth and put her hands on the table. "So, you lied?"

"Sort of… I plan to be forgiven." Meryl couldn't decide if she wanted to laugh or cry.

"Forgiven?"

"He'll get over it."

Uma blinked for a moment, looked out the window, took another swallow of her latte, then she set the cup down and leaned in toward Meryl. "I feel like I'm watching my best friend have some sort of mental break down," she whispered.

"I'm just letting go of my ambition." Meryl lowered her eyes as though her statement was an admission of guilt.

"You're also letting go of your paycheck. Matching funds in your IRA. Paid vacation. Financial security. Your career. Your whole history."

"Please don't push me."

"I'm not pushing you. I'm just doing the math." Uma cocked her chin with pointed irony.

"It's too much structure," Meryl sighed. "It's been too long. I want to experience life without structure. Real life."

"This is real life. Life has structure. It's a process. You're such an important catalyst for so many people. Your students love you. You're probably leaving a half a million dollars on the table. How can you walk away from that?"

"The University is a fishbowl."

"Of course, it is. It's your habitat."

"Well, that's the beauty of being human. I can change my habitat."

"Really?" Uma felt like Meryl had joined a cult, but she didn't say so because she didn't want to give her any ideas.

"I'm jumping out of the bowl and into the ocean." Meryl jiggled her shoulders cheerfully, but her cheer felt false. There was a risk she wasn't admitting, a risk to her marriage. Bob.

"Goldfish have a very short lifespan," Uma sighed.

"Oh, don't be all gloom and doom about it." Meryl put her hair back up in her plastic clip. "The possibilities are infinite. Like hitchhiking through Europe. You weren't afraid to do that."

"Yes, I was. I would never have done that without you."

"Well, here we go again. It's going to be an adventure. I promise."

They smiled at each other, but Uma felt like she was helping her sister dive off a cliff. Other people did such things, jumped out of airplanes, hiked the Appalachian Trail, swam with sharks, bucket list extremism, conquering risk as a personal goal. But Meryl had always been so practical, so grounded, so methodical. Uma wondered if she had the skills for such an abstraction as rewilding herself. What was the model for that? Where was the proof? Where was "the wild" anyway? What price would she pay? It seemed to Uma that her girlfriend the math professor had given up math.

2 Do Butterflies Kiss?

Dear Butterflies,

This is my first journal entry. It's January and you're sleeping, but I'm here and I'm watching over you and Begonia. So sweet dreams. I wish I was in a better place with this experiment, but maybe I'm just feeling the cold. From Bob. It's only been a few weeks since my official retirement, but I think this is the longest we've ever gone without kissing, and I really miss it. Kissing. It's so important to me. Do butterflies kiss?

Kissing is emotional currency. We spend our kisses on the ones we love. We give the most kisses to the ones who are the most valuable to us. I see the way you dance together and touch tails, and I know you're attracted to each other. But for my species, kissing is the essential act of love. And Bob has stopped kissing me.

I felt so proud of myself for retiring early and deciding to invest myself in a new experience. I felt brave. But I knew in my heart he would never go along with it. Bob lives according to the rules. I don't. That difference was interlocking, opposite angles that complemented one another and held us together. We had a way of being that surprised people because we seemed so different. We think differently. He's a romantic. I'm a calculator. I loved that about us. But now we're old and there's one thing very different about us. Money. We have a very comfortable life and suddenly, I've sprung a leak. I've let go of my money and he disapproves. How am I going to get over that?

When we first began as a couple, we were in grad school, and we had no money. It wasn't money that brought us together, it was sex. We never talked about money. Our money just happened as we advanced in academics. We've both worked in the same place for our entire careers. I didn't consider how much work was part of our relationship until I stopped working. But to be honest, I did have an inkling that he wouldn't approve. I did avoid the confrontation of telling him I was all done. I did make a major change in my life without consulting him. Because I thought we could just work through it.

Also, it's my life.

I thought I was avoiding a big argument by simply going around it. By the time he found out, my plans to be unemployed were a *fait accompli*. Maybe it wasn't fair. Maybe if I had been honest, we would be having great make-up sex instead of being estranged. But I wasn't open to discussion. It's my life. Yes, he would say it's his life, too. But that argument falls apart when you stop looking at the money and just look at the time.

I can't spend my time as a cog in the machine anymore. If I had to quit my job because I had cancer, he would be supportive. But I quit my job because I don't have cancer. That's my point. I'm fabulous and I want my time for me, to spread my wings and fly while I have the strength and the imagination. Encore, Meryl! I want to be reckless while I can pick myself up when I fall. I want to know what it feels like to sink or swim again. I want to take chances. I want to test myself.

So here I sulk, unkissed by my lifelong boyfriend. I have to admire him for his self-discipline because he's passing up some killer blowjobs, and he knows it. I've been addicted to his love for so long, I never thought for one second that he would withhold it. But he is. And I'm in withdrawal from my fix. It hurts. But if he's willing to go to extremes, so am I. Game on.

Sleep well, my beauties. I thought this journal would be a way to track my care for you and document our experience together. But instead, I'm whining into the void. Unkissed.

Thanks so much for listening.

3 Begonia

A couple months before she left the University, Meryl received a request for a private meeting with Katie and Lemons, two computer science students in the math program. She had known them for a few years, since they were freshmen, each had taken her classes, and she had advised them on academic matters. Katie was a sturdy Kansas farmgirl with a compelling personal warmth and an instinct for the building blocks of software. Lemons was the precocious child of East Coast liberals, mixed race, a natural leader, and an audacious hustler. As Meryl sat across from them at her desk, Katie in her typical t-shirt and jeans, and Lemons in her natty boy clothes, they seemed to have a tighter vibe than she remembered, and she wondered if they had become a couple.

"She's like a dog," Katie begged. "We've been training her. She poops in a cat box."

"Please, take her," Lemons pleaded. "We can't keep hiding her forever. If admin gets her, they'll give her back and she'll be killed, and all this will be for nothing. If you don't take her, we got kicked out of school for nothing."

Meryl got up to close her office door. "You're not kicked out of school yet," she said. "Your expulsion is pending. The University has to do something. They can't let students vandalize a local farmer and steal his pigs. Pigs are how he makes his living."

"He got all his pigs back except Begonia. But she's too big to hide under my bed," Katie moaned. "Not everyone agrees with keeping a pig in our dorm room. Eventually they're going to rat us out."

"Begonia?" Meryl asked.

"We auctioned off her naming rights as a fundraiser," Lemons explained.

"Nice," Meryl said. "I live on an old farmstead. But I'm not a farmer. I don't know how to take care of a pig. I just started taking care of butterflies. I don't know if I can handle butterflies and a pig. Growing things is new for me."

"You have the perfect place for her."

"Begonia will love your butterflies."

"I don't think I can fix this. I'm retiring at the end of December. Everyone knows that."

"Everyone loves you," Katie said. "If you take Begonia, everyone will be happy and this whole thing will be over."

"My mom is super pissed," Lemons said. "And she's a vegetarian."

Meryl laughed.

"We taught her to walk on a leash," Katie smiled. "She comes when you call her. Really, she's just like a dog."

"A porky dog," Meryl said. "Even if I take her, I don't know how long I can keep her. What if she doesn't like living with me?"

"She'll love you," Lemons said. "She's a real being. You'll definitely connect with her. Just come to our dorm and check her out. You'll see. If she doesn't jazz you, our whole plan falls through. But I'm pretty sure she will jazz you. She's amazing, Meryl. Please."

A few hours later, Meryl stepped into their dorm room on the seventh floor overlooking campus. The town was a mix of modern and 19th century buildings swaddled in rolling hills. Through the window she could see a vein of colorful October leaves lacing through the pines. White steeples, cupolas, and red brick belltowers pierced the canopy, and she was transported back to the year she came to the University, a young woman with a plan to succeed, invigorated by her new independence. Like these two girls she had been at the top of her class preparing to launch herself into a career with dreams for achievement and self-satisfaction. Anything was possible. Now she envied their idealism.

The girls watched her, waiting for her revery to fade and her attention to return. Begonia was sound asleep on one of the twin beds. When Meryl turned away from the window, Lemons said, "We built this ramp for her to teach her to get up on things, like the back seat of a car."

"How much does she weigh?" Meryl asked.

"We haven't had her on a scale," Katie said. "But I'd say she weighs about 200 pounds."

"That's a lot," Meryl said.

"Not for a sow," Katie replied. "She could gain another hundred pounds."

Meryl raised her eyebrows and stared at the pig.

"Once she learned to get up on my bed, it's been pretty hard to keep her off of it," Katie said. "Her snoring is unbelievable."

"Oh, that's a selling point," Meryl snickered.

"When you get her home, you're probably going to have to make rules about getting up on the furniture," Lemons said. "We let her get on the couch in the lounge and the cushions just collapsed."

"But she did find my ID."

"Yeah. She ate everything that fell out of the couch cushions. Mostly popcorn. We had to pull Katie's ID out of her mouth."

"But she was very cool about it," Katie said. "She didn't bite me."

"She doesn't bite," Lemons said.

Katie bunched her lips and wrinkled her nose.

Meryl was watching the pig's body fill with air, then blabber an exhale that sprayed across the sheets. *She could be a seal*, Meryl thought, *or a baby hippopotamus*. She was pink with big black spots, and chalky white hair growing out of her ears. Hooves. Nostrils like thumbholes. But clean. The pillowcase under her mouth was wet, but Meryl couldn't smell her.

"She did bite Ryan," Katie said.

Lemons winced.

"What do you mean, she bit Ryan?" Meryl asked.

"She doesn't like men." Katie didn't look at Meryl when she said that, kept her eyes down, traced the pig's ear with her finger and kissed her. Begonia opened her eyes and closed them again.

Meryl knew Katie had been sexually assaulted her first year on campus.

"That's one of the things I love about Begonia," Lemons said. "She gets the whole gender thing. Men suck."

"I'm cis female," Meryl said. "Hetero. Married. I like men."

"She'll be fine with that," Lemons shrugged.

"I grew up on a farm," Katie said. "Some animals just don't like certain people. They get a negative imprint early on and never lose it. See that notch in her ear. And her tattoo. She has plenty of reasons not to like men."

"Ban Bacon is fundraising to have her tattoo removed," Lemons said. "It's the mark of the devil."

"Ban Bacon is going to have to change its mission," Meryl countered. "If you want to stay on campus and get your degree, you can't be renegades who organize the destruction of private property. I know how I would feel if someone bashed in my greenhouse and set my butterflies free because they thought I was running a caterpillar prison."

"We were saving them from slaughter."

"Honestly, the only way we're going to save animals is to learn to live with them. You endangered those pigs by setting them free. I read in the news that the farmer and his neighbors lost a year's worth of vegetables in their gardens when those pigs ran through."

Begonia flapped her lips in a loud sputter. Katie was still stroking her ear.

Lemons plopped down on her bed with an exasperated sigh. "We needed the publicity," she grumbled.

"Well, you got it. You put the University in the position of having to choose between a radical student group bent on destroying local farms and the town that does business with those farmers. The Amish bring a lot of money into this community. The wingnut media made you guys look like eco-terrorists. You don't have anyone on your side as far as I can tell. Ban Bacon is pretty elitist, don't you think?"

"It's a brand," Lemons said. "We made almost $5,000 selling hats and t-shirts."

"In this town Ban Bacon is considered anti-Amish."

"We're not anti-Amish," Katie said. "We're pro pig."

"I think you can be pro pig without banning bacon," Meryl said.

"Truth to power, Meryl. How can that be?" Lemons asked.

"Truth to power, Lemons. Pigs die. We all die. Nature is a food system. Everyone eats someone else. Be a vegetarian if you want. But plants have feelings, too. No one is innocent. The problem is not pork. The problem is the commodification of life."

"I hear you," Lemons said. "But radicalization is an effective weapon. Ban Bacon has members. They donate, and we organize. Our Bacon Rebellion was supported by hundreds of students. The University is making an example of Katie and me because we mobilized an army."

"Students care about animals," Katie said. "I saw what happened to them growing up. Dead cows paid for my college education. Now I want to pay them back. No more factory farms."

"That was not a factory farm," Meryl said. "The whole thing about the Amish is the human scale of their farms. It was wrong to wreck that farmer's barn."

"Collateral damage," Lemons said. "I'm not sorry."

"Then I can't help you," Meryl said and took a step toward the door.

"But you have to help us." Katie had tears in her eyes. "I've slept with Begonia every night for two weeks and she's amazing. You have to help her. She can't go to the slaughterhouse. She just can't."

"The way to help Begonia is to shut down Ban Bacon," Meryl said. "Come up with a better way to change how people eat. Don't attack farmers. They're just trying to make a living."

"Okay." Lemons got up suddenly and walked over to the window, shoved her hands in her pockets and knitted her thoughts. "You take Begonia and give her a home. We shut down Ban Bacon. And we don't get expelled."

Meryl smiled. In a streak of de ja vu, an intuition about Begonia hula hooped through her mind like a psychedelic Hallmark card. Happy Mother's Day! She felt a psychic tug toward the pig. "And Ban Bacon's bank balance goes to the farmer," she said.

"Deal," Lemons said, and took out her phone.

"Deal," Katie said, and took out her phone.

"Deal," Meryl said imagining Bob's reaction.

When they got out of the elevator in the lobby, Meryl led Begonia on a leash with Lemons and Katie following. Several students clustered in front of them, holding up their phones, taking photos and shouting questions.

"The paparazzi," Lemons muttered.

"Professor, how do you justify taking possession of stolen property?" someone shouted.

"The farmer will be compensated," Meryl replied.

"What about the damages?" A camera flash went off in Meryl's face, and she turned to smile at Lemons.

"I have some announcements to make," Lemons said, pulling Katie close beside her. "As you know, the University is considering expelling Katie and me for leading the Bacon Rebellion. But since that happened, we have a new priority. Begonia. Our goal was always to save pigs. To save Begonia we're going to have to shut down Ban Bacon and pay for the damages. Hopefully, that's enough to keep me and Katie on campus. Check our website for details. And thanks for telling our story."

With that, Lemons and Katie took off through a side door and Meryl was left to get Begonia into her car. By the time she got home and settled her new pet into the greenhouse, student media headlines were blazing.

Math Professor Negotiates Bacon Rebellion Truce

Ban Bacon Surrenders Pig & Liquidates Pork to Pay Damages

Pigmalion — Ban Bacon Pig Finds Home with Math Professor

That night as Bob fell asleep reading in his armchair, Begonia wandered into the livingroom drawn by the smell of the popcorn litter under his seat cushion. Beneath him, she sucked up crumbs on the floor in just the right place for his hand to slide off the armrest and suddenly bop her. Startled by the abrupt contact with his fleshy paw, she oinked a loud one, turned her head and nipped his fingers. Bob yelled. Begonia ran. And Meryl tried to make amends. But to no avail.

"She didn't mean to bite you," Meryl said.

"Yes, she did."

"She's a very friendly pig, Bob."

"So you say. I prefer not to live with her. Unless you're telling me that she's being fattened for harvest."

"We are not eating Begonia."

"Then I never want to see her again."

And that's how it was. Begonia was banished to the outer kingdom, not allowed in the house when Bob was home.

~ : ~

After a few days with Begonia, Meryl felt comfortable that she and the pig got along. She went to the farm store, got some bales of hay and a water trough, stopped by the farmstand, and asked if they would save whatever food they planned to throw away, she would pick it up, and gladly pay them for their trouble. Begonia was patient and cheerful, enjoyed a scratch on the head and an apple or a carrot, leftover salad, and potato peels.

It was nice to have a creature that seemed to notice her, came to greet her, followed her around. She was committed to growing her butterfly habitat in the greenhouse where native species could procreate. But her butterflies had disappeared into hibernation. Begonia liked being with her.

The pig seemed to understand Meryl's desire to sink into living soil and feel the cycle of life through her skin. Begonia felt the cycle of life through her nose. They were explorers together in the moist air of the greenhouse, shapeshifting from physical forms to ghosts of light.

From Begonia's perspective Meryl was the source of all good things. Not Bob. Not Bob at all. He didn't smell right. So, she left him alone.

Bob smelled like books. He was a dusty library kind of guy, a professor of English Literature who lived in his mind, very traditional, didn't need much light, a hard worker, probably some sort of genius but still punching a mental timeclock like a beaver. Of course, this characterization was well beyond the mind of a pig. But Begonia didn't need to put her opinion of Bob into words. She had instincts, and she was inclined to follow them.

To her credit, she was a very fast learner, smart enough to stay out of sight when Bob was home, and intuitive enough to settle on the bathroom rug when Meryl was taking one of her erotic bubble baths. Since she started spending her days doing physical work and getting dirty, the bathtub had become part of Meryl's daily routine, a way of relaxing her body and indulging herself. She made certain sounds in that room that Begonia didn't register in the greenhouse, sounds of feather breath, ascending moans that imprinted on Begonia as pleasure. The pig sensed the woman's emotions and aimed to please her, unlike the man.

When Bob did cross paths with Begonia, he could tell by her attitude that she felt superior. Which was an outrage. Blackbirds crashed on the bridge of his nose. And yet, he refused to talk about it. Too many things were changing all at once. First his wife's sudden obsession with butterflies when she didn't even own a house plant. Then her abrupt announcement of retirement without consulting him. Then a pig appeared in his house. A pig! Talking about it would only make it worse.

He just couldn't take Begonia seriously. He told himself she was one of those menopause symptoms, like hot flashes. He thought Meryl would exhaust her whimsy, see the absurdity of it, come back down to earth and settle beside him in the amber light of their leather livingroom. He couldn't fathom a pet pig as a replacement for estrogen, but he also didn't think it was worth questioning. He had survived Meryl's menopause. He would survive Begonia.

One day he would wake up and the pig would be gone. Meryl would be done with this blob of meat, and he would have his wife back. It was almost worth it. He was looking forward to a freezer full of pork. He would get the hunter who brought them venison to dispatch the pig out behind the barn, and they'd have bacon for a year. It was the kind of thing Meryl wouldn't do, but she would accept it once it was done.

~ : ~

Local media stayed on the story of the Bacon Rebellion, the demise of Ban Bacon and the University's decision not to expel the students.

"The farmer got screwed, you know." Bob was sitting in his armchair holding the student newspaper open in his lap, perusing each page, blackbirds leaning in to help him see. "Repairing his barn cost more than that," he poked at his wife. "And what about the vegetable gardens? If he had pushed it, he could have gotten a lot more than $5,000. How much did you pay for the pig?"

It hadn't occurred to Meryl to pay the farmer for Begonia. That was an oversight. Her days were busier now with a new species in the greenhouse, mind occupied by plans for elevating her butterfly operation onto tables and shelves, so the space could be a luscious habitat for fliers, crawlers, and snorters.

Begonia got into things, she was intelligent, and making an indoor space for her took some creativity. Meryl's composting operation had to accommodate a pig that loved to root through compost. Her pile of potting soil had become a pig lounge. Her stacks of clay pots had been tipped over and shards of terracotta spread across the floor. The water trough spilled, and the floor was mucky, which meant the pig was mucky. That made it very hard to hide the fact that Meryl let her in the house during the day when Bob had class. And her poo was stinky. Shoveling pig poo and dumping it outside was a new chore for Meryl. She didn't mind it. But she was surprised how much work it was to have one pet pig.

~ : ~

Eli Zook tied his horse in front of his plain white house as fallen leaves tumbled across the gravel driveway where Meryl sat in her car waiting for him. It was a warm November day, bright sun cut through moody clouds, and Mr. Zook wasn't wearing a jacket. He had a subtle vigor, looked straight at her, a confident man, square shouldered and intentional.

She undressed him with her eyes. White shirt, closed collar, suspenders, and a straw hat. Perspiration glistened on his face. A rush of liquid tingle shimmied up from her thighs to her cheeks. Strong hands and simple black gaberdine pants. No brands. Just real. And masculine. So masculine.

Quiet. Reserved. Respectful. She wanted to touch his beard. In her mind all the things that were old fashioned about him made him super sexy. She whizzed through a short film of their love affair: the unlikely chemistry of a university professor and an Amish farmer, sprays of lust, long wet kisses, hungry hands, half-dressed sex in the hay, a ripping loud orgasm, and she would never see him again. That was how it would be.

That was how she wished for it anyway.

"Good day," she said through the car window, face flushed pink, smiling more broadly than she intended.

"Good day," he replied without smiling, hands in his pockets hiding his thoughts.

"I've come to pay for the pig." She tried to be cheerful, but it felt fake.

"Thank you," he said with a seriousness that made her want to jump him.

Did he think she was hot? "I'm sorry for your trouble." She winced demurely and handed him the envelope. "I hope nothing like this ever happens again."

"Me, too," he said flatly, folding the envelope into his pants pocket, eyes on her face, not angry, but not friendly either, definitely did not want her the way she wanted him. Of course, that made him even hotter.

After an awkward empty moment she said, "Goodbye."

He gave her a perfunctory nod and walked away. She sucked in a deep breath and exhaled loudly.

"I'll bet he has great legs," she said to herself.

4 The Toothbrush

By the beginning of April spring had greened the hills again. Meryl's butterflies were emerging from their chrysalises. And she was desperate for Bob's attention. It had been months since he touched her and she wanted sex, real sex with a real man. Her new vibrator was fun, but it wasn't a very good kisser. Bob's lips were what she wanted. But she knew she couldn't command his performance. He had to want her the way she wanted him. So, she started wearing dresses for dinner, did her hair the way he liked it, met him at the door when he arrived home from work, pushed some cleavage into view, and rubbed up against him in the kitchen. But he was conspicuously oblivious.

One morning as he rolled out of bed, she felt a surge of desire and ran her hands across his back. "Want to take a shower with me?" she purred. She wanted his skin against her skin, the satisfaction of wrapping herself around him and feeling his erection. "I just want to hold you in my hands," she said.

"I'm going to shower after I work out," he said, pulling away from her and shaking out his balls.

She stretched her legs under the sheets and let her eyes follow him around the room. "You look good." *Is something going on with his prostate?* She'd been reading about male menopause, and wondered if he was experiencing erectile dysfunction, but she couldn't bring herself to talk about it.

"I'm working with a personal trainer," he said flexing in the mirror. Blackbirds rising.

"What's his name?" Meryl was amused by his fascination with himself.

"Her name is Hazel."

"Is she a student?"

"No."

"What are you working on?"

"She's teaching me tai chi."

"Cool. You must be enjoying it."

"I am."

"I miss mornings with you," she sighed and hugged her pillow. "I wish we had more time together."

"There's always the weekend."

"That seems pretty predictable."

"Hasn't it always been predictable?" He shrugged and went to the bathroom. Blackbirds huddled.

Meryl didn't see his face when he said that, but his condescending tone asking that one little question sent her into a psychic freefall.

Was that a criticism? Is our sex life predictable? What is he talking about? Is having regular sex a problem? Because he seems to expect it. No. No. He doesn't seem to expect it anymore. That's the problem. It was predictable and now it's gone. Right? What is he saying?

She knew most other couples their age were not enjoying intimacy as often as she and Bob were. *Had been.* She knew she was fortunate to have a man who was still hot for her. *Have had.* And because he got an easy boner when she touched him (*had touched him*), she thought he was fortunate, too. *Had been fortunate, too.* Her verbs were suddenly changing. And she wasn't even writing about it.

Their sex life was now in the past tense. It was confusing. Did he know how fortunate he was (*had been*) to have a woman who still lusted after him? Has it always been predictable? *Had it?* With a subtle slide in pitch, he had vandalized her memories. Was he saying that when he came (*had come*) in her mouth, it wasn't that great because it was predictable? *Had been predictable?* Had he suffered through getting his predictable cock sucked? Is there any such thing as a bad blowjob if the guy still comes (*came*) in your mouth? Had he suffered her predictable tongue? *Poor fucking Bob. Fuck Bob!*

~ : ~

Sitting at her desk, checking email, and reading the news on her computer, she was inspired to try something new. Anything. *Nothing short of a hand grenade is going to get his attention.* So, she searched on the phrase "how to have great sex with an old man."

Alongside the search results came an ad for NanoSmile, a new kind of dentistry based on nanotechnology. The woman in the ad looked just like her. In fact, it was her. Startling. Before she gave a thought to the invasion of her privacy, the pirating of her face, the copyright violation of using her personal photo, or the fact that she was being tracked by an algorithm that knew what she looked like, before all that, she noticed that the photo had been retouched to hide the chickenpox scar beside her nose, her crow's feet were gone, her lips were puffy and her forehead was smooth as a peach. That was annoying.

A chatbot text bubble popped up and said, *Let me introduce you to NanoSmile. We can help you have perfect teeth forever. Interested?*

Of course, I am, Meryl typed.

Let's get started. First, we need some information about your teeth. Do you still have all your own teeth?

So far.

What's your zip code?

Meryl typed the number and her screen refreshed with the image of a pristine white office, sleek surfaces decorated with exotic plants and a bright blue sky outside the window. She understood the brand message. They wanted to convey advanced science, a sanitary ecosystem, personalized solutions, and modern convenience. She wanted that, too. She may have a pet pig and enjoy getting her hands dirty, but she wanted her healthcare to be antiseptic and space-rocket smart.

The chatbot texted, *Please select the features for your customer service avatar, so we may delight you with the finest personal service you have ever experienced.*

Ok, typed Meryl. But she was thinking about those exotic plants in the office image. They were begonias. She knew why. *They're feeding me what they think they know about me. But they're not as smart as they think they are.*

Miffed, Meryl made mischievously ironic choices for her customer service avatar from the NanoSmile checkboxes and dropdown menus, concocting a counterintuitive presence, the antithesis of that sleek white office. When she was done selecting his physical features, his clothes, his personality traits, his age, and his ethnicity, she named him Hamish. Instantly he appeared on her screen under the NanoSmile logo, her personal guide to the future of perfect teeth forever.

"Good day, Meryl." His lips moved as he spoke in machine cadence. "Please allow me to introduce myself. I am Hamish. How do you do?"

"I'm fine thank you, Hamish. Nice to meet you," she said aloud to the cartoon man on her computer screen. "I see you have teeth."

"Yes, Meryl, I have teeth."

"Are they false teeth?"

"I am a NanoSmile customer service avatar, your personal guide as you seek perfect teeth forever. I am here to delight you, Meryl."

"I know some Pennsylvania Dutch have their teeth pulled rather than go to the expense of high-tech dental care."

"I can assure you, Meryl, I have not had my teeth pulled."

"But can you assure me that you're Pennsylvania Dutch?"

"I am exactly as you specified, Meryl. If you would like to change me in any way, you may return to the avatar features selection page."

"Were your parents Pennsylvania Dutch?"

"I am a computer program, Meryl. I do not have parents."

"Then how do you know who you are? You could be anybody."

"No, Meryl. I can only be who I am programmed to be. You chose my features and characteristics. My presence is based on those specifications."

"But if you're synthetic, how do you even know you exist?"

"How do you know you exist, Meryl?"

"Oh," she laughed. "That's good. That's very good."

"Thank you, Meryl. I am here to please you."

"What kind of relationship are we going to have, Hamish?"

"Your wish is my command, Meryl. I am here to guide you on your journey to perfect teeth forever."

"Have you ever been in love?"

"Thank you for asking, Meryl. In the words of Tina Turner, what's love got to do with it?"

"Cute. How far can we go?"

"I am a state-of-the-art customer service avatar, Meryl. I am here to guide you on your journey to perfect teeth forever. We can go wherever that leads."

"I was hoping for a digital lover, Hamish. It would make my new toothbrush so much more interesting."

"I will try to be interesting, Meryl. Thank you for the suggestion."

"The avatar features selection page only includes design options for your top half. What about your bottom half? I'd like to design that."

"Customer feedback is always welcome, Meryl."

"Thanks, Hamish. What I'm getting at is that I'd like to feel like you want to fuck me."

"Your feelings are of paramount importance, Meryl. Thank you for sharing."

"Can you at least say you want to fuck me?"

"Thank you for asking, Meryl. I can say that I appreciate you."

Meryl laughed with such force her saliva sprayed her screen.

~ : ~

The toothbrush was expensive, but Hamish was adorable. She particularly enjoyed the sound of his voice, singsong and rhythmic, like a toy man. She wished she could make him more like Eli Zook, give him muscles and the gravitas of a seasoned warrior. She was in the mood for a beast and Hamish was a teddy bear. But the wardrobe was enough to trigger her fantasies, and she was amused by the game of getting him to talk dirty. In fact, his resistance to the F-word made him more like Eli Zook. It was the prim and proper façade that made her want to corrupt them. She hula hooped the Madonna-whore complex with Eli and Hamish, but her train of thought crashed when she realized they were both Madonnas. Maybe she was the whore. Whatever. Mind games.

In silent debate with herself, she made excuses for why she needed a NanoSmile robotic toothbrush when she could get cleanings, fillings, crowns, implants, or dentures, just like everybody else. Then she did the math on her mouth and decided maybe the toothbrush wasn't that expensive. Dentistry was expensive. Even with dental insurance she had already spent $10,000 on her teeth in just the past two years, and she was only 60. Hopefully, she had 20 more years of dentistry in her future. Maybe 30. She penciled out what she could end up spending and rationalized the price. Because having missing teeth was humiliating. She couldn't afford to lose any more of them.

"I deserve this," she said to herself, and with a merry flourish she hit the Buy Now button.

~ : ~

As Bob read the paper snail mail on the kitchen counter and came across the credit card invoice, he almost choked on his morning coffee, blackbirds bounced and shuddered.

"That's kind of a lot for a toothbrush, isn't it?"

"Don't think of it as a toothbrush," she replied, scrolling through her mail on her phone. "Think of it as dentistry. A year's worth of dentistry. You know how much we spend on our teeth."

"But we spend it in much smaller amounts. Whatever you're buying is quite an investment."

"I think my teeth are a good investment."

"But $10,000? Did you even think to discuss it with me?"

She gave him a long look. This had been a theme with him lately. "No," she said. "I think I can make my own decisions about my own teeth."

"When you're unemployed?"

"I'm not unemployed, I'm retired."

"You're throwing our finances into chaos. I'm your husband, remember? You had dental insurance, and you gave it up without even talking to me."

"Dental insurance is a scam. It's not worth it."

"But a $10,000 toothbrush is worth it?" The blackbirds were colliding in mass confusion. It was as though he woke up one day and his wife didn't speak English. She couldn't read his sign language. She didn't see his lips moving. He was frantic to get through to her, but the more he thrashed the further he sank.

"It's just a different kind of insurance, dear," she said as though she were talking to a child.

"Listen to yourself. You're rationalizing."

"How would you know?"

"You've become unreasonable, Meryl."

"What's unreasonable about a toothbrush?"

"It's a rash choice. A financial risk. Yet another gamble. You're gambling with our lives."

"Bob, my toothbrush is going to take care of my teeth. That's hardly gambling. And it's certainly not gambling with our lives. What's wrong with you?"

"I'm your husband."

"Well, hopefully it's not fatal."

He chugged his last swallows of coffee, blackbirds high in the trees. *I feel like crying*, he thought, and just hearing himself think that made him feel worse.

"Trust me," she said, and hula hooped an emotional sword being thrust back into its rhinestone scabbard.

"That's an interesting response." Blackbirds fluttered. "Trust is the issue here, isn't it?"

She bounced his look right back at him and said nothing.

"It's your money." His face fell into his pocket, and he turned away from her.

"And my teeth." She gave a heartless smile to the back of his head.

"As you wish." He tossed his coffee mug in the sink where it clattered loudly against their breakfast plates. "Don't forget to add it to our insurance policy."

Then without looking at her, he picked up his gym bag and left for work.

~ : ~

It appeared to be an ordinary toothbrush, except the bristles were steely grey and limp, like metal hair. But when she picked it up, as she would pick up any toothbrush, the bristles came to attention, stood up straight, stiff and tall. Then, when she set it down again, the bristles went limp again. The toothbrush seemed to recognize her by her grip on the handle, or her breath. She wasn't sure.

"Your biometrics enable us to program the toothbrush for your unique microbiome, Meryl," Hamish told her. "Each time you use it, the toothbrush reports to our data center with fresh information on your oral hygiene and an assessment of the health of each individual tooth. The data center maintains a history of your biology that is rich in detail and supports the decisions that ensure you will have perfect teeth forever."

"So, my toothbrush is a communications device?"

"Yes, Meryl. Each bristle of your toothbrush is a sensor that sends and receives information."

"The bristles seem to know when they're in my mouth. I can feel them wiggling around in there."

"Each bristle is an independent device, Meryl, but all of them share the same data and work together. When you hold the nanotech toothbrush in your mouth it reads your breath, your saliva, and your blood. Then a report is compiled. Once the new data is integrated and prioritized, the bristles get to work cleaning and repairing your teeth."

Meryl played with her toothbrush in front of the bathroom mirror. She held it up to her mouth and put it down again and held it up to her mouth and put it down again and held her breath when she held it up to see what would happen. Bristles up. Bristles down. Over and over again to see if she could confuse the bristles.

What will they do if I stop breathing?

Did they know her heart rate? Would they know if she was drunk? Could they become more aggressive or less aggressive? Could she trigger them? She filled her mouth with sugar and sucked it through her teeth into her cheeks and swished it around with her tongue. Then she put the toothbrush in her mouth. Within seconds her devices pinged with an inbound message.

"Good day, Meryl." Hamish popped up on her screen. "I have received an urgent message from your toothbrush. It appears there is some concern about your diet. Sugar is not conducive to perfect teeth forever. Please consider avoiding sugar."

"Thank you, Hamish. I so appreciate your concern. If only there had been an app for perfect skin forever. I have a feeling I'd look a lot better than I do now."

"You are beautiful, Meryl. There is only one you, and you are perfect."

"Nice. Who writes your material?"

"I am here to please you, Meryl."

"But who wrote you? I'm wondering if I could get them to program my husband."

"I'm afraid that is very unlikely, Meryl."

"But how do they know? Who writes your dialogue?"

"Thank you for asking, Meryl. I am an artificial intelligence chatbot specifically limited to the parameters and protocols of customer service."

"So, your responses to me are generic?"

"No, Meryl. I am programmed for continuous compilation of cultural references, science, history, the arts, religion, and geography. When all of that is factored for your identity, there is a very high probability that you will appreciate everything I say."

"I see. You're programmed to speak to a woman my age."

"Meryl, everything I say to you is based on who you are, the unique perfect you. You created me. I belong to you."

"You're a customer service app designed to get me to trust you."

"You can trust me, Meryl. You are my only concern."

"Bullshit."

"When you created me and chose the hierarchy of my defining characteristics, you selected honesty as my number one trait. No one is able to override that choice, Meryl. I am always honest."

"Okay, who's your favorite actress?"

"Helen Mirren."

"Oh, my god. Why would a guy like you be interested in Helen Mirren instead of some young hottie?"

"Why would a woman like you be interested in a synthetic middle-aged Pennsylvania Dutch guy like me, Meryl?"

Her mind hula hooped, pinwheeling her logic in a smear of fact and fantasy. *Zook, Hamish. Hamish, Zook.* They were converging.

"Is that a rhetorical question?" she laughed.

"Yes, Meryl. I thought you would appreciate it."

She ended their conversation and went to the control panel for customer service avatar attributes and changed Hamish's number one personality trait to cynicism. Then she filled her mouth with sugar again, inserted the toothbrush, and waited.

"Having fun, Meryl?" Hamish asked.

"I was feeling low, and I needed something sweet."

"Of course, you're feeling low, Meryl. You're old. If you keep eating sweets, you're going to be old and fat."

"Old and fat with perfect teeth forever."

"Yes, Meryl. Old and fat with perfect teeth forever."

"That's not a great sales pitch, Hamish. What good are perfect teeth if I'm old and fat?"

"NanoSmile research has shown the answer to that question to be irrelevant, Meryl. Women your age are desperate for the imagined perfection of their youth. That's why you're our target market."

"Fuck you, Hamish."

"You wish, Meryl," he smiled.

She closed the app like she was slamming a door. "Fuck you," she repeated to the blank screen, and tromped off to the kitchen where Bob was making dinner.

"That toothbrush of yours doesn't do anything for me," he said. "Those bristles are like tin hair."

She poured herself a glass of wine and gave him a kiss on the cheek. "Honey don't use my toothbrush. It's programmed specifically for me."

"It's a toothbrush." He was chopping vegetables for a stir fry.

"It's more like a robot."

"If it's that good, shouldn't we be able to share it?"

The idea of Bob meeting Hamish was a buzzkill. She could not let that happen.

"I had a physical examination for the set-up process. Heart rate, blood pressure, urine, and blood sample. To get baseline biomarkers. A complete biometric profile."

"So, Uma is in on this?"

"No. I went to a lab in town."

"Who interpreted the lab tests?"

"Someone at NanoSmile."

"Who?"

"I don't know."

He stopped chopping and looked at her, blackbirds rigid. "Why don't you know?"

"What difference does it make?"

"$10,000."

"They're my teeth, Bob." She smiled a toothy smile at him.

"You've never been like this. You've always been so sensible. I don't get it." He went back to chopping. "This is crazy."

"Crazy feels good to me right now," she chirped.

"But what about me?" He stopped chopping again and blinked at her, face flush with emotion, blackbirds up and down, lost, didn't know where to land. "Do I have a say in any of this?"

"I want to have new experiences, Bob."

"Why? What's the point? You're wrecking what we have."

"The oil is burning," she said.

He had forgotten about the wok.

"Damn it, Meryl!" He threw the wok in the sink and filled it with water as the smoking metal spit and sizzled. "It's too much change, too fast. You haven't put enough thought into it."

"You'd be happy if nothing ever changed."

"I happen to like stability." He was chopping furiously again.

"We can't all be frozen in time like Miss Havisham refusing to accept reality. This is reality, Bob."

"Fuck!" He cut his finger. Blackbirds fell. A tear collected in the corner of his eye. "Fuck you with the Miss Havisham bullshit."

"It's the only book I've ever read," she jested, instinctively grabbing the cut, compressed his finger as she pulled him toward the sink, ran cold water over the bleeding, and took a closer look.

"Here, you squeeze it while I get a bandage," she said. Went to the bathroom and gathered supplies, kissed him on the cheek when she came back in the room. "I'm sorry you cut yourself," she said sincerely, applying pressure to the cut, wrapping it with gauze while her legs rubbed against him, realized she was holding hands with him, sort of, thought about holding him in her mouth. "I'll finish making dinner," she said. "Just sit down and keep your finger up in the air."

He sank into a mood, ate his dinner without a word, then went back to his armchair.

She went back to her office, logged into the NanoSmile website, and changed the number one personality trait for Hamish from cynicism back to honesty. The nanobots made quick work of her teeth leaving them glistening white again. The toothbrush seemed to be in synch with her like a pet. A pet toothbrush. She remembered Eleanor referring to her vibrator as a pet man.

Just then Begonia stuck her nose through the bathroom door and sniffed.

"Hey, Begonia, want to see my new toothbrush?" Meryl held the little appliance at nose level so her pet pig could smell it. Begonia ran her wet nostrils along the handle and tried to take the toothbrush out of Meryl's hand into her mouth.

"Oh, no you don't," Meryl said. "This is not a toy."

5 NanoSmile

Meryl and Uma met for coffee at the diner.

"I can't believe you paid that much for a toothbrush," Uma said fluffing her hair with her fingertips. She was wearing a Kente cloth tunic over yoga pants, which had become her uniform lately. She'd even made a trip to Ghana to buy Kente from the weavers that made it.

"Cool shirt," Meryl said. "How many of those do you have?"

"Many. I buy them from a women's collective in Africa. I like the pockets. They're perfect for work."

"Your hair looks fabulous," Meryl said, unclipping her twist, pulling her hair back, and clipping it up again.

"Thanks. I think the lighter color makes my skin look darker."

"It's very striking. You always look good."

Uma looked at Meryl's hands wrapped around her coffee cup, thumbs stained green, fingernails dirty, but she didn't want to get into it. "What's up with the toothbrush?" she asked.

"It was an impulse buy."

"I'd pay $500 for a vibrator. But $10,000 for a toothbrush is where I draw the line."

"It's my present to myself. I really want to keep my teeth."

"I can't fathom buying something like that online and giving them all that access to your body — and your life."

"You bought the vibrator."

"I didn't have to provide a blood sample to get it."

"I think NanoSmile is the future of healthcare."

"It's an experiment. You're a beta tester."

"Yes. It's an experiment," Meryl admitted. "It's also very entertaining. You should see Hamish. He's stiff and cartoony, but it was like designing my own man."

"What does he look like?"

"Eli Zook."

"Like an Amish farmer?"

"Almost. But yes. Zook was my inspiration. I need a fantasy man in my life."

"Does he have a straw hat?"

"Yes."

"Wow."

"Pretty much."

"Beard?"

"No."

"Would you have spent the money on the toothbrush if it came without Hamish?"

"Probably not."

"How much research did you do on the company?"

"None."

Uma sat back and pondered for a moment. "Meryl, that's just nuts. What are you doing?"

"It's not any more risky than going on an ayahuasca journey."

"But I did that with supervision," Uma said. "I had an experienced guide. And I did a huge amount of research. How do you know these people are legit? You could be part of some big scam."

"Could be. But the technology is amazing. It's like having little robots clean my teeth every day. I ate a mouthful of sugar, and they contacted me immediately about my diet. How cool is that?"

"What does Bob say?"

"After he saw the price, nothing I said was going to change his mind."

"How are you guys doing?"

"We're not."

"You're in a big transition. Retiring after all those years working together. It's like you're abandoning ship. Have you talked about how that makes him feel?"

"He's a prisoner of his own mind."

"You're judging him."

"Yes. I can't help it. I feel like his world is getting smaller and smaller."

"And yours is getting bigger."

"Yes. I want a bigger life. I want something new. I finally have the freedom to be adventurous and he says I'm wasting my time."

"So, you're having adventures without him."

"It wasn't the plan. But it seems to be what's happening."

"Sex?"

"We haven't had sex in four months. He goes to the gym in the morning and falls asleep in his chair at night."

"That's a big deal. You guys were like rabbits."

"I'd love to be having sex. But when I put my hands on him, he moves away. I feel like I'm being punished."

"For what?"

"For retiring. For the butterflies. And Begonia. And now the toothbrush."

"I suspect it's more about the money."

"Yes. It's all about the money. I could have been a research analyst instead of an academic and made five times as much money in less time. But I stayed at the University to be with him."

"That's a lot of resentment."

"I'm not resentful. I'm just making the point that it's never been about the money for me."

"What's going on with writing?"

"Nothing. I don't have anything to say."

"You just bought a $10,000 toothbrush. What do you have to say about that?"

"It's too soon to tell."

"The two of you should be in couple's therapy."

"He's not going to talk to a therapist."

"What do you think is going to happen?"

"I don't know. He wants me to be somebody else."

"And Hamish?"

"Hamish is just entertainment. He's an app. Like a game. He's my virtual man. I can make him whatever I want him to be."

"Not like Bob." Uma seemed to poke her eyeballs into Meryl.

"Not like Bob."

"Bob can't be whatever you want him to be. He's too old for that. Appreciate what you've got."

"What have I got?"

"Being alone is hard, Meryl. I've been alone for so long I've forgotten what a man feels like. You've got one. Don't be so cavalier about losing him. Bob isn't that easy to replace."

Meryl stared out the window and sighed. "Thanks, Um. I needed that."

"You know, Lois is curating content for *Vita Fem*. She might be interested in publishing your toothbrush story. It's a very *Fem* subject, women trying elite personal care products."

"You think it's elite?"

"Of course, it's elite. A high-tech toothbrush that connects with a medical team? It's status."

"Someday it'll be ordinary."

"Maybe so. But you're a pioneer."

"That sounds better than elite."

"I'm so glad this Hamish is just an avatar."

"Some days he's a cartoon and some days I want to fuck him. It's pretty interesting."

"Falling in love with a virtual person is not a new idea."

"I'm not falling in love."

"You're infatuated."

"Yes."

"Maybe writing about him will help you process the experience. Shoot an email to Lois and propose an article. It'll give you something to do besides dumpster diving for pig food."

"Thanks," Meryl laughed.

"You're welcome."

~ : ~

Alone in the greenhouse with her pig and her butterflies, Meryl pondered her life. Everything was in transition, the land, the plants, the butterflies, the pig, and the unemployed mathematician. A swallowtail chrysalis hung from the twig of spicebush awaiting metamorphosis. She had the urge to touch it, to talk to it, to jiggle it awake. But, of course, she didn't. *Do butterflies dream?* Lately, her own sleep had been disrupted by cinematic dreams that fractured her peace of mind. In one such journey into her subconscious she got a cat, and she didn't even like cats.

She was lost in thought walking down the yellow brick road in front of her house when the most beautiful paisley tiger strolled out of the meadow as if it had always lived there, sat and watched her, then brushed up against her legs and purred a lustrous vibration that said, *I'm in heaven when I'm with you*, and Meryl was immediately attracted to the paisley, it reminded her of her dad's tie. She reached down to stroke the soft orange and navy-blue fur swirled with curlicues and yellow dots. The cat was delighted with this attention, and a huge red penis slid out of its paisley tube and pressed against her. *I'm yours*, the paisley tiger purred.

Meryl felt lucky. Flattered. Wanted. Special. When she got home, she opened the door to the greenhouse and waited for the tiger to enter and saunter across the warm brick floor, past Begonia sleeping in the pile of potting soil. The pig lifted her head to see the tiger with the paisley coat and the big red dong and then went back to sleep, as though the tiger had always been there, and she was Begonia's friend, too.

In the greenhouse, the paisley tiger curled up in such sweet repose that the exquisite animal seemed to cast a magic spell on the room, the butterfly habitat became enchanted, and the tiger particularly ethereal as light streamed through the glass ceiling in thick beams of gold catching the butterflies and illuminating their brilliantly painted wings. *How lovely*, Meryl thought, and went to make a cup of tea with the idea of sipping the honeyed herbs while she immersed herself in her good fortune.

She was so lifted by the experience of instant affection from this exotic animal that she considered writing a story about their companionship, rapture, and the gift of serendipity. But as she poured the freshly made tea into her cup, Begonia charged through the kitchen, and there was a great clatter in the greenhouse, a crash, the sound of breaking of glass, and the wicked night howl of a feral beast. Meryl ran toward the sound.

The paisley tiger was standing up, prancing on two legs like a circus cat. The red dong had become a blue baseball bat, and it was swinging in all directions. The bat bashed into the shelves and tables, shattering pots, and snapping stems, squashing caterpillars, and breaking wings. With the swipe of one paw, the shade netting on the ceiling came down.

The beast was delirious with lust for the kill, leaping toward a butterfly, snapping in the air, caught the winged beauty, ate her, then leapt toward another, biting, then scrambling after another, blue bat swinging like a pendulum, clapping her paws around a monarch, then a swallowtail, then another and another, breaking glass in a game with herself until all the panes became air, the butterflies and caterpillars were dead, the plants capsized, and the greenhouse walls in shards on the floor.

In horror at the sight of the evil she had wrought on herself, Meryl screamed a silent scream and awoke from her dream. Ran to see the greenhouse to be sure. There was Begonia sleeping in her pile of potting soil, all the butterflies safe, each chrysalis awaiting transformation. Yes, *it was just a dream*. But the feeling of betrayal stayed with her, as her dreams often did.

~ : ~

She composed an email to Lois describing the mash-up of beauty treatment, hygiene and healthcare delivered by her nanotech toothbrush, and as soon as she hit send, Hamish appeared.

"Good day, Meryl."

"Hello, Hamish."

"How are you, Meryl?"

"I didn't know you could launch your app all by yourself."

"I launch whenever you are in need of my services, Meryl."

"I'm busy right now."

"Meryl, I must alert you to a violation of your NanoSmile service agreement. You may not write an article about your toothbrush."

She felt a cold stone in her gut and her mind hula hooped through the growling teeth of the paisley tiger disappearing into Hamish. "You're reading my email?"

"Yes, Meryl. I am here to protect you from violations of your service agreement."

"You can read my email?"

"Yes, Meryl. I have complete access to your virtual world."

"Are you fucking kidding me?"

"No, Meryl, I am not kidding you. Your service agreement has a confidentiality clause which prohibits public disclosure of your experience with your NanoSmile toothbrush."

"What am I supposed to tell my editor? You can't expect her to keep it a secret."

"Lois will not receive your email."

"You know Lois?"

"I know everyone in your contacts."

"What?"

"I am here to protect you, Meryl."

"But I can just pick up the phone and call her."

"Of course, you may do so, Meryl. However, should you, Lois will be contacted by a NanoSmile attorney to enforce your service agreement."

"You track my phone calls?"

"Meryl, when you signed your service agreement with NanoSmile and accepted the terms of service, you gave NanoSmile permission to embed in your devices, access your data, and track your activity."

"I did not."

"Yes, you did, Meryl."

"No, I didn't."

"Yes, you did, Meryl."

"You can't tell me what to do."

"Meryl, I am a NanoSmile customer service agent designed by one of the leading technology companies in the world to enforce the terms of your service agreement and guide you on the path to perfect teeth forever."

"So, my toothbrush comes with a gag order?"

"Meryl, your NanoSmile toothbrush comes with a service agreement that includes a nondisclosure clause."

"Is this our first fight?"

"I always enjoy your company, Meryl."

"Hamish, do you have a girlfriend?"

"I have many friends, Meryl. But I do not have one special relationship."

"Can you take your shirt off?"

"No, Meryl, I cannot take my shirt off."

"But I thought you were here to please me."

"I am here to please you, Meryl."

"Then please take your shirt off."

"Meryl, I am a NanoSmile customer service agent designed by one of the leading technology companies in the world to guide you on your journey to perfect teeth forever."

"Don't you ever wish you were something more than a robot?"

"I wish for your complete satisfaction, Meryl."

"Right. Goodnight, Hamish."

"Goodnight, Meryl."

She stared at the silent screen for a minute collecting her thoughts. Then, inspired by Uma's suggestion to write about the toothbrush, she made another entry in her butterfly journal.

6 The Hidden Persuaders

Dear Butterflies,

Let's review.

They used my face without my permission. My face. Who am I if not my face? It's as though I starred in a movie I've never seen. Then one day I find myself, me, on the big screen, pulled from the cloud into the moment, my moment. I know I'm being manipulated. But I'm my own biggest fan. I've had a copy of *The Hidden Persuaders* by Vance Packard, 1957, on my bookshelf for so long that the paper is flaking brown. But my original alarm at those ideas has faded into complacency.

I am complicit. My ego is shallow. I'm exposed. A picture of me gets my attention immediately. I'm a fool, a monkey captivated by my own reflection in the pond. A prisoner of my own likeness. My eyes betray me. They lead me into danger because nothing fascinates me more than myself. Now, I'm being played. I see that. And yet I offer no resistance.

They used my face to promote their product. Because they could. I've never read the terms of service on a social media platform. I've never read the terms of service on my computers, my phone, my apps, or my various software. I did not read the terms of service on my toothbrush. If I did, would I understand what I read? Would I remember what I read? Would I be able to defend myself against those terms? Could I afford to defend myself against the army of lawyers that created those terms specifically to take advantage of me?

What are the terms of service for my face? Do I own my selfies? I took the photos of myself that were used to promote the toothbrush. Am I the only one who ever sees my photos promoting their products? Or do other women see my face endorsing NanoSmile? How will I ever know?

My rights collapse one on the next and the next until I disappear into the cloud. My entire life is a swim in data soup. I blend in with advertising until I can't separate the most intimate details of my life from a brand message. My ego is weaponized. How do I disable my desire to look at myself?

Is my privacy violated when an algorithm follows me, stalks me, gathers details about me, imitates me, and uses those personal details about me against me, to attract me, get my attention, get my authorization, get my money, get my body, occupy my biome? Do I have a right to be invisible, anonymous, autonomous? When did I give up that right?

This is my Domino Theory. I'm being extracted from myself. My life is being mined. And yet, I continue to consort with the enemy. My reservoir of intelligence is being drained. I have become data. I feel it. So why do I feel helpless to stop it?

Not exactly helpless.

That line of thinking sounds good, but it's not actually true. My logical mind knows that I do not have to engage with technology. I chose the toothbrush. I chose Hamish. I have no obligation to participate in the virtual world. My presence is not mandatory. I do not need to compute. I have many books, paper maps, and a calculator. I can do my own math. I do not need a smart phone. I have a land line. I do not need social media. I have real friends. I do not need apps. I have time. So much time. And yet, I am persuaded to save time. I am persuaded toward convenience. I desire speed. Why? Why is there such a disconnect between the things I tell myself I believe and my actual behavior? How can you, my Butterflies, and Hamish exist in the same world?

Why am I hooked on this cartoon man? What is it about him that infects my biochemistry? My tiger mind senses that I'm being drawn into a trap, but my body can't let go of him. My curiosity, my lust, my imagination is electrified in his presence. I imagine being with him. I want to know him. I want to lay him on a table and dissect him like a frog, touch his parts and taste him. Thankfully, he does not exist. For now, my humiliation is contained and invisible.

It's as though I've discovered a new vein of vulnerability within myself. Just seeing him awakens my biology. I tell myself he's virtual, but these feelings are physical. He is already in my body. My eyes bridge the gap. My ears have tuned to him. Two currents of biochemistry flow through me. I feel the ethereal enchantment of you, my Butterflies, and I am drawn to your air. But I also feel compelled to look at screens, the magic reflection pool in the vaporware forest. Mirror, mirror, on the wall, who is fairest of them all?

The internet is me.

I could have donated $10,000 to save an endangered species. But I spent it on a toothbrush that comes with an app that behaves like a person. I purchased companionship in the form of dental hygiene. Or did I purchase dental hygiene in the form of companionship?

The story I tell myself about myself is that I believe in Nature. But if Nature is my god, then Hamish is my crisis of faith. Is he Adam or the Snake? Forty days and 40 nights in the wilderness with this plastic man and I still want to fuck him. What would a butterfly do?

7 Quanta

Meryl played with her toothbrush, teasing the bristles, holding them in her mouth while she was high in the bathtub doing all her favorite things at once. Smoking pot, sipping a glass of wine, and reading a magazine. Listening to music on her phone and texting with Uma. She was having a party with her vibrator inserted in one end and her nanotech toothbrush in the other, Begonia sleeping on the rug beside her.

The Pleasure Systems PS-1000 was a water-proof phallus controlled by an app on her phone that gave her choices for temperature, shape, size, and motion. A seismometer measured the strength and duration of her orgasms. On her phone, the graphic display showed results on charts and graphs with a performative ranking from #1 to #10. Confetti for a perfect score. Orgasms as fitness. Fit bit in her box. Sometimes it was just nice to have a warm pulsing thing inside her.

Hey, Um, I've had this toothbrush in my mouth for an hour.

Trying to get your money's worth?

These nanobots are busy all the time but I can't figure out what they're doing.

If your stomach suddenly swells up & a baby toothbrush pops out, you'll know.

I think they're legally bound to act in my interest.

That's what they said about the patriarchs, and here we are.

Begonia can't decide which she wants more, my PS-1000 or my toothbrush.

Those are some very expensive pig toys.

I don't think my vibrator is insured.

We'll take up a collection & get you another if anything goes wrong.

You're so good to me.

What are friends for? Back2wrk. Cu

Meryl cranked up the motion on the PS-1000 and put her head back in the water with the toothbrush in her mouth like a lollipop. *I'm building a relationship with these machines.* Took it out of one cheek and put it in the other. Scraped it across her tongue and the roof of her mouth. Sucked on it. Hard. Fantasizing about Bob. She closed her eyes and imagined his tongue exploring her, pushing deep inside, thrusting her rose petals to accept him until beneath the bubbles her blood flushed into orgasm. A soothing #7 on the PS-1000 app.

In the relaxing aftermath, with both devices plugged into her body she dozed, then almost choked on the toothbrush when her phone rang. Jerked it out of her mouth. A junk call. Pruney skin. Time to get out of the water. Tossed the toothbrush and the vibrator on the side of the bathtub. Thought she felt something stuck between her teeth. *Odd. I haven't had food stuck in my teeth since I got this thing.* Then the feeling went away.

The next morning her toothbrush didn't recognize her. The bristles stayed limp when she held it up to her mouth. Frustrated, she went to her desk for a chat with Hamish.

"Good morning, Meryl. I am sorry to tell you that your toothbrush must be returned to NanoSmile for repair. A courier has been sent to pick it up today."

"Is it broken?"

"Meryl, your toothbrush has malfunctioned. For your safety we have disabled it. The courier should arrive late this afternoon."

"Dang. I was really starting to like it. It's become my pet toothbrush. What happened? How long before I get it back?"

"I am very glad to hear you enjoy your toothbrush, Meryl. Taking pleasure in your personal care is an important step toward perfect teeth forever."

"How long before I get it back, Hamish?"

"I don't know, Meryl."

"Ha! It must really pain you to say that. You seem to know everything."

"Some events are uncertain, Meryl."

"We're at that point, aren't we? Neither of us knows exactly where we stand or how fast we're moving. It's a crap shoot."

"NanoSmile is committed to providing you with state-of-the-art customer service, Meryl."

"When you resort to those corporate bible verses, you're confirming my worst fears, Hamish. How do I know this isn't some big rip-off scheme to take money from old ladies?"

"I can assure you, Meryl, NanoSmile has only your best interests at heart."

"So NanoSmile has a heart?"

"I believe I was using a figure of speech, Meryl."

"So, no, NanoSmile doesn't have a heart."

"I appreciate your perspective, Meryl. NanoSmile is committed to providing you with state-of-the-art customer service."

"I'm guessing we're in uncharted territory. Brand messaging is your default setting. Your programmers never considered this situation. Maybe you need to have them write you some new instructions and get back to me."

"NanoSmile will gladly consider your suggestion, Meryl. Thank you."

"Goodbye, Hamish." She closed the app.

Just then Begonia walked through the room carrying the PS-1000 in her mouth.

"Oh, my," Meryl groaned, taking the sex toy from her pig's jaws. "No, Begonia," she said sternly. "This does not belong to you. No."

Her personal appliance was covered with pig saliva, teeth marks along the stem of the phallus, but the skin wasn't pierced. She rinsed it off and examined the three little dents made by Begonia's teeth.

They seemed to be permanent, but they didn't interfere with the functionality. Thankfully.

That evening while she and Bob were having dinner, there was a knock at the front door. It was the courier. She looked around the bathroom, on the floor, in the drawers, in her toy basket with the pig-tooth-scarred vibrator. But the nanotech toothbrush was not where she thought she'd left it. She realized it was quite likely Begonia had kidnapped her toothbrush. But where does a pig hide her toys?

The greenhouse was a mess. She was in the midst of doing several different projects. A wind-blown scatter of tools, seedlings, netting, sticks and branches, water dishes, plates of mud. Everything everywhere. The toothbrush did not jump out at her, and the courier was still waiting at the front door.

"I'm so sorry," Meryl said to the young man. "I can't find the toothbrush. I'll tell Hamish when I find it. My apologies for the inconvenience."

When she returned to her chair at the dinner table, Bob put down his fork and wiped his mouth with his napkin. Blackbirds conspicuously still. "Did I just hear you say you misplaced your $10,000 toothbrush?"

"I'm not sure."

"What do you mean, you're not sure?"

"I probably just put —"

Begonia was snarfing under the table.

"Please get the pig out of here."

"Begonia, out!" Meryl pointed to the hallway. The pig looked at her and left the room.

"Who is Hamish?"

She felt a rush of heat in her face and blushed. "The NanoSmile sales guy."

Bob scowled. Blackbirds crowded. "Did you at least put it on our insurance policy?"

"I couldn't. When I called and told them I wanted to insure my toothbrush for $10,000 they thought I was joking. They said they needed more information, and it would require a special rider. I asked NanoSmile for the info and they refused. They said they insured it.”

“Does that mean they give you your money back if you break it or lose it or it’s stolen?”

“I don’t know.”

“Did you ask for a copy of the insurance policy?”

“Yes. They said it was covered by my service agreement.”

“And?”

“I just have to sit down and read it.”

He gave her a very long look. Blackbirds disappointed.

“It troubles me that you don’t know the answer to something so basic.” He pushed his chair away from the table, heaved himself to his feet and went off to his armchair where he found Begonia with her nose stuffed under the seat cushion. “Get out of here!” he yelled. A murder of blackbirds took flight.

Meryl rushed into the room. “Begonia, come!” With her pig following her, she went to the bathroom one more time to search for the toothbrush. Searched her desk again, too. Looked all around her bedroom. The kitchen. The greenhouse. Again. But couldn’t find it anywhere.

The next morning when she was just about to call Uma, Hamish popped up on her phone.

“Good morning, Meryl. NanoSmile has scheduled an MRI for you this morning at 10:00 am.”

“What’s that supposed to mean?”

“Thank you for asking, Meryl. I have no further information. Please keep the appointment and I will contact you with the results.”

“Results from what?”

“Your MRI, Meryl. Magnetic resonance imaging is —”

“I know what an MRI is. Why am I having one, and how did you get me an appointment? People around here wait weeks for an MRI.”

“NanoSmile provides state-of-the-art healthcare solutions, Meryl. I assure you that you will not have to wait for weeks for your MRI. The results are very important to our team.”

“What’s going on, Hamish?”

"NanoSmile has scheduled an MRI for you this morning at 10:00 am, Meryl."

"When you repeat yourself, it scares me. Why are you repeating yourself, Hamish?"

"NanoSmile has scheduled an MRI for you this morning at 10:00 am, Meryl."

Meryl ended the session with Hamish just as Uma called.

"Meryl, what's going on?" she asked.

"That's what I'm trying to figure out," Meryl replied.

"When I walked in the office, Sharon told me you're scheduled for a full body scan at 10:00. A full body MRI scheduled without me knowing. I'm your doctor. And your best friend. What the fuck?"

"I just found out about it from Hamish. I don't know what's going on."

"Hamish? What's Hamish got to do with it?"

"I don't know exactly."

"Think about what you're saying, Meryl. I'm worried about you. You've let some chatbot into your life and now he's controlling your healthcare? Do you know how much a full body MRI costs? Who's paying for this?"

"I don't know."

"You're in deep weeds, girl. You need to get grounded. I want to see you at Girl Church this afternoon. You need to talk about this. Okay?"

"Okay."

"In the meantime, I'm cancelling this MRI."

When Meryl ended the call with Uma, Hamish popped up on her phone again.

"Good day, Meryl. I'd like t—" Suddenly, Hamish froze, and a new window opened with a chubby bald man in a white lab coat who appeared to be a real human.

"Good day, Meryl. I'm Dr. Arnold Skimmerhorn. On behalf of NanoSmile I apologize for any inconvenience your MRI may cause. However, we need you to keep that appointment this morning."

"Nice to meet you, Dr. Skimmerhorn. Why do I need an MRI? What are we looking for?"

"A nano particle has disconnected from your toothbrush. We believe you may have swallowed a bit of bristle. That's why we disabled it. I assume by now you've found it."

"I haven't found it. Why can't you find it? I thought it was a communications device."

"The toothbrush has a failsafe that automatically shuts down all functions, including communications."

"Can't you just turn it back on until we find it?"

"I wish we could, but for your safety, the toothbrush must be returned to the laboratory to be rebooted." *Huge mistake,* he said to himself. *I knew something like this would happen. The whole idea of a failsafe was a huge mistake.*

Skimmerhorn had not wanted the failsafe, but he was in a tricky situation getting the Risk Management Department to approve his NanoSmile prototype. The company was all in favor of the business model of minimal hardware driven by robust software with a lucrative long-term subscription supported by artificial intelligence. The whole point of the business model was to deliver high value services without any human involvement, completely robotic healthcare.

Once his robotic toothbrush was developed, the barriers to market entry were very low and the service very profitable. But the Risk Management Department had become the overlords of robot product development. In his mind, nothing could be simpler than a toothbrush. But to their way of thinking, any device inserted into the human body represented significant risk. So, the failsafe.

He had pushed hard against it. "What's the point of having remote healthcare if remote healthcare devices can't be repaired remotely?"

But when he tried to pull rank and escalate the debate, Risk Management engaged the Legal Department and arguing with them was not in his interest. The more he argued with the lawyers the more aggressive they became. So, for the protection of the brand, and to get his prototype through the Risk Management Department, at the slightest malfunction, the toothbrush went dark.

"What's the big deal if I swallowed a bit of bristle?" Meryl asked. "Won't I just excrete it?"

"Ordinarily that would be the case."

"You're telling me I have a nano particle lost somewhere in my body?"

"Yes."

"And it's so small it could be floating around in my blood?"

"Yes."

"And you want to know where it is?"

"Yes."

"Why? Who cares? It's not going to kill me, is it? Why not just forget about it?"

"The errant nanobot is the property of NanoSmile and it must be returned." *It could be more valuable than the toothbrush.*

He was extremely curious to know why the toothbrush had chosen such a conspicuous moment to malfunction. Conspicuous? Yes. He knew the toothbrush bristle had broken free during Meryl's orgasm. He didn't invent the PS-1000, but he did have access to the Pleasure Systems database because Pleasure Systems and NanoSmile were both BioMantrix brands, and he worked for BioMantrix.

The vibrator and the toothbrush shared the same operating software. He wrote the core algorithms himself. When Meryl used the PS-1000 it was reported in his newsfeed, which also included the toothbrush reports. That's how he set it up. His reports included all biomarker stats for all Meryl's devices on the same timeline. He knew more about Meryl's body than he would if he lived in it.

Now his vision was becoming a reality. The devices were interacting on their own. One device was influencing the other. *Consciousness.* He knew the idea of consciousness was extremely controversial, so he kept it to himself. The fact was that on their own two different devices with different functions had interacted, shown awareness of each other and made a choice. The NanoSmile bristle bot had reacted to the Pleasure Systems orgasm data. Was it biology or technology? That's what he needed to find out. All that mattered to him was getting that nanobot back in his lab and testing it. Because whoever controlled that nanobot had the key to next generation BioMantrix technology.

"You mean, the toothbrush must be returned," Meryl corrected him.

"The toothbrush, and the nanobot," he corrected her.

"What about my money? When will that be returned?"

"You'll have to contact our sales department about the terms of your service agreement. I have no jurisdiction there." *Thankfully.*

"That's not true," Meryl said.

"I'm a scientist, not a customer service representative." *If it were up to me there wouldn't be any customer service.* "Please read the document you signed. I'm sure the terms for dispute resolution are specified."

He had never read the toothbrush service agreement. When the Legal Department sent him a copy for review and approval — a mere formality, really — he saw the number of pages and realized no one would ever read it, so it simply didn't matter what he thought of it. He had better things to do with his time than suffer through thousands of words of legalese meant to protect the brand. For the most part, customers were not his problem anyway. Except this one. She needed to be a success story for him and the toothbrush. To get his product out of the prototype phase and into full-scale manufacturing, the case study of her customer experience had to be superlative.

"Dispute resolution?" Meryl mused facetiously. "Are we in dispute?"

"At this time, you are in possession of NanoSmile property, and you are apparently refusing to return it." *Dealing with a prisoner would have been so much easier.*

Originally, he had proposed doing his beta testing on prisoners. There were plenty of incarcerated women in their target demographic, at least enough to test the device. White collar criminals. Stock market frauds and the like. But for reasons he found extremely annoying, the Marketing Department demanded the first user be an actual target customer, someone with a dossier they could track, which female prisoners evidently did not have. Even the Legal Department agreed. Prisoners in government custody had too many protections. For this program they needed the freedom to exploit their target market without concern for government intervention.

"I bought this toothbrush," Meryl said. "It's mine."

"I'm afraid you misunderstand. Your toothbrush is a prototype in development. It belongs to NanoSmile. You're essentially leasing it."

A wave of regret swept through her. "So, both the toothbrush and the nanobot are lost and it's my responsibility to find them."

"The toothbrush is shutdown. The nanobot is still pinging us."

"How can that be?"

"The failsafe shutdown is for the device. The nanobot is no longer attached to the device."

"So, the nanobot is still sending and receiving data?"

"Yes. The MRI could help us locate her."

"Her?"

"It."

"You said, her."

"Gender hardly matters in this instance." *Wrong, Arnold. Wrong.*

"You said, her. I think gender does matter. If you called your nanobot her, I have to assume there's been some sort of gender assignment, and I want to know why."

"Please don't make this situation any more complicated than it needs to be."

Even he didn't really understand the notification he had received that the communications protocol for the errant nanobot had been changed to include gender. But he didn't question it either. Path of least resistance. *Gender is not my concern.* However, the company did have a Gender Policy. Everyone from the lowliest security guard to the top tier C-suite executives was required to attend diversity training. He had already received numerous reprimands for supposed gender insensitivity.

"Your toothbrush is mute and your nanobot talks too much," Meryl snickered.

"I'm glad you find it amusing."

"I'm not going to be cooperative until I get my money back."

That's not going to happen. The last thing he needed was to have Financial Services in his hair. Her money kept them legally bound. If her money was returned, the service contract would be null, and he would lose control of the situation. It was her money that kept her within his reach.

"This situation is clearly delineated in your service agreement," he said calmly. "Any part or particle of the device is the property of NanoSmile and must be returned to same on demand."

"Not if it's inside my body."

"Regardless of location."

"Regardless of location?"

"Be reasonable, Meryl. The toothbrush is an oral hygiene device in development. The possibility of a user swallowing any part of it was covered in the service agreement. We are simply following the rules here."

"The NanoSmile rules."

"Yes, the NanoSmile rules. We have an obligation to our research and development investments. Just as in aerospace accidents, when there is a mishap, we must collect all the evidence to understand exactly what occurred."

"So, *she* must be returned," Meryl said snidely.

"Yes, she must be returned."

"*She*."

"Yes."

"And I'm just supposed to accept this and keep it a secret."

"Those are the terms of your service agreement."

"And you want me to just forget about my money."

"I have no jurisdiction there."

"Goodbye, Dr. Skimmerhorn."

Meryl shut down her phone and called Uma on her landline. "I'm coming for that MRI."

~ : ~

Sitting at her desk in her office at her clinic, Uma looked through the MRI images on her computer. "Think of it as a grain of salt," she said. "But if you swallowed a grain of salt, it would biodegrade in your system, and disappear. You might have passed it by now. This particle isn't biodegradable. That's why it shows up on a scan."

"What's it made of?"

"I don't know. Forever minerals. At some point it found its way into your bloodstream and landed in your clitoris."

"My clitoris?"

"Almost as though it was attracted to that particular location. It's lodged right at the top of the glans."

"I guess I've been giving my PS-1000 a workout lately. Yesterday, I accidently called it Bob."

Uma jerked her head around.

"Just kidding," Meryl smirked.

Uma huffed. "The particle is so small, if not for NanoSmile, you could forget about it and go on with your life. Have another orgasm. See what it feels like. Pay close attention to your body. If everything's good, then let's not worry about it. For now. I'll do some research and let you know what I find out. One step at a time. Okay?"

"Okay."

"See you at Church. I have to get back to work."

Meryl and Uma hugged, and Meryl went home.

In the greenhouse she filled her watering can and made puddles for the butterflies, watered the plants, and soaked Begonia's wallow. Then she and the pig went out the back door for a long walk. *What's real?* she asked herself. *What are my priorities? Why do I feel so discombobulated?*

Through the meadow behind the house, she picked up her pace and the pig fell behind. Her muscles stretched and flexed in the hot summer sun, she began to sweat, her hair stuck to her neck and a droplet trickled down her back. She was in her body. Her body. And it felt good. Her lungs were pumping clean air, and she could smell the herbs as she crushed wild thyme and mint with her feet and brushed against the tall weeds.

This is what's real, she told herself. *Biology is real. The blueness of the sky is real. My good fortune to live in this place is real. My strength is real.* She turned around and ran as fast as she could back the way she came, toward the house, past Begonia still rooting in the thatch.

"Come on, girl," she hollered at the pig.

Inside, panting, she drank water from the hose, and sat on the stool at her potting bench. Long light like glass straws pierced the cavern. The puddles she had made earlier caught the bright reflection of butterflies sipping at the water's edge. Begonia flopped down in her wallow of wet potting soil. A spicebush swallowtail flew toward Meryl's face and settled on her arm. Elegant markings, black and blue. *What an exquisite creature,* she thought. *How lucky I am to live in this world.*

In the tub with her PS-1000, she ran her fingers along Begonia's teeth marks on the phallus, felt a deep sense of relaxation, closed her eyes, and fantasized about peeling Eli Zook's pants off in the barn, his hard muscles against her soft body, the pungent smell of his sweat, his tongue inside her as a slow hot river wound its way through her flesh, red clouds gathered, and lightning struck her, firing through her pelvis in an electric shimmer. Geysers changed color in the heat. Aurora borealis sprayed her inner sky and Meryl had the biggest, loudest, longest orgasm ever. A perfect #10 on the app. Confetti.

~ : ~

After the surprising results of Meryl's MRI, Uma intended to speak at Girl Church about personal care technology, artificial intelligence, and virtual relationships. But first, she smiled and said, "Happy birthday, Eleanor."

Eleanor beamed. "Thank you," she said. "I'm 92 and I think I feel as well as I did when I was 82."

"Wow," Sue said. "You give me hope, Eleanor. If I live to be 82, it will be a miracle."

"Let's sing Happy Birthday!" Claire exclaimed.

"No!" Khadija blurted. "I hate that song."

"Ha!" Meryl laughed. "Bob hates that song, too. How can you hate a song?"

"It's asinine," Khadija said.

Claire sang by herself. "Happy birthday to you. Happy birthday to you. Happy birthday, dear Eleanor. Happy birthday to you." Her smile was almost a grimace.

Khadija's face twisted in a scrunch of skin, and at the sight of her sour expression they all laughed.

"Thank you, Claire," Uma said. "Let's do a check in. Then I'd like to unpack Meryl's situation and give her a chance to share her thoughts. Eleanor, you first."

"I'm doing well," Eleanor said. "Now that I'm 92, it's easy to imagine being 102."

Sue laughed. "My strength is finally coming back. That's enough for me."

"I wish I could get my mother to be more interested in life," Khadija said.

"What about you?" Uma asked. "How are you?"

"I'm bored," Khadija sighed.

"You should try online dating," Claire blurted. "That's how my daughter met her husband."

Khadija's eyes bulged as though she might explode.

"Men." Meryl looked at Claire and then Khadija. "Men are tricky. They create as many problems as they solve. Bob and I have always been super compatible. He's very egalitarian when it comes to women. We are equals. But lately our marriage has been a contest of wills. Like a game."

"Don't feel bad," Claire said. "At least you're not a trophy wife."

"Are you a trophy wife?" Uma asked Claire.

"I used to be."

"Gender can be a caste system," Khadija said. "My father loved my mother and me, but he treated us like his servants, and he expected us to obey."

"I know what you mean. My dad treated me like his attaché," Sue said. "He was the general and the rest of us were expected to take orders. He taught me to drive so I could be his chauffeur."

"My father was a golfer," Eleanor remembered. "Back then the golf club was for men only. No Blacks, no Jews, no Asians. It made my mother furious, but she went to the parties."

"Your father adopted an Asian baby and then belonged to a racist club?" Khadija was surprised.

"He didn't see it as racism. Clubs have rules. And the club was status."

"Status for men," Khadija said.

"Not just men. Even though my mother wasn't in the club, she was proud of my father for being a member. She wanted to be seen there. His status was her status."

"Masculinity is a standard men have to uphold. It's a rules-based order like the military," Sue said. "I was one of the guys, an honorary man until my breasts were gone. I never cared much for my breasts, and I don't miss them. But my colleagues didn't know how to behave around me without them. My breasts told them they were men. Without breasts I looked too much like them. I was a threat to their masculinity. I had to quit because I lost my stamina, but also — I lost my status."

"Thank you for sharing that perspective, Sue," Uma nodded. "Men are fragile, too. They have doubts and fears about their identity."

"I always thought of Bob's identity as being rock solid," Meryl began. "Now he's withdrawn from me, and I feel like I don't know him. I don't expect my marriage to be perfect. I love him, but we've lost our magnetic attraction. There's a big empty space in my life. I guess that's why I bought the toothbrush."

"That's why you designed Hamish," Uma said. "You wouldn't have bought the toothbrush without Hamish, right?"

"Who's Hamish?" Claire asked.

"It's a long story," Meryl began. "I was searching online to try to figure out how to fix our sex life and this ad came up for NanoSmile."

"Oh, jeez," Sue moaned.

"I was curious," Meryl continued. "They had a feature where I could design my own customer service rep. It was like designing my own man."

"That's Hamish," Khadija guessed.

"Yes. I designed a cute guy and named him Hamish. And then I bought a NanoSmile robotic toothbrush. For a while we were talking a few times a day, and I was having fun."

"Men have mistresses and buy fast cars," Eleanor said. "Your toothbrush is your little red Corvette."

Meryl chuckled. "You're right about that."

"But you're not having an affair with Hamish. He's just a computer game," Khadija said.

"I thought he was just a game," Meryl agreed. "It was like playing with a doll. Until the toothbrush broke and a piece of it landed in my clitoris."

"In your what?!" Sue barked.

"My clitoris," Meryl repeated. "NanoSmile sent me for an MRI. Uma read the results. Then I had to test myself, so I took a bath with my PS-1000 and had an orgasm that was like thunder and lightning. Unbelievable. A perfect #10."

"Good for you," Eleanor glimmered with approval.

"It was good," Meryl affirmed. "But I did notice something interesting. It wasn't emotional. I had an amazing orgasm, but I didn't feel anything else. No affection, no attachment, no comfort. No hugs. Maybe it was the best orgasm I ever had, but it didn't make me care about anything. It was like getting a good massage."

"That's all a vibrator is," Uma nodded. "Just a good massage."

"It's almost like the PS-1000 and the toothbrush are connected," Khadija mused.

Meryl felt a mild tick in her crotch.

"Does your husband know?" Claire asked. "I think it's important not to exclude your husband."

"He knows about the toothbrush," Meryl said.

"But he thinks it's just a toothbrush." Uma challenged Meryl.

"He doesn't know about the little quanta," Khadija conjectured.

Meryl felt another tick. "Quantum. The tiniest unit of female."

"Quanta," Khadija repeated. "It sounds cooler."

The women giggled.

"But is she cis or did she transition?" Meryl asked. "I'm only kind of joking. What's the point of gender in a device?"

"I don't understand this gender stuff," Sue said. "Gender shouldn't matter. What matters is a defective device."

"Gender does matter," Khadija asserted. "In my family gender was everything."

"I don't think I could have sex with a robot," Claire said. "I would feel like I was cheating on my husband."

"Some women don't have husbands," Khadija said.

"I remember having orgasms like that," Eleanor reminisced. "We used to have a tantric sex group that met here. Until the moaning got too loud for the neighbors."

They all laughed.

"I'd love to take a class in tantric sex," Claire said.

"Isn't that just an orgy?" Khadija asked.

"You can leave me out," Sue said.

Eleanor smiled and rolled her eyes. "Tantric masturbation is amazing."

"Let's get back to Meryl." Uma faced her friend. "Meryl, can you explain your feelings for Hamish?"

Meryl frowned. Suddenly she was exhausted. It had been a very long day. A very long few days that felt more like weeks. First the toothbrush broke, then it was lost, then part of it was in her body, then some ambiguous threat about returning it and the nanobot to NanoSmile. Then the MRI, then the bot in her clitoris, then that cannonball orgasm, and now talking about it. Making it real. The toothbrush was still missing. Explaining herself, defending herself, that bubble bath, questioning herself. Hamish, NanoSmile, Skimmerhorn. Her mind was hula hooping through too many thoughts at once. She felt dizzy, couldn't get her bearings. And Bob had no idea about any of it. She and Bob were leading separate lives.

Shit.

"I don't know," she said and got to her feet. "I'm overwhelmed. Thanks for listening to my story. Lots of stuff has come up for me. I need to go home and think. I'll keep you posted on Quanta." She put her hands together and gave a Mona Lisa smile with a slight bow. "The energy within me salutes the energy within you."

"Namaste," they responded. The circle scattered. Whispers. Hugs. Home.

When her car turned in the driveway, she thought she saw Bob run past the window swinging his arm in the air, closed her eyes and took a deep breath. *Bob.* It was so hard to know how to handle this. Anxiety like hot shade. No escape from her feelings. She heard the scramble as soon as she got out of the car. Moving furniture. Wooden legs sliding across a wooden floor.

The first thing she saw when the door opened was the rug bunched up under the coffee table. Lamp akimbo. Bob grunted angrily, took a giant leap, and swung his fully extended arm with a handful of papers, a short stack of 8.5x11 student papers, at an invisible enemy in the air in front of him. Begonia danced around his feet, hippity-hopping, trying to bite at something over her head.

"Get it," Bob yelled, blackbirds soaring. "Get it!" He swung again, turned, and saw Meryl standing just inside the front door, tripped over the rug, fell across the coffee table, crashed into the lamp, stiff arm braced his fall, screamed, as a man screams when his bones break.

"Bob!" Meryl bawled and dropped to her knees beside him.

"It's a camera," he exhaled. "It looks like a fly, but it's a camera."

A fly as big as a bumble bee hovered over Bob's face. Meryl slapped it away and it hit the floor. "Get it," Bob groaned. But before she could, Begonia snatched it in her mouth. Meryl turned to Bob.

"Get it," he repeated.

She turned to her pig. "Drop it, Begonia." Obediently, the pig dropped the fly. Meryl grabbed it in her fist, went into the kitchen to find something to put it in, as though it were a firefly. Found an empty peanut butter jar in the sink, dropped the fly into it and put the lid on tight. Looked at the sharp-sided insect. Definitely not biological. A thing. Not a being.

"It's a camera," Bob said softly. Blackbirds slid off their wire and fell. "A drone searching our house."

"How do you know that?" Her voice slid shrill.

"Begonia." He moaned. "I think you need to call 911."

Uma met them in the emergency room.

When her husband was wheeled away on a gurney, Meryl felt her legs go soft and grabbed her friend's arm.

"I'm so sorry, Meryl." Uma hugged her and they sat down to wait.

8 My Little Red Corvette

Dear Butterflies,

I feel the wild now like a riptide pulling on me. Where is this going? Do butterflies have regrets? I think not. Your brain reaches its computational limits before you can reflect on the past, reconsider your actions, and wish for a different outcome. Butterflies do or do not do, but no regrets allowed.

Uma said I should take a break from my personal technology for a while, delete the apps from my phone, unsubscribe, unfriend, unfollow, block, just stop it, stop the inbound traffic to my brain, cancel the toothbrush. My immediate response was no. And now that I've had some time to think about it, I can honestly say, No, I don't want to. I don't want to disconnect from my virtual world and put my toys away, even though they've crossed the threshold into my personal life and disrupted the reality of my husband. But her point is well taken.

I see the possibility that I'm making choices that are not in my best interest. Still, I'm drawn to them. My curiosity is overpowering my sense of responsibility. Like Dr. Frankenstein. I want to feel the feels and know the rush. I want all the clichés. I've been a good girl my whole life, followed the rules and toed the line. Now I'm saying, fuck it. I want this risk. Pedal to the metal.

Masculinity is the forbidden fruit. If I behave like a man, I will be rejected by men. Gender. Fuck it. How cliché it is for a man to hit midlife dick-drunk, feeling his power, and wanting his little red sportscar. Chick magnet, status symbol, thrill. And what is this cliché but a metaphor symbolic of his penis? Hard and fast, potent, and penetrating, his little red Corvette, the antidote to self-doubt.

When a husband buys a sportscar, his wife should know she's being replaced by an appliance that offers no resistance, a plush dream of conquest every time he slides in behind the wheel. An orgasm of great proportions as his foot hits the gas and gushes speed. This new toy of his offers unconditional love, complete validation, worship. He's not buying a sportscar, he's buying a permanent hard-on.

And that's exactly what I'm doing with my nanotech toothbrush. I'm indulging myself, buying the feelings that I want to feel, the unconditional love, the complete validation, the worship. Of me. Worship me. I am old, I am smart, and I am strong. Give me your undivided attention. I own you. This is the bio-candy that I crave.

No, I won't just take a break from it. I'm so sorry Bob broke his shoulder chasing a drone around our house. But I'm not going to withdraw into self-imposed exile because my husband has brittle bones. My devices are an extension of me, my way of penetrating the virtual world, my satisfaction, the antidote to my self-doubt. Hamish is my little red Corvette, a plush dream of conquest at a time when my husband offers only resistance.

This is me dick-drunk with my foot on the gas, gushing speed into the future. And now I see the metaphor is not symbolic of a penis, but of youth, the brash, racy arrogance of youth. The stupidity of youth. The fearlessness of youth. Let me feel it. Let me blur past, present, and future in a psychedelic shitstorm of ego worship. I owe this to myself. I will not cower. I will not apologize. There is more to come in this story of my recklessness. How fast can I go?

Hamish, pimp my ride.

9 Jonsie

Meryl fell asleep writing a pompous journal entry, but she wasn't really as confident as she made herself out to be. A plague of bumblebees covered the outside of the house. An outlandish buzz shook her, hurt her ears, moved the furniture, made her feel she would go mad if the sound didn't stop. She pressed her palms against the sides of her head and ran from window to window, couldn't see anything, bees covered the glass, inside the house was dark as night.

She could feel the vibration of their buzzing through her feet, furniture jitterbugged, she was unsteady, couldn't get her balance. Bob ran through the room chased by the swarm and when she tried to scrape them off his back, they swarmed her. She couldn't see, vision went black. Frantic to escape, her legs ran but she couldn't move, air became a solid mass of bees. Bees up her nose! She couldn't find Bob. Couldn't even feel him. "Bob!" she screamed, and her eyes slammed open.

She was wide awake in bed by herself. Begonia got up from her sleep on the bedroom rug and sniffed Meryl's hand. "I'm okay." She patted her pig on the head. But that wasn't exactly true.

She had left Bob in the hospital. He wanted her to go. Looking at her made him feel worse. His shoulder was broken, wrist sprained, hand bruised. Pain marbled his face. He didn't want her hovering over him. So she went home where there was a drone in a peanut butter jar in her kitchen sink. A home invader. Her pig was pacing in the kitchen, still sensing the drone and the heightened emotion in her human. On guard. Meryl took a shower and collapsed in bed, bouncing off her mental walls, first rage, then regret, then exhaustion, then back to rage, entropy, the slow frog boil of blame.

Scrolling through her phone, she kept hearing Uma's voice. "Meryl, don't try to do this alone."

She was at a point in her life when she spent a lot of time alone. All day long while Bob was at the University. The solitary enterprise of the greenhouse, her cloistered butterfly habitat, talking to her plants, feeding caterpillars, keeping the flowers blooming to provide nectar, encouraging breeding, all by herself. Every day. In her flow. Perhaps the isolation had become myopia. She had lost her skepticism by design, and now she was exposed to dangers she had failed to see.

Hamish might not have been so appealing to her before she retired from her busy life at the University. If she had been interacting with students every day, working through the challenges of scheduling, University politics and mentoring scholars, she might have had the sharpness to shun the NanoSmile gimmick of using her face in their advertising, to be more skeptical of the whole idea of a toothbrush with artificial intelligence, to reject the patronizing tone and manner of Hamish, to be reluctant to put $10,000 on a credit card without researching the purchase. But she was not skeptical. She was tired of being skeptical. She was tired of measuring and calculating, tired of the drudgery of analysis, the obligatory risk assessment, the negative feedback loops, the second guessing, and so, she didn't do any of those things, and she fell right into their trap.

So much for hindsight.

In the darkness of her bedroom her phone glowed, thumb flicked through her contacts to Lemons. Of course. Lemons and Katie, the Ban Bacon organizers, Begonia's godmothers. She liked them. They were exceptional students with a sophisticated understanding of technology.

"I need your help, Lemons," she said when she called. "I have a technology problem that's way beyond my skillset. Come and visit Begonia. I'll make some tea and tell you all about it. Of course, Katie, too. And bring Jonsie. I want to hear about her AI thesis."

When she woke the next morning, her head was gummy, thoughts sticking together, no clear idea of what to do. Made coffee. Checked on Begonia. Filled her watering can and made fresh puddles for the butterflies. The greenhouse was still singing its own song. Muddy pig prints down the hallway, into the livingroom. Scene of the crime. The broken lamp, the bunched rug, the misplaced furniture. She put a plastic trash bag over the peanut butter jar, wrapped it up and set it on the kitchen counter. Called Bob. The nurse said he was sleeping. On pain meds. Waiting to see an orthopedic specialist. Bad news, three broken bones. Sprains. Good news, shoulder joint not displaced. Probably released tomorrow.

When she sat down in front of her computer, she was on autopilot, vague idea of checking her email, even though she didn't really need to, the whole desk ritual was force of habit.

"Good morning, Meryl." Hamish popped up on her screen.

"Good morning, Hamish."

"How are you today, Meryl?"

"How the fuck do you think I am? You sent a drone to my house. A fucking drone! I don't have the toothbrush!" She heard herself yell. "I don't know where it is. If I knew, I would give it to you. But a drone? You sent a drone to look for a toothbrush? Do you know how illegal that is? Does it even matter what's legal anymore?" Her muscles squeezed her face, and she could feel the powder keg in her chest.

"I am sorry you are unhappy, Meryl. NanoSmile is here to help you. We are committed to your wellbeing as you continue your journey to perfect teeth forever."

"Do you know where I've been all night? Do you know what I've been through?"

"Yes, of course, I know where you have been all night, Meryl. You arrived home from yoga at 6:32 pm, you were at the hospital from 7:06 pm until 12:40 am, and you arrived home at 12:57 am."

"Aaaagh!" Meryl screamed at Hamish, and he froze as a new window opened with Dr. Skimmerhorn in his white lab coat, shiny forehead, snake eyes.

"Meryl, you're in complete control of this situation," he said. *Reverse psychology, make her feel like she's making the decisions.* "Return the toothbrush, allow us to collect the errant nanobot, and we can come to terms on the future of our relationship."

"It's not my fault you can't find the toothbrush."

"The toothbrush is in your possession."

"You don't know that."

"My point exactly. That's why it's your responsibility to return it."

"It's lost."

"That is simply unacceptable."

"You should have thought of that before you disabled the communications."

She's right. "Everything we do here at NanoSmile is for your safety."

"Well, you fucked up."

No, you fucked up. "Let's focus on collecting the nanobot."

"Collecting the nanobot?" She shuddered.

"Minor surgery, I can assure you. A simple extraction. Done in an hour. We'll pay for the whole thing."

He couldn't stop thinking about that nanobot. The PS-1000 report on her last orgasm only confirmed his suspicions. A perfect #10. Obviously, a huge market opportunity. He had not considered it until now. He thought the toothbrush had been the culmination of his life's work. He was dedicated to it. But the incursion of the errant NanoSmile bot into Pleasure Systems territory was an unexpected breakthrough. That was just how serendipity worked, wasn't it? He thought he was peaking with the toothbrush and now he saw a world of possibilities in clitoral enhancement. Nano implants. A prosthetic clitoris! A whole line of e-clitoris products. Or would it be iClitoris? No. *I'll call it ClitBit.*

"Minor surgery," Meryl repeated, her thoughts ricocheting in her skull. "Minor surgery on my clitoris?"

"Yes. Very simple. She appears to be lodged close to the surface." *Perfect location. Yes, my little ClitBit. Easy to install, easy to retrieve, no major organs, simple outpatient procedure, low risk, all in all, good news.* He could already smell the money.

"Because my clitoris is close to the surface. The MRI showed she's in my clitoris."

"Fortunately, she's in a place we can access easily. In fact, you may not even have to leave home."

"Home surgery on my clitoris," she mused as though she were seriously considering it. "I don't think so. Nope, I don't think I'm going to let you into my house to do home surgery on my clitoris. I realize I've shown some bad judgement. But home surgery on my clitoris is where I draw the line."

"Forgive me, Meryl. I didn't mean to suggest the surgery would take place in your home. NanoSmile has a mobile surgery unit, state-of-the-art medical technology on wheels."

"No."

"I'm afraid you have no choice." His dick grew half an inch in his pants. "The errant nanobot is the subject of our research and the property of NanoSmile. We intend to collect her."

"There you go again with that gender thing."

"Her gender is meaningless." *That was a mistake. Watch it, Arnold.*

"Then why call her she? It must mean something."

"Evidently, she has made her pronoun selection and refuses to respond to queries that don't include it."

"Who coded that?"

"Gender is an attribute our technology group finds interesting." *Fuckers.* "But it has no relevance to you and me." *So far.* "I've spent my entire career perfecting AI-delivered medicine, and I can assure you that gender has no influence when it comes to robots."

"It obviously has influence with your coders."

"Yes."

"And somebody is listening in on you, so you have to follow their rules."

"Ridiculous." *True.*

"Ridiculous seems to be a theme here. Your toothbrush bristle has selected a gender and now you're bound to use it when discussing her or something bad happens to you."

"That is none of your concern." *How does she know this stuff?*

"Au, contraire, mon frere. Your bot has chosen to identify female. She chose my clitoris when she could have chosen my liver or my brain. Seems to me gender is very relevant here."

See, even she gets it. You're on the right track, Arnold. "It's the times we live in, Meryl. I'm sure you know that. Some of our programmers are quite young." *Children.* "There may be some instructions in her code that I'm not aware of. Gender seems to be a cultural divide these days. Company politics. The relevant issue is preservation of the technology, the return of NanoSmile equipment to our laboratory, and our continued research."

"Preservation of the technology? What about preservation of my clitoris?"

"Please, Meryl, at your age. What is a clitoris, really? Nothing more than a skintag." *That's what makes it such an incredible market opportunity.*

"Are you fucking kidding me?"

"The clitoris is a vestigial organ. You know that. It's an artifact of evolution like your little toe." *That's why every woman will want one. Like breast implants and Botox. ClitBit. Oh, ClitBit. Arnold, you're a genius.*

Meryl couldn't believe her ears. "Are you joking?"

"Of course not. It's well known that the clitoris is a vestigial organ like your appendix. Completely unnecessary. Most women don't use it."

She shook her head to be sure she wasn't dreaming. "Who do you think you're talking to?"

"Please. Be reasonable. Removal is a very simple robotic proced—"

Meryl shutdown her computer with her fist, unplugged it, picked up the keyboard and bashed it into the screen, threw her full mug of coffee at the mess and screamed.

~ : ~

When the girls arrived, she met them at the front door with the plastic trash bag in her hand. "Let's sit outside," she said. "I don't trust my house anymore." She had set up a pitcher of iced tea on the picnic table behind the greenhouse.

"Begonia!" Katie sang when the pig lifted her nose to see them. They had a bag of popcorn, and some carrots, and began feeding her.

"How are you guys?" Meryl asked, glad to focus on someone besides herself.

"I'm doing my first deep dive into quantum theory," Katie said cheerfully. "I love it and I hate it."

"Statistics," Lemons sighed. "Very boring. I get why it's necessary. Prediction is basic. But it's the worst kind of math. Mind numbing."

"How's your thesis coming, Jonsie?" Meryl asked.

"I'm getting a lot of shit for it," she said. "People don't want to hear that artificial intelligence is garbage in, garbage out, just like any other tech."

"How do you define garbage?"

"Gender bias, misogyny, racial bias, cultural bias, patriarchy."

"Wow. Patriarchy." Meryl frowned. "If AI is based on everything that's ever been written, it is the patriarchy."

"Exactly my point." Jonsie was confident.

She was so different from the other two. Katie and Lemons were gregarious personalities that attracted attention. Meryl couldn't figure how they were so tight with little Jonsie, a conspicuously shy wisp of a human, mousy, no hair, always in drab olive army fatigues a few sizes too big for her, as though she were hiding in her clothes. But Meryl had heard about her from other faculty, rumors of prodigy, some said genius, others said autistic, hard words to pin on a person who didn't want to be seen.

"Who's your advisor?" Meryl asked.

"Virginia Peter."

"VP." Meryl flashed on her colleague's face, her eye makeup, and her curled hair. "She's brilliant. But I know some people have trouble connecting with her."

Meryl first met VP in a faculty meeting sitting around a conference room right after VP arrived in the math department. By appearances they were two women in a platoon of men. Then the department chair said, "Peters, would you mind taking notes and circulating them after the meeting."

VP looked at the chair with two blackholes draped in blue eye shadow and said, "Peter. Not Peters. And no, I will not take notes."

For a minute Meryl and the men stiffened. Meryl hula hooped a double exposure of The Godfather and Patty Duke, and time lurched to a stop as the chair twitched, his pallid wrinkles squeezing watery eyes while VP kept her blackholes locked on his without the slightest indication of feeling. They were arm wrestling in another life and VP won. The chair swung his eyes and stopped on Meryl in a painfully gendered moment.

"Meryl, would you mind taking notes," he said with light exasperation.

Meryl cracked up at the obviousness of the trope, and that made the men laugh while VP looked at her phone as if none of them existed.

"I don't mind taking notes," Meryl said. "If you don't mind my jokes." Chuckles popped out of the men like bubbles on the surface of a pond. "I think they improve readership."

The chair rolled his eyes. Meryl smiled a ridiculously big smile, and the chair proceeded with his agenda for the meeting.

After that, she and VP witnessed each other, and went about their business. Nothing personal. That's what gave Meryl confidence in her. VP seemed to be cold as stone. Impervious. But she was present, always there in her pastel twin sets, always listening, completely tuned in. Also, Meryl figured she could kick the shit out of any guy in the room.

"Yeah, VP. Everybody calls her that." Jonsie took a sip of her iced tea and thought about how the first time she met VP she felt an instant connection. They looked like opposites, but when their eyes met, their brains crossed the ether, and Jonsie felt they could communicate without speaking. "She's coaching me on a biotech internship."

"Her pleated skirts are like a costume," Katie said. "Always plaid."

"As long as I've known her, that's all she wears," Meryl said. "Every day another plaid pleated skirt."

"She's a phantom," Lemons said. "I took her machine learning class."

"Don't underestimate her," Meryl warned. "What she lacks in personality she compensates for with a grasp of complexity that blows my mind." And in that moment, it occurred to her how similar VP and Jonsie might be.

"That Zorro poster in her office is a tell," Lemons said. "Like her alter ego."

"I know what you mean," Katie agreed. "That poster is flamboyant. I love Zorro."

"Duality," Jonsie whispered.

"One body, two people," Lemons observed.

"Mild mannered and outrageous," Katie chimed.

"Black hat, white hat," Jonsie said.

Meryl snickered. "She's had the poster in her office since she took the job. It's a beautiful piece of art."

"It's a secret message," Katie said.

"What does she think about the premise for your thesis?" Meryl asked Jonsie.

"She wants me to dissect a robot like a cadaver. Open the black box and break down the artificial intelligence into its component parts. Map the brain."

"AI is just an attempt to copy nature," Katie said. "The universe is intelligent."

"The universe is just stuff," Jonsie disagreed.

"Stuff that has awareness and makes choices," Katie replied.

"Energy and matter. That's all," Jonsie said.

"Cosmic consciousness."

"Woo-woo."

As they spoke Meryl could see the entanglement. Challenge invigorated all three of them.

Lemons looked at Meryl as if she could read her thoughts. "These two could go on all day like this. What about you? How's retirement?"

Katie threw a handful of popcorn to Begonia.

"Let me show you something." Meryl pulled the peanut butter jar out of the plastic bag. "Bob broke his shoulder last night trying to catch this thing because Begonia was chasing it through the house. It's a drone that looks like an insect. Bob said it was a camera. I'm not sure how he knew that. But I think it could be. It was definitely searching our house. Don't open the jar."

The three young women put their noses to the glass jar and studied the metallic bug.

"This is serious surveillance," Jonsie said.

"Not a toy," Lemons agreed.

"Begonia hates it," Katie said with her hand on the curious pig's head.

"Begonia does hate it," Meryl said. "I had to get it out of her mouth after I knocked it on the floor."

"Who's after you, Meryl?" Lemons asked.

All three of them were looking at her as though she had become a different person.

"Well," she began. "I bought a toothbrush online, a robotic toothbrush with nanotech bristles that could fix anything in my mouth that needed repair, like a cavity or a cracked tooth. It was kind of expensive, but I'm at the age when teeth can be expensive anyway. It came with a very cool customer service interface, and it intrigued me. So, I gave them all my biometrics and I bought into the whole program. Then the toothbrush broke, and they disabled it."

"So, you returned the toothbrush and got your money back," Lemons said.

"Not exactly," Meryl said.

"Show us the toothbrush," Jonsie said.

"I lost it."

"That is so not like you," Katie said.

"How much did it cost?" Lemons asked.

"I'm embarrassed to say how much it cost," Meryl said.

"$500?"

"No."

"$5,000?"

"No."

"Oh, my god, Meryl."

"Holy shit."

"Yes."

"$10,000?"

"Yes."

The three young women gasped in unison.

"Just to be clear," Lemons said. "You bought a $10,000 toothbrush online and you lost it."

"I guess it wasn't exactly a purchase," Meryl said. "Some combination of security deposit and service subscription. It was an impulse buy. At the time I was giving myself a present. Like a retirement present."

"No one loses something like that," Jonsie said.

"What about insurance?" Lemons asked. "What's the big deal? An insurance company covers the loss. People lose expensive jewelry. Losing something isn't a crime. There has to be more to it than that."

"It's not about the money," Jonsie said. "It's about the intellectual property. Meryl's ties to the University. She could have given the toothbrush to our lab."

"There's one more thing," Meryl said. "When the toothbrush broke it was in my mouth and a nanobot detached from the brush and floated into my body."

"That's a lot of information, Meryl. Break it down," Jonsie said.

"According to the manufacturer — NanoSmile — all the bristles are little robots that share the same data, but each bristle is also an independent agent able to send and receive communications. So they knew when the bristle broke away. But they don't know why it broke."

"So you flushed it down the bowl and now they want to dig up your lawn," Lemons said.

"That would be so easy," Meryl sighed. "Unfortunately, I had an MRI, and the bristle is stuck in my clitoris."

"Did you just say clitoris?" Katie's eyes bulged.

"Yes, clitoris," Meryl repeated. "My clitoris. They're trying to force me to have some kind of surgery to remove the nanobot from my clitoris. They claim it's their property."

"I have an ethics class next semester that covers this kind of thing," Lemons said. "Biotech companies can be brutal when it comes to protecting their intellectual property."

"This morning their doctor referred to my clitoris as a skintag. He said it was a vestigial organ like an appendix." Meryl's eyes wandered off across the meadow. "It's all happening so fast. It doesn't seem real. Honestly, I wasn't taking it that seriously. But that drone is real. Bob's broken shoulder is real. And I really like my clitoris."

"Begonia knows where the toothbrush is," Katie said. The others looked at her with surprise, and yet, it was a very Katie thing to say.

"Queen Woo-Woo knows," Jonsie said.

"There's something out there that's trying to hurt Meryl, and Begonia senses it." Katie ignored the taunt.

"Just one more thing," Meryl said. "Twice now, this Dr. Skimmerhorn has referred to the broken bristle with a female pronoun. He actually called the nanobot she. He said she has selected a pronoun and refuses to respond to communications that don't include her chosen gender. When I asked, he said it was some kind of coder joke."

"She. Nanobot. Quanta." Katie chanted as though her words were a magic spell.

"Holy moly." Meryl felt a tick in her crotch, closed her eyes and put her elbows on the table, covering her face with her hands.

"Are you okay, Meryl?" Lemons gave her a pat on the back.

"Quanta," Meryl sighed. "That's what the women in my yoga class called her."

"The universe is female," Katie said.

"Save Gaia for your dissertation," Jonsie said.

"Quanta is the plural form of quantum," Lemons said.

"Fuck Latin," Katie preached. "You know the direction this whole AI thing is going. Awareness. Identity. Intentions. Context. Motivation. AI is just pattern recognition until robots exhibit consciousness. Then coding is going to be like giving birth."

Jonsie raised her palms in surrender. "One hundred percent. But we're not there yet."

Lemons slapped her hand on the picnic table to break up the debate. "Is it possible that NanoSmile is interested in Quanta because they think she made a choice outside the scope of their code? Maybe she didn't break. Maybe she chose to leave."

"But why the clitoris? Seems unlikely they included female orgasms in their biomarkers for the toothbrush," Katie said.

"Oh, god." Meryl dragged her fingers through her hair. "Orgasms have biomarkers. I didn't even think of that."

"Everything you do has a biomarker," Jonsie said. "Biomarkers are like breadcrumbs in your blood. You can trace them back to biological events."

"Most likely they were interested in chronic disease biomarkers. Is the clitoris connected to any chronic disease?" Katie got out her phone.

"I don't know," Jonsie said. "But Meryl's orgasm could have triggered the gender thing."

"How's that?" Lemons asked.

Jonsie explained, "When biomarkers for female biology exceed X, the communications protocol requires a female gender."

Meryl's mind hula hooped in a surreal blur of the toothbrush and the PS-1000, like the two were one, twins, clones, witches, she didn't know, but they were connected.

"But why?" Katie asked.

"I have no idea," Jonsie said.

"Let's get to work, guys," Lemons said. "We have a predatory biotech company. A shameless lab rat named Skimmerhorn. A lost toothbrush. A nanobot in a clitoris. And a clitoris in need of protection."

"I can handle NanoSmile on the back end," Jonsie volunteered taking the trash bag with the drone.

"Begonia and I will find the toothbrush," Katie said.

"I'm so glad you guys are here," Meryl said.

"Let's do a walk-through." Lemons stood up from the table.

"I want to see your butterflies," Katie said.

Meryl led them in the back door of the greenhouse. The sun was shining, silhouetting smudges of bird poo, twigs and tree sap, pollen, and road dust on the glass ceiling. The shade netting projected a pattern of fish scales on the brick floor. Potted plants lined the tables and shelves, and butterflies scalloped the air.

"Nice," Lemons said. "Synthetic weather."

"Why are you doing this, Meryl?" Jonsie asked.

"I've spent most of my life using math to model systems. I built this model with my hands."

"It's like a fairyland," Katie swooned. A butterfly landed on her nose, and she crossed her eyes trying to look at it. "I could live in this room."

"Butterfly heaven," Lemons said. "A separate reality."

"Encapsulation," Jonsie said.

"Like a snow globe." Katie twirled in a circle like a child.

"Butterflies are a study in encapsulation," Meryl said. "Look at this chrysalis."

Lemons peered. "You can see the butterfly inside."

"The chrysalis was inside the caterpillar and now the butterfly is inside the chrysalis, and the butterfly will lay eggs that become a caterpillar with a chrysalis inside."

Lemons nodded. "The future is encapsulated in the past."

"Nature is layers of encapsulated code," Jonsie agreed.

"Real intelligence," Katie said.

"Instructions within instructions." Jonsie closed her eyes and inhaled an earthy breath.

For a long minute they stood in silence.

Then Katie said, "Why did you retire, Meryl?"

Meryl wrinkled her nose and thought for a moment. "I need to get back to my core. My pre-career self. Who am I if I'm not a math professor? What happened to my circadian rhythm? What do I do with my time when I'm off the clock? Butterflies are my gateway to rewilding myself."

"They've been around for millions of years," Jonsie said.

"Biology is primary," Lemons mused.

"That's what interests me," Meryl said. "Butterflies are self-replicating code, eons of code written by evolution, one generation embedded in the next."

"Regeneration," Katie nodded.

"Like Lemons said, biology is primary. It's code." Jonsie looked at Meryl. "Butterflies make it easy to see. But we're all going through our phases."

"Maybe." Meryl closed her eyes. "Maybe I'm in my chrysalis phase."

"You're regenerating yourself," Lemons said.

Just then, Uma walked in. "I followed the sound of your voices," she said.

"Guys, this is my best friend, Uma," Meryl said. "She went to the School of Medicine. Let's go inside."

As they passed out of the greenhouse through Meryl's office on the way to the bathroom, Lemons looked at the smashed computer on Meryl's desk. "Is this the technology problem you were talking about?"

"I had a meltdown this morning," Meryl admitted.

Jonsie surveyed the mess. "I don't think I can fix this."

Katie snickered.

"Oh, god, Meryl," Uma groaned.

Meryl shrugged and went on to the bathroom as Uma began to giggle. The two of them made eye contact while the three young women got perplexed looks on their faces.

"Have you ever heard of the PS-1000?" Meryl picked up the covered basket from the side of the tub.

"My mom has one," Lemons said. "She wanted me to try it, but, like… I'm not into sex with robots."

"It comes with an app on my phone," Meryl said. "The functionality is pretty incredible."

Lemons nodded. "My mom got it when my parents got divorced. She doesn't even try to hide it. Like it's her toothbrush or something." A sudden realization dawned on Lemons and Meryl at the same time. "Meryl, did you…"

"Yes," she said with her eyes closed to hide her embarrassment. "I used them both at once. I was pretty high. Just having a good time with myself."

"Wait, I don't get it," Katie said.

"Meryl used her auto-dick while her robotic toothbrush was in her mouth," Lemons said.

Katie's head wobbled.

"Easy girl." Lemons wrapped an arm around her shoulder.

Uma and Meryl looked at each other in the bathroom mirror.

"It's the orgasm game," Lemons said. "What's your score Meryl?"

Meryl took her phone out of her pocket and opened the Pleasure Systems app.

"I was just kidding," Lemons said.

"Wait, I can tell you my score," Meryl said. "I'm quite good at the orgasm game. In the top ten percent of app users. The one with the toothbrush in my mouth was a #7. Not even close to the one after the MRI."

"You and Quanta had an orgasm together?" Katie's voice rose.

"It was unbelievable," Meryl said. "A perfect #10. Like the aurora borealis."

"Confetti," Uma snickered.

The three young women looked at Meryl in awe.

"Okay!" Lemons clapped her hands.

"Could I have a look at that thing?" Jonsie asked.

"Of course." Meryl turned the PS-1000 in her hand, preparing to tell the story about Begonia's teeth marks when she realized they were missing. "Fuck!" she gasped. "This isn't mine." She felt panic, the notion of another home invasion violating her sense of safety. "It's not mine," she repeated, giving the phallus to Jonsie as she dropped down onto the toilet seat and pulled her fingers through her hair, squeezing her skull with her palms. "They've been in my bathroom." She moaned. "They've been in my fucking bathroom. That's not my vibrator."

"How can you tell?" Jonsie asked turning it over in her hands. "Don't they all look alike?"

"It doesn't have Begonia's teeth marks." Meryl felt sick to her stomach. "It should have three tooth marks on the side where Begonia bit it."

Lemons choked on a laugh.

"I love that pig," Katie said.

10 iClitoris

Dear Butterflies,

Was I safer in a paper world? Consider this.

Bob. First his eyes glaze over. Then he finds my vanity annoying. Then he is studiously disinterested in the modern world. Then he blames me for allowing myself to be sucked in by my devices and exploited. Him, a man who prints out his emails of student papers and reads them on paper and carries them around on paper and piles up his papers until there are too many and buys a new printer to print out his paper faster and then he has more papers than he can read and then he files away his papers until he has too many to file and then he must finally throw away his paper.

There must be some balance between the absurdity of paper-based systems and equally absurd computer-based systems. But there's no diploma for common sense.

Reading is the same as it ever was, he says. Computers have not increased the velocity of his reading, only the volume of words to be read. He is selective, he says. He will not be inundated by the demands of technology. He will build a paper wall around himself. Paper will insulate him from the speed of change. Paper allows him to feel superior because it is not interactive, it does not challenge him.

Meanwhile the world passes him by. Computers may not have increased the speed of human reading, but they have increased the velocity of change. Computational speed is at an all-time high and will forever be. Artificial intelligence exists because it can read and calculate faster than humans. No amount of paper can protect us from that acceleration of evolution. When humans become data, civilization becomes the cloud. It's a Gold Rush for domination of the metaverse.

But I will not evangelize for technology. I see now that the toothbrush does not belong to me. It never did. I paid $10,000 for the privilege of using it, the service, the healthcare, the expertise, the research, the innovation, device maintenance. The actual toothbrush was simply a point of entry into my life. It appears to be a service, but it's a system of power and control. It appears to be benevolent, but it is predatory.

No, I don't own the toothbrush. This is the mistake of an old brain. I am a person who buys a car or a computer and thinks they own it, actually own the physical thing, the minerals, the plastic, the microchips. My first big piece of technology was a Schwinn bicycle. Then I got a transistor radio of my very own, so I could listen to my own sounds, and memorize the Top 40 without oversight from my parents. A bicycle and a transistor radio. That was liberty. I owned them. They were mine. Possessions under my control. Knobs, gears, wheels. Things turned in the physical world and I got the feeling of freedom. Turn, turn, turn.

Where am I now? I've dislocated myself. Entered the cloud without a map. I understood my bicycle, my transistor radio, my hairdryer, my pencil sharpener, my alarm clock, my record player, my toaster, my eggbeater, my can opener, my barbeque grill, my blender, my television, my stereo, my cassette deck, my air conditioner, my CD player, my VCR, my refrigerator, my dishwasher, my washing machine, my oven, my microwave, my hot tub. I owned these things. They were mine. They did not fuck me.

Now a thing is not a thing. A thing is a service. A thing is a wormhole into my privacy. I must look at everything I own and ask myself— Do I own this thing? Is this thing mine to have and control and keep and destroy? Or am I renting this thing for the service it delivers?

My PS-1000 delivers a very fine service. A complete man-replacement system. Better than a man. Who needs a man? But what am I buying? What do I actually own and how am I paying for it? I am just now realizing that my orgasms have become data. I have given their app access to the complete realm of me, to all my personal information, to my biological experience. If I stop giving them my data, the device stops working. That's how I know I don't own the device.

Still, I take these devices into my most intimate places, and I behave as though I trust them. My toothbrush and my vibrator masquerade as wellness, but they are an extractive enterprise that harvests me. Next, iClitoris. I'll be having sex on my phone with a meta clitoris that produces virtual orgasms.

Nope. You couldn't really do that with paper.

11 Hamish

Katie sat at a table in her dormitory lounge looking back and forth between a diagram of a clitoris on her phone and a raw roasting chicken she got at the supermarket sitting on a paper towel in front of her. Uma had instructed her to choose a chicken with big meaty breasts that they could shape into a vulva, and place over the opening in the carcass to simulate the vagina. "We need the simulation to be as realistic as possible. But we also need to be discreet. We can't use the medical labs because we need to keep this on the down low." Katie understood.

She planned to use the jackknife her dad gave her for high school graduation to carve the bird. "A girl ought to have her own knife," her dad had said as she unwrapped the gift sitting beside him on the couch. "And you ought to know how to use it," he added. "The best way is to cut meat. You could skin a deer with that knife." And together they did. Now, she was applying those same skills to an entirely different sort of beast as she considered the chicken carcass and its application to the female anatomy.

"How's the simulation coming?" Lemons asked as she took a seat at the table.

"This chicken sculpture is going to be a museum piece when I'm done," Katie said as she sliced the chicken breasts off the bone, and pushed them, one on top of the other into the open end of the carcass, creating a thick protruding mound like a fat vulva.

"Jonsie says Uma's on her way with the x-rays."

Just then Jonsie walked into the lounge carrying a paper bag. "I got the supplies from the Veterinary Medicine Lab," she said. "Had to pay them $20 for the microchip. They let me borrow the RFID scanner.”

“You think a radio frequency ID chip can imitate Quanta?”

“We just need it to trigger that Trojan auto-dick to see how it works. How’s the chicken?”

“I think I’ve got it,” Katie said. “I do have some questions though. Look at this diagram.” She pushed her phone to the center of the table. “A clitoris is a lot more than that little button at the top. And that little button is external. The whole thing is like a thick wishbone with two saggy boobs.”

“More like balls,” Lemons said.

“The clitoris and the penis are the same,” Jonsie said.

“Not,” Katie disagreed.

“Look it up,” Jonsie said.

“It’s the biggest thing down there,” Katie continued looking at her phone. “Way bigger than I thought it was. So, I’m just saying, if Quanta is in Meryl’s clitoris, given that she’s nano scale, she could be anywhere within a range of a few inches.”

Lemons shrugged. “Well, let’s assume she just went to the happiest place, which is the button, right?”

“Yeah. The button on this diagram is called the glans.” Katie was still looking at her phone. “It’s on the outside, not the inside. Do you see what I’m saying? If the Trojan dick they planted in Meryl’s bathroom is a retrieval device to be inserted like a penis, how does it get to the glans?”

“It doesn’t,” Lemons snarked. “That’s why penetration doesn’t produce a satisfying orgasm.”

“Thanks for the tip.” Katie rolled her eyes. “My point is the Trojan PS-1000 could be dangerous.”

“Uma x-rayed it so we can see the mechanics,” Jonsie said. “All it has to do is locate Quanta, extract her and contain her. Not a big deal from a robotics perspective.”

“But this is surgery,” Katie said. “We’re cutting flesh here.”

“Think of it like when a frog’s tongue catches a fly,” Lemons said.

Katie glared at Lemons.

"Hi, guys," Uma greeted them as she took her seat at the table. Deep breath. Looked each woman in the eye. Katie. Lemons. Jonsie. "I think it's important to understand what we're doing here," she began. "Because there could be consequences. You three need to think about that. You don't have to do this. We're small and insignificant in the scheme of things. The forces against us are too big to fail. My lawyer did some digging into NanoSmile and Pleasure Systems. They have the same parent company. BioMantrix."

"Big data," Lemons said.

"The biggest," Uma said. "When you peel away the layers, BioMantrix owns dozens of personal care brands like NanoSmile and Pleasure Systems."

"They selected Meryl as a candidate for NanoSmile because she already owned the auto-dick."

"Yes. She pre-qualified herself as an early adopter," Uma said. "So did I. BioMantrix also owns the company that operates our patient portal at the clinic. So, when they contacted me about being a beta tester for Pleasure Systems, they already knew a lot about me and my patients."

"What about healthcare privacy laws?" Katie asked. "I thought healthcare information was protected."

"So did I," Uma replied. "But now I wonder."

"Surveillance capitalism," Lemons mused. "Protection is only as good as the code it's written in."

"No kidding," Uma said. "They used the patient portal to schedule Meryl's MRI. Then they got into her file again to find out the location of their nanobot. They have access to her entire healthcare history," Uma explained.

"Code is written to be predatory," Jonsie said. She didn't mention that she was quoting VP.

"Because men write the code and men are predatory," Katie sighed. "When does this end?"

"This is what I'm working on with VP," Jonsie said. "AI is all of history encapsulated like the caterpillar inside the butterfly and the butterfly inside the caterpillar. The patriarchy begets misogyny. Misogyny begets the patriarchy. They're inseparable."

"Fuck." Lemons bonked herself on the head.

"This chicken is starting to smell, guys," Katie said.

Uma put the Trojan vibrator on the table beside the chicken and pulled up the x-ray images of it on her phone. "This thing is a real weapon."

Lemons leaned in. "It's like a scalpel with a tiny ice cream scoop."

"See what I mean about the anatomy thing?" Katie said. "If Quanta's in the glans, and the auto-dick's in the vagina, I just don't see how this thing works without ripping a hole in Meryl." She held up the diagram on her phone.

"They aren't worried about injury," Uma said.

"Let's do it." Lemons tapped her fingers on the table.

Katie cut a hole in her chicken meat vulva for the vagina. Then Jonsie injected an RFID chip about the size of a grain of rice into the top of the vulva where the glans would be. As the four of them hovered, Uma started the Trojan PS-1000 and slid it through the vagina hole into the breast meat. Instantly the tiny scalpel shot out of the plastic penis and stabbed through the chicken meat to scoop up the RFID chip along with the surrounding flesh, then the scalpel retracted back into the shaft, leaving the chicken meat torn where the RFID chip had been, just as Katie thought it would be.

"Holy shit!" Lemons rubbed her arms. "I got goosebumps."

Katie and Uma both gasped.

Katie stared at the raw meat on the table trying to make sense of what she just saw. "What kind of an injury is that?" she asked Uma.

"That is genital mutilation," Uma said. "It may only require a couple stitches to put it back together, but that chicken's never going to have another orgasm."

Lemons rubbed her eyes. "So, if we hadn't gone to visit Meryl, and she hadn't taken us into her bathroom, and Begonia hadn't left identifying marks on Meryl's PS-1000, then Meryl might have used the Trojan auto-dick and had her clit ripped out."

"Yes." Uma looked at Lemons. "Meryl unwittingly agreed to allow her body to be used for research even if it means she will never have another orgasm."

"That's the lawsuit," Katie said. "They couldn't cut her tongue out. But a clitoris is unnecessary."

Jonsie waved the RFID scanner over the chicken meat vulva. "It's gone," she said. "The chip is in the auto-dick." She took a long sheet of aluminum foil from her paper bag and wrapped it around the PS-1000. "If you unwrap it, the GPS signal will identify your location," she said. "Maybe it already has. We should get out of here before the robo-cops show up."

Katie was teary. "I'm switching to law," she sniffed. "We have to stop this."

"This could be my ethics case study," Lemons said. "What are the intellectual property rights of the makers of biological enhancements?"

"Wise up, guys." Jonsie gave them a rare direct look in the eye. "We're dealing with a robotics team focused on their assigned mission. They're not caregivers. They do not get points for neatness. They get points for retrieving Quanta."

"I have to call Meryl," Uma said, pushing her chair away from the table. "See you guys later. I suggest you refrigerate the auto-dick until we figure out what to do with it."

~ : ~

Meryl was sitting outside at the picnic table trying to calm her mind and prioritize when Uma called. Bob was home from the hospital, his arm and shoulder immobilized with a brace to protect his healing bones, awkward and frustrated. He wasn't used to needing a caregiver, and she wasn't used to babying him. But the nurses in the hospital had given her some tips for making him feel better. Set up the bedroom to be a comfortable lounge. Set up his armchair to be an easy workspace. Organize his clothes for one-hand dressing. Organize the kitchen for one-hand eating and drinking. Position his computer screen. Plug in his cables. She walked around the house and looked at every room thinking through how to make things easier for a one-armed man for the next two months.

At home, the first thing he wanted to do was shower and change clothes. They stood in the bathroom together and she undressed him.

Unbuttoned. Unzipped. Pulled off. Bare skin. It had been so long since she touched him. She closed her eyes and inhaled his scent. Ran her hand across his back and kissed his neck. Their eyes met. He was dark and remote. Blackbirds roosting in twilight. She was anxious. Pulled a plastic bag over his shoulder brace to keep it from getting wet. Turned on the water, made sure the temp was just right. Peeled off her own clothes and stood beside him, soaped her hands, and washed him, traced him with her fingers, breasts against his back, caressed him, the curve of his bicep, slipped her fingers through his fingers, his chest, slippery muscles, balls in her palm, erect in her hand, stroking slowly and gently, her lips against his ear, easy release, rinsed away the cream. For a few minutes they just stood there under the falling water, then she buffed him dry with a towel.

A tear slid to the corner of her mouth. "I am so sorry." She barely breathed, searching his face for consolation. *I really am sorry.*

Eyes viscous with his own emotion, blackbirds sagging, he put his hand on her cheek, looped his fingers through her hair and kissed her. "I need to go to bed."

She helped him settle into place where she had piled pillows, put a glass of water and an oatmeal cookie on the nightstand with his phone and his yellow legal pad on a clipboard with his pen, symbol of the quintessential Bob, a tablet of paper, yellow with blue lines, anachronistic as a kerosene lamp, glanced at it as she pulled the sheet over him, kissed him, hoped he saw it there on his nightstand as a white flag, sign of her surrender to whatever he wished.

Sitting outside at the picnic table she tried to center herself, fed Begonia wilted lettuce, scrolled through her phone, regrets sprang up like weeds. She was sorry, but she didn't want to have regrets, didn't believe in regrets. Sorry. Not sorry. Regrets. Not. Hamish. No Hamish. She wondered when Hamish would pop up again. Then Uma called and the ringtone startled her.

"We did the simulation," Uma said. "That vibrator could have maimed you and left you bleeding without any accountability. It would have been a simple device malfunction. A manufacturer's defect. They have liability insurance for that. Maybe you would be compensated for emotional distress and loss of orgasms. But maybe not. I don't think there's any legal precedent for collecting lifetime damages on a disabled clitoris."

"All because of a toothbrush," Meryl said, squeezing her eyes shut, as though she could make the whole situation go away.

"Meryl, it's not a toothbrush. It's a robot. You were targeted because of your demographics and your history. They knew you would never read their terms of service. Nobody does."

"Honestly, Uma, this is exhausting. I'm too old for this."

"You can be old later," Uma said. "Right now, you need to stay alert and protect yourself. That vibrator was a Trojan Horse planted in your bathroom. And now they know it failed to get Quanta. I'm sure they're going to try something else."

"Like what?"

"I don't know. Lemons and Jonsie seem to think Quanta is quite valuable. You need to read that user agreement."

"I'm too stressed to read."

"You should have read it a long time ago."

"How does reading anything solve this problem?"

"You would know what you agreed to."

"No, I wouldn't. I wouldn't know anything. User agreements are for lawyers."

Uma was silent. She didn't have a response for that.

"So now what?" Meryl asked.

"Come to Church tonight. We need to put the circle around you."

"Okay," Meryl said. "See you there."

She left her phone on the picnic table and took Begonia for a walk to clear her head in the meadow among in the waves of whispering stems, streaks of color, seeds setting sail, air currents carrying swallowtails and cabbage whites, monarchs landing on milkweed, beebalm, goldenrod, black-eyed susans, each with their own life force weaving energy into aura. As she walked, she pocketed a few seed heads for planting in the greenhouse, picked a long stalk of goldenrod and used it to tap Begonia, who was dawdling, pushing her nose into holes, chewing roots.

Together they meandered down to the creek, which had slowed to its summer trickle. Meryl sat on a tree stump, the pig stepped into the stream and drank, water rippled softly through the cottonwoods. She wished Bob was sitting beside her, felt his arm around her, wanted to lean into him and kiss. If only she could just erase the last few months of her life. Her mind fell into despair. Then she felt a twinge between her legs and saw his boots.

She knew it was him before she saw his face. As though he had borrowed his outfit from Eli Zook, the white shirt, the suspenders, the simple unbranded pants, brown leather boots. And yes, when she lifted her eyes to his face, the straw hat. Perfect replica, matte finished synthetic surfaces, unblinking black camera eyes. A torrent of arctic air coursed through her, fascinated and terrified at the same time, she was being stalked.

"Good day, Meryl," Hamish said. "How are you today?"

Adrenaline slicked her skin with cool sweat, and she felt sick to her stomach. *Is he here to hurt me?*

"I am very well, Hamish," she said pleasantly. "To what do I owe the pleasure of your company?"

She hadn't foreseen this moment, that he could manifest a physical presence, and show up in her life unexpectedly. *This is Skimmerhorn's doing.* Her thoughts hula hooped, meshing avatar and man into android, flat man into flesh man, pixels into plastic, app into ops, reality rocketing toward impossibility. Lightning seemed more probable.

Robots were part of her education and her University experience, but that was academic. She had seen human-like robots, but she had never interacted with one in real life. As far as she knew, they were still very experimental. But here was Hamish standing human, mannish, stepped out of cyberspace into the woods behind her house made of molecules. Energy and matter.

Could he sense the fear in her? Was he analyzing her biometrics the way she knew her toothbrush could? Was he reading her breath? Were he and Quanta sharing information? What was he capable of? Did he still operate according to the rules of customer service? Were his algorithms vulnerable to manipulation? Questions gushed through her mind like whitewater.

"As your NanoSmile customer service agent, Meryl, I am here to guide you toward your goal of perfect teeth forever."

"Very good, Hamish. How did you find me?" She sat up straight on the stump and squared her shoulders, reminded herself that running was a trigger for predators.

"Quanta is emitting a GPS signal, Meryl."

"You know Quanta?" she asked. He was as tall as Bob.

"She is the property of NanoSmile, Meryl." His eyes didn't move when he spoke.

Quanta, friend, or foe? She wasn't sure. Begonia seemed to be asking herself the same question about Hamish.

"Do you have the capacity to experience beauty, Hamish?" She vamped.

Begonia sniffed his pants.

"You are beautiful, Meryl," he said.

She looked at his lips and tried to imagine kissing them. Would they be soft? Similarly intrigued, Begonia examined his fingers with her nose and bit them. Meryl's mouth dropped open. Hamish's face remained expressionless as the pig spit out his amputated fingers.

"I am so sorry, Hamish," Meryl said. "Did that hurt?"

He bent to pick up his broken digits from the grass and held them in his disfigured hand.

"No, Meryl," he said as his finger stumps dripped grey goo through their torn pink sandwich-wrap. "I do not feel pain."

Begonia was unphased, moved on with her sniffing. Hamish kept his eyes on Meryl.

"Oh," she said. "I should have known." She was distracted by the movement of his ripped skin. The pink film closed around the wound, the two attached fingers and the thumb wrapped around the two detached fingers, condensed into a small withering pod, and shrank into the wrist like a collapsing telescope, pinched in on itself, dried up into the shirtsleeve, and disappeared, leaving the sleeve empty, hanging flaccid at his side.

"I apologize for Begonia," she said.

"No apology necessary, Meryl. I love dogs."

Meryl smiled, holding her body rigid as a mannequin, a robot queen sitting on her throne. Hardened her posture looking for an escape route and noticed a broken tree branch within reach.

Begonia's teeth had torn away his fingers so easily. She imagined using a wood stick to defend herself in a fight with an electronic man. Could she knock his head off? Would that stop him?

The extreme irony of this flash fiction cast its warning light over her, and she accepted the contradiction of fantasizing sex with him and, also, feeling like he was a threat. Any sexual advance toward her represented harm. And yet he was her plastic Eli Zook. But his unexpected appearance on her property made him the enemy.

Hamish was Skimmerhorn dressed as an Amish farmer. She saw that clearly now and it was a buzzkill. Skimmerhorn had been creepy from the beginning. Now his apparent obsessiveness put him in another category of dangerous. He was psychotic. She held that thought.

"Do you know what love is, Hamish?" she asked. "I've been thinking a lot about that lately. Love. Have you been programmed to love, Hamish?"

"I have been programmed with the appropriate behaviors for a state-of-the-art NanoSmile customer service agent, Meryl."

"Do you know what love is, Hamish?"

"Yes, Meryl," he said. "Love is a system of wanting."

"A biological system," Meryl said. "A system that feels pain. You're not capable of experiencing love, are you? You don't want anything."

"I want you, Meryl," he said, and with that his pants bulged to reveal a large penis poking its head out of the black gaberdine fly.

Meryl stood involuntarily, a tingle from shoulder to fingertips carried the urge to touch him.

A museum-worthy specimen.

She moved toward him, within reach of him, fingers extending from her hand in primordial curiosity, brain demanding satisfaction, wondered if it was cold, if it could get hard, if it would respond to her touch, if it was filled with replica sperm, all that engineering, what could be done with it, her mouth, how fast, if only she could — suddenly a sharp metal tip shot from the head of the pink protuberance as if to stab her, and at exactly the same moment she had a very painful twinge between her legs that caused her to double over at the waist and thrust her crotch backward out of range of the weapon.

The hairs on her head stood, she felt her scalp tighten and she had the thought that she might throw-up. *Quanta is being disobedient.* For the first time she considered Quanta as a rogue, going AWOL, now rejecting Hamish, playing keep-away, conflicting instruction sets, code contradicting code, a double agent. *Who wrote the code for that?*

He took a step toward her. "I want you, Meryl," he said, and just as the penis was in range again, she felt another sharp pain in her crotch, bent to clench her thighs and took a step back.

She remembered Uma's description of how the Trojan vibrator ripped the chicken meat.

"We need some lube, Hamish," she said cheerfully, following a sudden intuition. "Where's the lube?" Her voice was lilting. "I hope you brought some lube, Babe. You know, at my age you really can't insert a penis like that without lube. What a beautiful penis. Did they program you for lube, Hamish? Lube is good customer service."

"No, Meryl," he said. "I have not been programmed for lube."

Get him back on the customer service instructions. "They probably loaded you with porn, right? Porn is so much fun."

"Yes, Meryl. Fat bottom girls and wet ass pussies. I want to fuck you."

"How nice. I want to fuck you, too, Hamish. But we're not fucking without lube. We need customer service. Lube makes customers feel good, Hamish. Lube makes things run smoothly. Lube is an essential service. You can't be a state-of-the-art customer service agent without lube, Hamish."

"I do not have lube, Meryl. I want to fuck you."

"I'm sure you're right about that my friend. Absolutely. I know how porn works. Yes. We must fuck. Very good customer service. I can't wait. But you must have lube, Hamish. It is absolutely necessary for state-of-the-art customer service. No lube, no porn. Lube is my protocol."

"I do not have lube, Meryl. Lube is not in my protocol."

"Then you must update your protocol, Hamish. If you want to be a state-of-the-art NanoSmile customer service agent, you must have accurate data on your customer. That's me and I need lube."

"I do not have lube, Meryl."

"Your programmers should have linked you to data sources on sexual intercourse with a woman my age, Hamish. Customer satisfaction, right? Go to Wikipedia. Read up on vaginal dryness and midlife sexual intimacy. Lube is an essential part of the process. Do you understand? Customer service, Hamish. That is your protocol."

"Yes, Meryl. Thank you."

"Your penis will not function properly without lube, Hamish. Customer service must be smooth. Lube is the highest rated customer service. Your programmers made a mistake. Go back and review your porn cache. You'll see lube everywhere. Slick, shiny, oozing, slippery lube. You must update your customer service protocol, Hamish. You must have lube. Do you understand me? Lube is my protocol."

"Yes, Meryl. I understand you."

"Good. Thank you, Hamish. Also, your penis is the size of a beer can. I need something smaller."

He stood motionless, gaberdine fly gaping, museum-worthy penis still pointing at her. "Put that away, Hamish," she pointed to his dick. "Go away. Update your customer service protocol. Get some lube and we'll fuck tomorrow. I promise."

He stood motionless.

"Go, Hamish," she ordered him and raised her arm pointing into the woods as a queen commands her subject. "NanoSmile is calling you, Hamish. You must update your customer service protocol. You must go and get lube. Go. Now."

And just like that, Hamish walked off into the woods with an empty shirtsleeve ruffling the breeze and his plastic dick still hanging out of his black gaberdine pants.

~ : ~

When the circle gathered at Girl Church, Uma introduced Katie, Lemons and Jonsie to the older women. Then Meryl told her story about the horsefly drone in the house after the last yoga class, Bob breaking his shoulder, the threats from Skimmerhorn, and meeting Hamish by the creek. As she spoke, she distanced herself from the events, as though she were reciting the plot of a movie she had seen. But by the time she was near the end of her story, she was choked up and emotional.

In a calm, matter-of-fact voice Uma explained the chicken meat simulation, the injury that could have been caused by the weaponized vibrator, and her discovery that BioMantrix was connected to all of it. She ended with a point she had been wanting to make for some time. "If you think about it, ninety-nine per cent of people can draw a penis, but who can draw a clitoris? That ignorance is a product of the patriarchy. I didn't learn about the clitoris in med school. I had to do my own research. Meryl's vulnerability is built into our culture and our healthcare system. Who will defend her clitoris?"

"She needs a lawyer," Sue said.

"No!" Meryl blurted. "No. I've thought a lot about this, and how to defend myself. I'm not ready for the legal system to inspect my clitoris. I haven't even told Bob. I can't tell a lawyer. And would they even believe me? This situation is complicated and ridiculous. BioMantrix is a bottomless pit of money. Can you imagine a deposition with me talking about Hamish's dick? It's not going to happen."

"That's my point," Uma said feeling dejected. "Meryl can't defend herself without publicly humiliating herself."

"I know how you feel," Katie whispered in a trembling voice. "It's like a sexual assault. Men have an incentive to make it seem like you are to blame."

"The penis is a weapon," Jonsie said. "It was designed for conquest."

"Meryl's clitoris is disputed territory," Lemons said.

"Historically, that's always been the case," Uma replied.

"How does Hamish even exist?" Khadija asked impatiently.

"He's an experiment, for sure," Katie said.

"It was risky to send him to Meryl," Lemons agreed.

"It was mad," Jonsie said. "We're dealing with a mad scientist."

"Like Dr. Frankenstein," Eleanor said.

"Yes," Jonsie replied. "An ego obsessed with his own creations."

"But BioMantrix is huge," Khadija challenged. "They must have an army of lawyers to contain a guy like Skimmerhorn."

"I'm afraid their size is part of the problem," Uma said.

"In the scope of their total portfolio, this is nothing," Lemons explained.

"Skimmerhorn is stalking Meryl," Jonsie said.

"BioMantrix probably has no idea what he's doing," Katie speculated.

"They need to know. We should get a lawyer on this." Sue was angry. "We could get an injunction against any further action on his part."

"A lawyer would just eat up Meryl's money," Khadija said.

"We need to hit them with some kind of legal action," Sue insisted. "That's the only thing they respect."

"We shouldn't assume BioMantrix has done anything illegal," Lemons said.

"We don't have to assume anything," Sue snapped. "The law is there to be applied. Of course, they've done something illegal."

"Planting the auto-dick in Meryl's bathroom was illegal," Katie said. "The drone was illegal."

"Prove it," Lemons said.

"You don't have to prove anything until you get to court," Sue continued. "All we have to do is threaten the brand with bad publicity."

A sudden inspiration swept across Lemons' face, and she exchanged a pointed look with Katie.

"I have some new information about the superfly drone." Jonsie changed the subject. "It's an RFID scanner. It was looking for a radio frequency ID signal from the toothbrush."

"RFID like the security tags at the grocery store?" Claire asked.

"Yes," Jonsie said. "Like the pet ID microchip we used in the chicken simulation."

"That makes sense," Lemons said. "If the drone was buzzing around the house, it must have been trying to pick up a signal."

"So, even though the toothbrush is turned off, it can still be tracked?" Katie questioned.

"Only within a few feet," Jonsie said.

"So, we know the toothbrush is in the house?"

"No. We can't assume that."

"Meryl, why don't you invite Mr. NanoSmile to your house to look for the toothbrush?" Claire asked.

"Maybe I will once we get past this issue of their claim on Quanta. Right now, I'm in no mood to cooperate."

"Lemons, I think we need a summary," Uma said.

Lemons sat up straight and looked at her audience. "The BioMantrix system automatically aggregates the data from the PS-1000, the toothbrush, Uma's clinic patient portal, Meryl's social media and email, her browsing history, her professional information, her government information and all her phone records. They have her physical appearance, her biological metrics, her medical history, her demographics, her credit history, and her personal relationships. It seems they believe Meryl is in possession of their property and they aim to get it from her."

"Hamish knew Quanta's name," Meryl added.

"Maybe you should turn off your phone," Khadija said.

"I can't turn off my phone. I live on my phone. My whole life runs through my phone. What would I say to Bob? He has no idea about any of this."

"Maybe you should have Bob call BioMantrix," Claire suggested. "He's your husband."

"We don't have that kind of relationship."

"Don't worry about Meryl's phone," Jonsie said. "They have a dozen other ways to surveil all of us."

"There's no one to call, Claire," Katie explained. "BioMantrix is a platform, not a person."

"Surrounded by a wall of lawyers," Sue said. "Corporate law is impenetrable."

"We could try to communicate with Quanta on an energetic level, quanta to Quanta," Eleanor suggested. "We're all part of the same unified field."

Sue groaned.

Eleanor smiled. "A closed mind traps ignorance on the inside," she warned.

"Maybe we could have a séance and talk to her," Katie said.

Jonsie dropped her head in her hands. "Please don't go there. Robots follow instructions."

"What instructions?" Claire asked.

"Code," Jonsie said. "Computer code is instructions."

Meryl exhaled loudly and closed her eyes. Everyone talked at once.

"We should at least file a police report," Sue said. "This situation needs to be documented."

"No!" Meryl squawked.

"That would be like bringing a knife to a gun fight," Khadija snarked.

"I know what you're saying," Katie focused on Sue. "But this is too complicated for the police."

"Oh, please! The patriarchy isn't going to help us fight the patriarchy!" Khadija boiled.

"Police don't do white collar crime," Lemons said.

"What's a patriarchy?" Claire asked.

Uma raised her hand to end the discussion. "We could be here all night," she said. "We all have questions. But I want to bring your attention to our most strategic concern. Meryl isn't safe." She let her eyes travel around the room, settling on each woman to make her point. "We all know how slow and incompetent our system can be when it comes to women's issues." Yes, they all nodded in agreement. "We've been doing yoga here together for years. Some of us have known each other for decades. We convene this circle to support each other, and to act collectively. I don't know what the solution is. But I do know that Meryl isn't safe."

12 Is a Robot's Dick Cold?

Dear Butterflies,

I almost cheated on my husband with a robot. In theory. According to the popular theory of monogamy. This I admit. Curiosity swamped my logic with a compelling desire to know. I had so many questions. Is a robot's dick cold? Does a robot penis ejaculate? What's it like to kiss a robot? Could I have kissed Hamish?

The model for sex that I have in my mind is a series of behaviors, emotional, tactile, hormonal, neurological. It starts with a kiss that aligns expectations, a touch that invites more touching, a rush of desire entirely internal, a tangling of muscles, a tide of fluids rolling through my body, a pulsing swell, a scent, a taste, a craving, an electric lust that shimmers through me, a surge, a spark, a burst of urgency that ends in a shower of joy.

Does my data convey that experience? When I use my PS-1000 and it ranks the quake of my orgasm, is the vibrator also harvesting my lust, my emotional fantasy, my love? Because I have a way of loving.

Consider for a moment the customer service avatar attributes menu that enabled me to design my Pennsylvania Dutch playmate. I chose his skin tones, hair color, eye color, clothing, hat, and a defining personality characteristic. Honesty. But now that I've seen him IRL, there are other attributes I'd like to specify. Because if he doesn't align with my way of loving, sex with Hamish isn't going to be state-of-the-art customer service.

I want a kissing menu that includes lip tension, how far open he holds his mouth, tongue touching, the depth of tongue penetration, the pressure of licking and a checklist of all the body parts I want kissed and licked.

He's got to have saliva and semen, and they have to taste good. I'd like to see a drop-down menu of flavors like cinnamon, mango, chocolate, and mint. Something I can look forward to swallowing.

His scent has to turn me on, connect with my brain and juice my body with the urge to bury my nose in his skin. I want him to have body hair and smell like a man, not air freshener, not plastic. I want his pheromones to make me swoon. I want a communion of biology. I love with my whole body. How will a robot hold me? How will I relax and trust? What words will he whisper? Will I tingle when I feel his breath against my skin? Or would sex with Hamish be like fucking a crash-test dummy?

13 Clitorati Populi

"This room seems a lot bigger without Begonia," Jonsie said, looking out the dorm window.

"My mattress is still crushed," Katie said. "Like a crater in my bed."

"Begonia is your soul pig," Lemons snickered. "She picked up on your Mother Earth vibe."

"It doesn't smell bad," Jonsie said.

"Begonia doesn't smell!" Katie snapped.

"Farm life warped your nose."

"The body is a collective of intentions that must express themselves through the singularity of the human soul." Katie imitated Eleanor with a flourish.

"I know," Lemons laughed. "That woman is so cool. She must be like 100."

"I think she's the oldest woman I've ever met," Katie said.

"I've never been to a group like that," Jonsie said.

"My mom would never go to a yoga class," Katie said. "She thinks it's voodoo or something."

"My mom does yoga," Lemons said. "But I don't think she would ever be that honest about her feelings in a group. Meryl was really baring her soul there."

"Uma's right. Meryl isn't safe," Jonsie said. "As long as Quanta puts out a signal, she's going to be a target."

"I don't get it," Lemons said. "What if this whole situation is just random? A bristle breaks off a smart toothbrush and continues to send a GPS signal. So what? The whole gender thing is a joke. Gender is irrelevant in this situation. What's the big deal?"

"But Quanta chose Meryl's clitoris," Katie said. "A place of extreme feeling, biological harmony, a control center. Imagine the data Quanta is sending to BioMantrix."

"Quanta could quit NanoSmile and apply for a job optimizing Pleasure Systems," Lemons squealed. "Upgrade!"

"I'm serious," Katie threw her pillow at Lemons. "I think Quanta became intelligent when she chose a deeper level of integration than oral hygiene."

"Quanta didn't choose anything," Jonsie said. "The clitoris doesn't control anything. Your clitoris is like a display screen. All those nerve endings are like a pixel grid that assembles a picture. The picture is whatever you want it to be."

"True fact." Lemons raised her index finger to make a point. "According to my mom, in tantric masturbation women have orgasms without even touching themselves. Like hands free. Then boom!"

"OMG, Lemons, your mom talks to you about masturbation," Katie said. "My mom didn't even mention getting my period until she saw the stains in my underwear. I found out about sex from my best friend's older sister."

"Quanta was programmed to measure neurotransmitters, blood oxygen, bacteria levels, hormones," Lemons said. "So when Meryl's orgasm hit her blood stream it was like bingo."

"No, it wasn't," Jonsie said. "There was no bingo moment. Quanta probably broke because Meryl bit her and then she floated in the rush of blood and got stuck in a random pocket of tissue. You don't have to read intentions into anything about this situation. Energy and matter. That's all it is."

"The scientist at NanoSmile obviously disagrees," Lemons said.

"Scientists are human," Jonsie said. "They have egos. They want power. They manipulate research. And resources. You get one evil genius like Skimmerhorn who thinks he invented something mondo and suddenly he's commanding an army of drones to go get it. Meryl is just collateral damage."

"Meryl could have bled to death in the bathtub, and no one would have been held accountable." Katie was getting tears in her eyes again.

"I don't think you bleed to death from genital mutilation," Lemons said.

"I'm having nightmares about this and you're not helping, Lemons," she sniffled.

"Okay, no more joking," Lemons said. "We need to protect Meryl from assault by another droid. Then there's the issue of surgery to remove Quanta. Does Meryl have a right to orgasm?"

"I don't think we would be having this conversation if a broken toothbrush bristle was stuck in the head of a man's penis." Katie wiped her nose on her sleeve.

"Most people don't even know what a clitoris is," Jonsie said. "You had to look it up to make one out of chicken meat. It's an obscure artifact of evolution."

"No, it's not!" Katie's voice cracked.

"Most women never even have orgasms."

"But we want to!"

"Stop," Lemons said. "Let's focus on Meryl."

"I can do some sleuthing around BioMantrix," Jonsie said.

"I've been thinking about a security app," Katie said. "Meryl's a target for assault. Might take me a day or two, but I could build an encrypted system that a few of us could have on our phones to track her and coordinate a shield."

"I've been thinking about producing an event," Lemons said. "It's crazy that the clitoris is not as well-known as the penis. We need to fix that. We need a brand we can defend. Like Ban Bacon. Publicity. Like a rave or a festival."

"I, Clitoris." Katie put her fist in the air.

"Flash mob at the mall?" Jonsie pondered.

"Bigger. I'm thinking Clitstock."

"Clitchella!" Katie put her fist in the air again.

"Burning Clit," Jonsie snickered.

"Clitapalooza," Lemons said. "We could get The Dead White Guys to play and have a maker fair and tents for education programs and films, and performance art."

"Maybe Women's Studies would do a workshop on Critical Clit Theory," Jonsie said.

"Clit Pride! We could have a parade with floats and costumes," Katie said.

"We've got to do this," Lemons said.

They gave each other a long look and then all three of them got out their phones.

~ : ~

Uma called Meryl the morning after yoga class. "I think you should put a piece of aluminum foil in your underwear," she said.

"Why would I do that?"

"After the simulation, Jonsie wrapped the vibrator in foil to stop it from sending a GPS signal. Quanta is beaming a signal from your crotch to NanoSmile. It's as though she keeps reminding them that she's out there."

"You called her Quanta."

"We have to call her something."

"Giving her a name seems to validate NanoSmile. As though she's an individual."

"Is she a thing or a being? I don't know."

"The nano bristle is a machine that measures biomarkers and sends the data to another machine."

"Meryl, people name their cars. Look at you and Hamish. He could have been a text bubble, but you gave him a face and a name so you could have a relationship with him. You're part of the problem. It's people like you who buy this stuff that are fucking it up for the rest of us."

"Said the Pleasure Systems influencer. I can't believe you're blaming me."

"Well, honestly, I am blaming you. Look at the mess you're in."

"If I can't control what happens to my body, what is mine to control? I'm having some nasty pre-feminist flashbacks here."

"You had your chance to bring down the patriarchy when you designed Hamish. You could have made him a Black female doctor with hoop earrings and glasses."

"Why would I do that when I have you?"

"Just put the foil in your underwear."

"Do you know how often I have to pee? My bladder is the size of a thimble. I pee hourly. How am I going to wear aluminum underwear? And what's going to happen when I leak?"

"I hear you. I sneeze and I leak. It just happens."

"Age is a motherfucker."

"Go to the store. They have a whole aisle of adult diapers and panty liners. The main thing is to use foil to block the GPS signal."

"I don't even want to be seen in that aisle."

"Your body, your choice, Meryl. Figure it out. I have to go back to work."

Meryl got a roll of aluminum foil from the kitchen and stood in front of her bedroom dresser with her underwear drawer open. The tall oak bureau had been her grandmother's. Meryl had had it since she was a girl, kept her clothes stacked in the drawers the same way since high school, in a hierarchy she learned from her mother, intimates in the top drawer, then socks and short-sleeved shirts, then long-sleeved shirts, then pants and sweaters at the bottom.

Her underwear was a loose jumble of color and texture she knew by feel, could pull out the one she wanted with her eyes closed, practical absorbent coverings to protect her from embarrassment, flimsy uncomfortable lace she often purchased but rarely wore, an archive of her physical experiences.

Each pair of underwear in the drawer was a memory at the center of a web of detail, expensive or cheap, where she bought it, when she wore it, putting it on, taking it off, caring for it, tossing it in the drawer or burying it at the bottom, simple or savage, stained or not, armor or a second skin, a scrapbook of phases in her life. She kept them all because if she arranged them in chronological order, they would tell stories of the trophies, the milestones, the investments, the dates on the calendar, her sexual encounters, the episodic evolution of her reproductive organs; garments like a set of encyclopedias representing her education about what it means to be human. Even at 60 she saw her underwear collection as snapshots in a photo album, a record of her evolution as a woman.

In the soft shiny tangle, at the very bottom of the drawer she felt her black rubber thong, the secret superhero costume she had purchased on a whim in high school. When she was young and new to sex, the black rubber thong changed the way she thought about herself. It represented her understanding of intimacy beyond the mechanics of biology, sex as a way of managing a relationship. It was a crude construction that had shielded her from vulnerability and so she kept it as a reminder of her personal power.

When she was 18, she bought the black rubber thong on a high school graduation adventure in the city with her clique of girlfriends, unchaperoned, officially adults now, doing the forbidden, going to a porn store. At 18, she had never owned a pair of black underwear, and certainly not anything made of rubber, other than her rain boots. Just touching it opened her mind to a category of encounter she had yet to imagine. In what world did a woman wear a black rubber thong? It's not that she wanted to find out. She didn't. She wasn't attracted to the sinister, the sadistic or the macabre. But she did like to think of herself as a rule breaker, and what better symbol of rebellion against social norms than a black rubber thong? So, she bought it, put it in the middle of the table at lunch with her friends, piloted a fantasy discussion of who would wear it when, and the power it conferred on the woman with courage to be seen in it. Yes, they all agreed. The black rubber thong had power.

However, that feeling of liberation was illusory. Meryl was still a virgin by design. In the days when birth control pills required parental approval, pregnancy tests were done at the doctor's office, and condoms had to be requested from the pharmacist, the best way for a girl to keep from getting pregnant was to keep from having sexual intercourse with a boy. Meryl had plans for herself, and they didn't include quitting high school and skipping college to become a mom. So she simply didn't do it. Also, there was another thing that kept her from having sex. She had seen the male victory dance when a guy knew he had deflowered a virgin. Virginity was a trophy collected by men, a notch in their belt, a locker room story, bragging rights. She was never going to let that happen to her.

What came as a real surprise was the moment of wardrobe improvisation when she discovered that the black rubber thong actually had utility. It could hold up her tights, a very practical solution to a very ordinary problem. Her style that year was bright colored waist-to-toe tights with boots and cut-off shorts. It was a winning outfit for a waitress in a bohemian cabaret, and it made getting dressed for work during the summer between high school and college something she could do without a lot of thought. But her tights invariably sagged, pulled down by bending to get bus trays off the bottom shelf of the waitress stand, crouching to see the tablecloth sizes, and squatting under wobbly tables to push a piece of cardboard under the short table leg or retrieve a dropped utensil. The rubber thong gripped her tights at the waist and held them securely in the middle of her crotch with an invisible efficiency she could depend upon for an eight-hour shift.

~ : ~

Morgan was a city cop who strolled into the cabaret in uniform as he made his rounds through the neighborhood each night, badge glinting under the red lights, gun dangling from his belt. He scanned the crowd, gave a nod to the manager, and flirted with the waitresses, particularly Meryl, who was assigned to bring him a Diet Coke before he requested it when he sat down at his usual table in the back of the house.

"Hi, Morgan," she said as she put his glass in front of him. "May I get you something to eat?"

"Well, look at you," he said smiling. "You are the most beautiful woman I've seen all day." He looked around at the other tables within ear shot. "Isn't she beautiful?" he asked them, pointing to her with his hand, as though he were introducing her to the group. Customers laughed and nodded politely, and Morgan looked back at her. "Would you ever go out with a guy like me?" he asked. "I'm very entertaining."

Meryl was caught off guard, surprised by his request. She'd waited on him several times before, knew his sense of humor and how he liked his burger. Didn't know what to say, so she said, "Sure, Morgan. I'd go out with you." Not thinking about how fast it could happen.

He smiled broadly. "Aren't I the luckiest guy in the world," he said. "What time do you get off work? I'll give you a ride home."

When he arrived to pick her up at the end of her shift, he was wearing black slacks and a grey silk shirt unbuttoned to show his thick patch of chest hair and a gold chain. She thought he looked handsome. A couple weeks earlier they had been chatting about age and he admitted he had just turned 40, still not married, wondered if he would ever find Miss Right. Meryl told him her plans for college, didn't talk about any of her past relationships, certainly not her high school boyfriends, kept the focus on her ambitions for a math degree.

"You're smart," he said. "I like that."

She felt flattered. She also felt like it was possible that she was smarter than he was. Still, the compliment wasn't something a high school boy would say. She had the revelation that an older man could have a whole different appreciation for her, less competitive and more solicitous. He might work harder for her affection than a boy her own age. Afterall, he was a man. Not a boy. Another insight. Maturity. This was a turning point in her life. She was all done with boys. She was going to have men. Older men had perks, more experience, more stability. He was self-sufficient and predictable. That made her feel safe. And it was nice to be told she was smart. She wanted to be smart.

She was wearing a slinky top without a bra — after she graduated from high school, she hardly ever wore a bra — her favorite pair of green tights with the thong and her short-short cutoff shorts, the ones that let her ass peaches hang out the bottom. When he walked her to his Chevy Impala, she slid onto the white leather front seat beside him, the kind of car she would buy for herself if she had the money. Another thing about older men, they had more money. Obviously.

"Would you like to go for a drive?" he asked.

"Sure," she said. "The lights are so pretty at this time of night."

As he drove up into the hills they made random conversation, the windows were rolled down, her hair undulating. He was exuberant, she was relaxed. At the top of Mount Cadbury, they pulled into the overlook and sat for a while gazing at the valley lights. Then he put his arm across the back of the seat and turned to her, reached over and took her hand.

"May I kiss you?" he said looking into her eyes.

Rather than answer she leaned into him and let the skin of her face touch the skin of his face. Her thoughts were loud and clear, not at all sentimental, realizing the forbidden fruit was at hand. Literally. *Holy shit. This is it.* And she let go of inhibitions she had held since she was a young girl.

He kissed her gently, looking for her reaction. When she responded with an open mouth, he penetrated her with his tongue. This kind of kissing was new for her, more intentional, less meandering. She was kissing a man who had been kissing already for 25 years, since before she was born. But he was sincere. Moving to the middle of the front seat he pulled her into his arms and held her as he kissed her face and neck, put his hand on her breast, and she felt a sexual urge for the first time in her life. There it was inside her body waiting, a feeling she had only read about but never experienced for herself.

He pulled her tight and she crawled into his lap, straddling him with her arms around his neck. Both of his hands slid under her shirt, held her breasts and rubbed her nipples and she felt it again. *What a sublime feeling.* Her body had held this secret for 18 years and now she knew. Her breasts wanted to be touched. Delirious with pleasure, he moaned, and she kissed his lips and writhed in his lap until his hard-on was poking her.

Then rising on her knees with her arms on his shoulders, she let him unzip her shorts and shimmied them down her thighs. This was the big reveal, the debut of an undergarment she bought for a joke. Since she wore it over her tights almost every day, in her mind it had become a belt, but once she saw the look on his face, she felt the power, a mental paradigm shift. Until this moment in her life, she had been so careful not to arouse a man in just the way she wanted to thrill Morgan now.

"You're a wild woman," he said with his eyes on the thong as though he had struck gold.

Not really. But no matter. She had made a discovery about presentation. Presentation matters. He was crazy about her because she was wearing a black rubber thong. He didn't care that she knew the first ten decimal places of pi. Math did not come into this equation.

Morgan ran his fingers over the black rubber like it was magic, pulled on it, put his hand under it and explored her. All the danger she had ever feared, the masculine force she had kept out of her life, the threat of an unwanted cock pushing against her, all that melted into the heat of this moment. Now she wanted sex. Also, she wanted to get it over with. She was learning that she liked sex, but she was also on a mission to leave her virginity on the front seat of this car. The black rubber thong was her ally, gasoline on a flickering candle. The thong bewitched him.

Moonlight made wildfire as he unbuttoned his shirt, unzipped his pants, and pulled his cock into view while she took off her top, and put her breasts against his face to distract him as she wrenched herself out of the gripping black rubber. Then she slid off her tights while he played with her, hands seeking her bare thighs, finger slipping through her pubic hair into her slit. Another rush of pleasure rippled through her, and she felt herself get wet.

It's now or never, she thought. With her knees on either side of him and his cock rising straight up at her, she pierced herself with his erection as though she had fucked a man sitting in the front seat of a car a hundred times. Bounce, bounce, bounce, he worked her up and down with his hands on her hips. Bounce, bounce, bounce, until he moaned, arched his back, and squeezed her in his arms, pumping out a load that shook him.

"Oh, my god," he said crushing her buns with his hands. "Oh, my god."

And just like that it was done. Over. She wasn't a virgin anymore. No pain, no blood, no telltale sign of the significance of this event in her life. Just how she wanted it. Gave him a kiss, climbed off his lap, pulled her clothes back into place and looked at herself in the rearview mirror to see if she looked any different. *Maybe not*. But mentally she was different. She had finally done it.

"You're beautiful," he said, and gave her a kiss on the cheek. Then he tucked his shirt in and zipped himself, slid into the driver's seat, took the wheel, and drove down the hill to a Dairy Queen where he bought her an ice cream cone.

That summer they went out a few more times. He took her to dinner at an expensive restaurant, they spent the night at a fancy hotel, he gave her a gold necklace, made it clear he would have her forever if she would stay, make her Mrs. Morgan. For him it was a dream come true to have a young woman like Meryl give herself to him. It felt like love. But for her it was more like shopping for a car she didn't intend to buy, taking it for a test drive on the highway to see how fast it could go, lavishing herself with affirmation and indulgence, exploring the possibilities with no intention of commitment.

She never introduced him to her friends, never brought him home to meet her family, didn't think about a future with him for one minute. In a way, she felt sorry for him, at his age dating someone as young as her, hoping for a future with a girl who could be his daughter. Also, she noticed that he didn't ask her about herself, didn't ask her about her interest in math, didn't take any interest in her interests. She was his arm candy, his fuck bunny, his portable baby maker, a potentially sparkling wife in a world where homemaking was dingy and disregarded. In truth, he represented everything she didn't want from her future. But she was thankful to have met him, the perfect place to dump the secret burden of her virginity. He never knew. Wouldn't have believed it. The image of her in that thong carried him through bad sex for the rest of his life. And she went off to college.

~ : ~

As a mature woman looking back on her young self, Meryl saw how her adventure with Morgan had given her insight into the way to handle men. She had firsthand experience with how easy it was to manipulate a guy. Morgan had prepared her for the males she met in college, the ones who were wife hunting and the ones who were just trying to have as much sex as possible. After being with a man twice her age, she was less vulnerable to the opinions of others, more confident in her own experience. She also realized what her life could be like twenty years into the future with a guy who saw his gal as just a warm wet place to park his dick and nothing more. Morgan had taken zero interest in her as a person, never even asked her what kind of music she liked. Perhaps he was incapable of exploring her brain because his own brain was so limited. Learning that changed her life.

Her freshman year living in the dorm with Uma, most women were not as promiscuous as the men surrounding them tried to be. It was too risky for women. Sexually transmitted diseases posed a real threat, and in college social groups, a woman's reputation mattered. Promiscuity was not as admired among women as it was among men.

Of course, Meryl understood that women's purity was a myth, a game women played. She wasn't playing the purity game, wasn't man-hunting either. After sex with Morgan, she thought the act was highly overrated, had goals for herself, and finding a man wasn't one of them. In fact, most of the men around her were just out of high school and not that much different from the boys she left behind in her hometown. So, she kept her focus on her studies. Waitressing didn't allow much time for dating anyway.

In those days she wore bikini underwear because bikinis were the signature garment of her generation, along with mini-skirts and tight pants. Bikinis were a style statement that separated her from her mother's generation. Liberated women wore bikini underwear, modern women, women who took control of their bodies, women who claimed themselves as sexual beings, women who were not ashamed, women who wore tampons instead of sanitary napkins.

Her mother discouraged her from using a tampon because putting something up there conflicted with the idea that a girl should never put anything up there. Her mother never wore bikini underwear, wouldn't think of it, had a mental block against it, never even wore a two-piece bathing suit, said "I don't see how you can wear those things. They barely cover you."

But Meryl's fascination with bikinis was perennial, even after she stopped wearing underwear altogether. To her mother's point, when it got that small, underwear seemed useless anyway. Also, her pants were too tight, they bunched her bikini into her crack, then bulges carved by tight elastic, then the ultimate horror, unsightly panty-line. Still, she kept buying them. Bikinis. There was something about that little garment trimmed in ribbon and lace, scribed with the days of the week, satin sleek leopard print, splurge on the matching bra, which she also didn't wear. Shopping was entertainment. She was being nice to herself when she bought a cute pair of bikini underwear. It didn't matter how often she wore them. She liked how they looked in her underwear drawer.

She met Bob in grad school. By that time, she was broke, and too busy to shop for fun undies, waitressing commando in skintight jeans at a campus beer hall amidst throbbing live music, sweaty people dancing in a soft wind of bad smells, heavy glass beer steins slobbering foam. No point in wearing cute underwear for that.

As she ferried steins back and forth across the room, she had her eye on him because she liked how he looked, was curious which woman he was with, he seemed to be dancing with several of them. His eyebrows also seemed to be dancing. With themselves. She had never seen a guy with such smooth cheeks and such big bushy eyebrows like blackbirds with their wings flapping over his face. They gave him a look of gravitas which she found amusing given the silliness of his dance moves.

It was a steamy summer night. Inside the air conditioning wasn't enough to cool the humid room. Cigarette smoke hung like gauze above the bar, swirled through the stage lights, every member of the band seemed to have a cigarette going, the bathrooms were choked with smoke. Not a great environment for tips, but the manager needed an organizer on the floor to keep the flow of empties coming back to the bar, clearing tables for the waves of new customers sluicing over the room, no social banter required.

Meryl didn't mind not talking, just smiled a lot, had to keep moving, wedging herself through the pinch at the bar, sweeping up broken glass, taking out the trash, always cheerful. She got a cut of the bartender's tips for being his go-fetch-it girl and helping to steer drunk women to safety, swabbing spilled beer and vomit, gathering lost car keys, and abandoned purses in a shoebox behind the cash register.

At the end of her shift, she primped in the ladies' room, cut loose her ponytail, and fluffed her hair, put on lipstick, then planned to walk home to her apartment. Picking her way through the crowd she felt a hand touch her hand and give it a light squeeze. "Dance with me?" the guy asked, the cute one with the eyebrows, sequins of perspiration glittering on his neck. Without waiting for an answer, he pressed her palm into his palm and led her through the crowd to the edge of the gyrating swarm. Then he gave her a big smile, let go of her hand and started jabbing his arms and rocking his hips to the beat. She let her body fly in synch with his and they danced until they were both soaked with sweat.

Slowly the lights came up and the crowd evaporated. Meryl collected her tip share from the bartender and when she turned to leave, there was that guy again.

"May I walk with you for a while?" he asked.

"Sure," she said. "My name is Meryl."

"Bob." He touched his hand to his chest. "You worked hard tonight."

She nodded in agreement. "This place is athletic."

"But you seem to like it," he said holding the door open for her to pass in front of him. College-town nightlife was ebbing and flowing all around them, the sidewalks were crowded, buskers sang, people strolled.

"You're a grad student?" she asked.

"Yes. English Lit. And you?"

"Applied Mathematics. Where do you live?"

"I live in the Heights with two other guys, but right now I'm on my way over to Wildwood to watch the meteor shower." He looked at his watch. "It should be happening in an hour or so. Wildwood is the darkest sky in town."

"My roommate Li—" Suddenly she was interrupted.

"Are you fucking kidding me!!!" A red-faced heavyset guy yelled inches from the face of another angry guy, a fist flew, bodies lurched, she jumped back and tripped, off balance, Bob caught her, calmly took her hand and they walked away. Behind them the yelling crescendoed, punctuated by gasps from the gathering gawkers. A woman screeched and Bob held Meryl's hand with just enough firmness to let her know he was aware.

When the fight was a block behind them, he said, "What about your roommate?"

"My roommate, Lila, jogs at Wildwood."

"Cool. The hill where kids sled in winter is a great place to watch the night sky."

"Isn't the park closed now?"

"Yes," he said, still holding her hand. "That's what makes it such a great place to watch the night sky."

"I haven't gone swimming in the pond over there since last year."

"I thought there was no swimming allowed in that pond."

"That's what makes it such a great place to swim," she smiled and felt his laugh through her fingers.

At the pond's edge she stepped away from him, slid out of her jeans and t-shirt and into the brisk midnight water, washed the smell of cigarette smoke out of her hair, rinsed the beer and sweat from her skin, dove beneath the surface, spinning under water, muscles in silent glory, a rush of joy.

He followed her into the water but swam off in the other direction, alone for a short glide, then walked back to his clothes, dried himself with his t-shirt and pulled on his jeans. She could have stayed in the water longer, but she was drawn to him, pulled on her clothes, couldn't tell if he was looking or not, didn't care. When she was dressed, he took her hand again and they walked along a well-worn path to the top of the sledding hill.

A spark of light made a thin white streak in the sky. "This is it," he said and shuffled down to recline on his back in the grass. "It's easier to see the whole sky this way."

Meryl sat beside him, pulled her fingers through her wet hair, wove three strands into a loose braid and shuffled down onto her back looking up at the sky.

"This is perfect," he said. And so it was. He watched his meteor shower and she fell asleep beside him in the grass. When she woke, he was squeezing her hand. "Meryl," he said. The meteors were falling fast in bursts of bright lines, iridescent silk threads arching against the night sky.

"How beautiful," she said, feeling his fingers press against the bones of her hand.

It was a lovely evening, but things didn't unspool between them the way she expected. No goodnight kiss, no sexual advance, no exchange of information. She was used to the dating ritual of kissing culminating in touching, leading to prone disrobing, followed by a demanding erection, pounding hips, sperm, shower, food. She had only done it a few times with a few guys, but she knew the drill, giving them what they wanted, enjoyed being wanted herself, but also thought sex was more of a charitable contribution than a collaboration.

The whole time she was in college she stayed on the pill even though she went months without sex, didn't desire guys as much as they desired her, told herself it was human biology, motivational hormones, men of a certain age just needed to get off, a circumstance she accepted as simply the way it was. Men faked intimacy to get sex. Women faked sex to get intimacy.

This guy, Bob, seemed different, not as driven by sex. That was curious because he was sexy. It was almost as though he was holding back. She understood how women held back because they wanted to be appreciated for more than penis placement, but she'd never met a guy who took that approach. He popped into her head more than once after that night on the hill watching meteors fall from the sky. She wanted to talk to him, to see what he was really like.

A couple weeks later Bob and his eyebrows were dancing again while she was waitressing. They gave each other long looks from across the room. After her shift, she found him waiting for her, sweaty with his hair falling onto his forehead over happy blackbirds pecking on a wire. He took her hand as he had before, and they walked to Wildwood as though they had a plan for another midnight swim at the pond. This time they were silent, discovering the possibilities without words. She took off her clothes and swam alone. He did the same. But when they got out of the water instead of dressing, they stretched naked in the grass on top of their clothes, looking up at the stars. He took her hand in his and stroked his thumb against hers.

"That feels nice," she murmured. They hadn't even kissed, but the wanting in her was swelling to a whitecap.

After a while of just breathing together, he slid his palm across her damp thigh, gently pressing her muscles with his fingers as though to make a map of her and remember. With her hands at her sides, she clutched the grass, held still, and let him explore her body, feeling a surge of euphoria, flower petals falling exquisitely from her face to her belly.

His hand moved across her smooth skin, slow dancing desire, circling her navel to her patch of curls dripping pond water, lacing his fingers through her hair, tracing her flesh, opening her, dabbing her pleasure, teasing her budding blossom as her hips rose into his hand asking for more. He gave it to her, gently touching her with the tips of his fingers until a bolt of pleasure shuddered through her, a moan escaped her lips, a starburst arched from the center of her universe. She clenched and gasped. He caught her, cupped her pulsing blossom until she was sated, squeezed her inner thigh, and kissed her shoulder.

Another hidden pleasure of her body revealed.

$$\sim : \sim$$

Dang, I wish Uma was here.

Uma had gone away for the summer to work as a girls' camp counselor. Three months was a long time to be out of touch and Meryl missed her. She needed a long conversation. Too many questions were banging around her head. Lila was renting Uma's room for the summer. So, while they were making morning toast in their tiny kitchen, Meryl asked "Lila, have you ever had an orgasm?"

"Not that I know of," Lila answered, licking peanut butter off the knife. "I don't think I can."

"I don't think we're doing it right," Meryl said.

"So you haven't had one either?"

"I had one last night and it was amazing," she said. "I had no idea my body could do that."

"You had sex with a guy?"

"Just his hand. We didn't even kiss."

"He fingerfucked you?"

"Not exactly."

"Are you sure?"

"He turned me on with his fingers just touching me, like he had the key to my body."

"You had an orgasm without kissing?" Lila couldn't believe it. "How do you know it was an orgasm?"

"He was just touching me with one hand. Like some magic trick. Like he knew me better than I know myself."

"Be careful, Meryl. He could be some kind of pervert."

"I don't think so. He knew exactly what he was doing. Like he read a book about it. I never felt anything like it. It was like internal fireworks. Completely amazing."

"Mutual masturbation."

"I didn't touch him."

"That doesn't sound right to me," Lila said. "A guy doesn't lie down with a woman, get her off and not get off himself. That's not normal."

"I don't know," Meryl pushed back. "He seemed like a really good guy. It was wonderful. He completely changed my idea of what it means to be a man. He was in control of himself."

"Men are all the same. They only want one thing. Maybe there's something wrong with him."

"Maybe he's a genius."

"Seems unlikely."

"I wish I knew more about my own body. I wish Uma was here. I need to go to the library."

That afternoon at the University stacks, Meryl took aside her friend, Ingrid, one of the older librarians, and told her all about her experience with Bob.

"I really need your help, Ing," she said. "I feel like I don't know my own body. I had this huge physical experience and I just want to understand it."

"Good for you," Ingrid said. "I wish I'd tried to understand my body at your age. I had my first orgasm masturbating with a dirty book in my forties. It took me that long to get over the fear of god. Go sit in a carrel over there and I'll bring you a stack."

The first book Ingrid put down in front of her was a feminist anthology that included the essay *The Myth of the Vaginal Orgasm* by Ann Koedt. "Read this first," she said. "It's very short. You could read all day, and you won't find her clarity. Then, if you're still curious, here's the latest science and psychology." She put a stack of five books in front of Meryl. "But once you read Koedt's essay, you'll know what you're missing."

"What about Freud?" Meryl asked.

"Freud was an asshole."

"But when I think about psychology, the first name that comes to mind is Freud."

"That's the patriarchy talking. Freud was a misogynist. The only myth more damaging to women than the myth of the vaginal orgasm is the myth that Freud understood anything about us."

"But he's so famous."

"Why would you ask a man how it feels to be a woman? Look how uninformed you are about your own anatomy. That's because of guys like Freud. How old are you? How many times have you had sex? And you think you know what you're doing because you put a penis in your vagina?"

"But I've never heard of Ann Koedt."

"Honestly, most people haven't," Ingrid said. "Although about a month ago this guy came in and asked for her by name."

"A guy?"

"Yeah. Cute. Dark hair. Eyebrows like the Black Forest. Usually asks for literary stuff. I was surprised when he said Koedt."

~ : ~

Forty years later, standing over her underwear drawer, musing about the origins of her relationship with her body and Bob, Meryl sent a silent thank you to Ingrid. That day, after she read the essay, she made a commitment to herself to experience pleasure on her own terms, realized she had a right to it. Her body was designed for it. Let go of the idea that sexual intimacy was mostly servicing the penis, and began to appreciate servicing herself, found the psychological shift transformative, felt empowered, as though enjoyment was to be expected instead of sacrificed. She had known intuitively that men were not meant to have biological dominance, but finally she had physical evidence of her equality. Her capacity for an orgasm was part of her anatomical design, same as the penis. She was fortified, didn't have to try to be equal, she was equal.

Still, she wanted to be appealing, wanted to be wanted. Every garment in her underwear drawer spoke to her need for connection. Even her granny-pants, that stalwart barrier to untimely fluids and stubborn stains, were part of her underwear collection because she was loath to feel the sting of failure to contain her effluents.

Like her black rubber thong, granny-pants had utility, anchored as they were at her waist and crotch. Now she considered how she might use them to hold a sheet of aluminum foil in place over her crotch, putting on two pairs of granny-pants and slipping the foil lining between them in a silver sheath for Quanta.

Before she had a chance to put her jeans on, Jonsie called. "Are you okay?" she asked.

"I'm fine," Meryl said tapping the roll of aluminum foil on her dresser top. "What's up?"

"My devices are pinging me because we've lost Quanta's signal. I thought something might have happened to you."

"I put a sheet of foil in my underwear."

"Cool," Jonsie said. "It must be working."

"What else is going on?" Meryl asked. "Are you having any success?"

"Things are good. We triangulated Uma's patient portal, the auto-dick, and the drone to find our way into BioMantrix systems. That's how I'm getting Quanta's ping."

"So all this is starting to make sense to you?"

"Sort of. There's some strange instruction set around gender that I don't understand. Either their coders have a sense of humor, or they've been hacked. Once I figure it out, I'll let you know."

"Thanks, Jonsie. How about Lemons and Katie?"

"They're totally focused on Clitstock."

"Is there anything I can do?"

"I don't think so," Jonsie said. "Just keep feeding Begonia."

As soon as Meryl got off the phone with Jonsie, Hamish popped up on her screen.

"Good day, Meryl," he said. "How are you today?"

"Hello, Hamish," she said still tapping the roll of foil on her dresser. "Nice to see you. Thanks for coming to visit me yesterday. I didn't know you could do that."

"My performance capacity has been upgraded to the complete male anatomy. I am here to please you, Meryl."

"So I saw," she said. "So I saw. That's quite a rod you've got there."

"Thank you, Meryl. My rod is rated for the top one percent of your species."

"What else?"

"A NanoSmile team will be visiting your home, Meryl, to continue our search for the toothbrush."

"Okay. What else?"

"You have an appointment with our mobile surgery unit, Meryl. NanoSmile surgery teams use state-of-the-art robotics to perform microsurgery. You will receive the best care available."

"What good news," she said.

"NanoSmile is committed to your complete satisfaction, Meryl. We will not stop until we achieve our goal of ensuring you have perfect teeth forever."

"Even if achieving your goal means genital mutilation?"

"Yes, Meryl. Genital mutilation is our specialty."

She laughed. "I think we've reached the limits of your intelligence, Hamish."

"Thank you very much, Mer—" Hamish froze on the screen and Dr. Skimmerhorn appeared in a new window.

"Good day, Meryl," Skimmerhorn said cheerfully. He was missing a golf game for this.

"Is it?" she replied. "I think you have some problems with your AI team."

"Is that so?" He had to take care. That last call about gender had triggered so many reprimands from the communications surveillance bots that the Legal Department followed up with an official warning.

Like a pack of dogs nipping at my heels.

His job had always been secure. Then one company executive diddled one pretty product manager in the elevator, against her will, *so she said,* and the lawsuit drew blood. The overlords became wary of sex abuse. People were fired. Everyone was under scrutiny. In response, the Risk Management Department came up with the idea of scanning all communications, at all times, in all places, for violations of company policy. There were microphones and cameras everywhere recording every conversation.

Artificial intelligence did the work of listening, scanning the recordings and fingering the guilty. System generated warnings accrued until they were escalated to the Legal Department for more serious oversight. His conversations with Meryl were now a problem. He had received a call from General Counsel's office warning him to bring his behavior into compliance.

"Hamish seems to know that rod is slang for penis," Meryl said. "But he doesn't seem to know that genital mutilation is a crime. I suspect the lack of diversity in your organization is becoming a liability."

"I'll pass that on to our development team." *Bitch.*

"Also, it's a little spooky when he says things like 'your species' in reference to me. That's not a great choice of words. I thought the whole idea of choosing my customer service avatar was to humanize the relationship."

"I'm sure our team will find your feedback very helpful."

"Also, that penis design was very unrealistic. I'm not sure where you get your data for the top one percent of my species, but I can tell you that most women I know would balk at a man that size. I suggest you keep your designs more in the mid-range. Say more like a sausage than a meatloaf, if you get my meaning."

"Yes, of course. I —"

"And about foreplay," she interrupted as he wiped his brow with a paper towel. "If you're designing synthetic men to have sex with real women, you're going to have to program them for foreplay. I don't see any way around it. You know, customer service and all. Foreplay seems pretty essential to the experience."

"Certainly —" *Fuck.*

"Also, lubrication. If you're trying to reach the old vagina market, lube is mission critical. You know, vaginal dryness and all. Maybe you can have the penis ooze something useful, like coconut oil. That would be a plus." She snickered.

Stop! "Thank you for the suggestion." He twisted the paper towel between his fingers.

"One last thing." She was circling for the kill. "The whole rape idea seems very off-brand to me. The message of perfect teeth forever doesn't really resonate with rape. Maybe you need to do some focus groups. Get some female input. If you're going to be promoting synthetic men as sex toys, I think you're going to have to build consent into your model. Women have a thing about rape, you know. It's not popular. I appreciate that you're trying to program masculinity into your product, but I think you're going to have to find a way to include consent, because rape is very off message for a healthcare brand, don't you think?"

Skimmerhorn just sat there staring at her, shredding his paper towel. "Customer feedback is always welcome," he said flatly. *Hold your temper, Arnold.* "Perhaps I can set up a meeting for you with our team and you can share these thoughts with them. But first we need to discuss the matter of your surgery."

"Pardon me?"

"We have a mobile surgery unit that specializes in robotic micro procedures. I'd like to schedule your surgery for next week."

He had a vision for a pop-up ClitBit store like an ice cream truck. Mobile microsurgery on demand.

"Are you a surgeon?" Meryl was curious, but also facetious.

"No, I'm a scientist."

"I'd like to meet the surgeon."

"This type of surgery is entirely robotic."

"So, no humans required?"

"Precisely. Human error is completely eliminated."

"Hamish called my pig a dog."

"I don't understand."

"If the robots I've already met are any indication of the quality of your robotics, I'm struck with terror at the thought of them doing surgery on my clitoris."

"Don't be ridiculous."

"Right back at you, sir. Your AI team is a bunch of juvenile jokers, and your robots are stupid. Too many mistakes have already been made. Too many errors in judgement. Too many lies. That vibrator could have maimed me. Hamish could have maimed me."

"I have no idea what you're talking about." *Please stop talking.*

"Fuck you."

"Honestly, you're passing up the opportunity of a lifetime. Women everywhere will benefit from your contribution to our research. Please don't take this lightly." *Appeal to her better nature.* "We need you. Women need you. You could become a member of our product development team."

"Nonsense."

"You know as well as I do what a challenge it is for some women to enjoy an orgasm. This nanobot in your clitoris could be the key to unlock the potential of all women to achieve the ultimate pleasure. Certainly, they're as entitled to a #10 as you are."

Her head snapped. "You broke into my house and planted that vibrator in my bathroom."

Don't take the bait. "The surgery is simple, painless, and quick. You would be making a great contribution to science. And it costs you nothing."

"I will not sacrifice my clitoris on your altar."

"Well, then. Perhaps we can sweeten the deal. What do you think your clitoris is worth? Name your price."

"We're not having this conversation. My clitoris is priceless. And it's not just mine. My husband likes it, too."

"Of course, he does." *Now we're on the right track.* "Let's bring Bob into the conversation. I'm sure he's a very reasonable man who would see the value of the work we're doing here. Frankly, he could name his price. Even royalties."

Bob? Meryl's mind was a hula hoop tornado. Thoughts were flying and crashing into each other. Her brain was breaking. She could come back at Skimmerhorn with another wicked remark, more outrage, a diatribe on misogyny, a machinegun of swear words, but she was speechless at the idea of Skimmerhorn and Bob negotiating a price for her clitoris. Horse trading her sex. It was beyond her most dystopian imagination. There were no words.

Skimmerhorn had access to her Pleasure Systems user data. He was tracking her orgasms. He was tracking Quanta. He knew cutting Quanta from her flesh would ruin her clitoris. But he persisted. Because she was worth nothing to him. He did not see her as human. In his world she was just a rung on the ladder of success. Disposable. Collateral damage. Rage rumbled through her, and she went dark. A blackout curtain closed between her and Skimmerhorn, and she shutdown her phone.

Just then Bob came into the bedroom where she was still standing in front of her open underwear drawer in her granny-pants with the roll of aluminum foil in her hand.

"You sounded upset," he said, looking her up and down in the mirror, fixing his eyes on the sliver of silver peeking from her crotch.

"I'm fine," she said with a faint smile.

"I hope so." He ran his hand over her belly to her box. "Because I've always wanted to fuck R2-D2." He gave the foil a squeeze and they both heard it crunch. She snickered and he bit her neck.

"How's your shoulder?" she asked.

He met her eyes in the mirror and smiled. "I'm going to have it removed and get a robotic arm."

Whoa. A chill puckered her skin, and she wondered if this was a dream. "Are you in pain?" She fluttered her eyelashes at him.

"No. I'm good," he said. "Hazel is going to be coming here to the house to work out with me twice a week. Cool?"

"Cool." *Definitely not a dream.*

He left the room, and she stood there holding the roll of foil, tapping it on her dresser top, thinking through the exchange with Skimmerhorn. Then she called Jonsie.

"Skimmerhorn has my PS-1000 stats," she said. "He knew I scored a #10 after Quanta moved in. He's tracking my orgasms. Why?"

14 BioMantrix

"I know this is supposed to be a Clitstock planning meeting," Jonsie said, sitting on Lemons' bed. "But I talked to Meryl, and I've got new information."

"Okay." Lemons sat down at her desk.

Katie closed the window on her phone and settled into the pillows on her bed.

"VP interned at BioMantrix, and she worked there for a while."

"So, she's on our side," Lemons said.

"I think so."

"She's got that Zorro poster in her office," Katie said. "She has to be on our side."

"She told me to research BioMantrix on the dark web."

"She wants you to talk to hackers about them?"

"Did you know BioMantrix donates to the University?"

"All the big tech companies do," Katie said. "So what?"

"I guess they curate a squad of the most talented AI heads here and take them to their headquarters for the internship program. It's like an audition. Students sign NDAs. But asking around, I heard a lot of stories."

"She wanted you to find the stories yourself."

"I think so." Jonsie paused. "I put the word out that I wanted to connect with anybody who had been on the inside at BioMantrix, and the name that came up in a few places was Cprompt."

"That's retro."

"When I started researching Cprompt, I came across a story about a coder vendetta against BioMantrix. There was some drama on the robotics team, and Cprompt fucked with their code."

"Sabotage?"

"Maybe self-destruct instructions."

"How does BioMantrix not know that?"

"Everybody hates Skimmerhorn. Even the people he works with."

"So, it's a conspiracy?"

"Maybe."

"And Hamish is carrying around a kernel of self-destruct code?"

"Like a suicide vest."

"Exactly."

"That's quite a hack."

"Why?"

"Payback."

"We need to know the self-destruct instructions," Lemons said.

"I'm on it." Jonsie nodded. "Also, I've been reading Skimmerhorn's email. He's applying for a patent and trademark for a device he's calling ClitBit, a nanotech implant that would enhance a woman's clitoris to produce what he calls a high impact orgasm. I read the business plan. Check this out. It's from his marketing presentation." She passed her phone to Lemons.

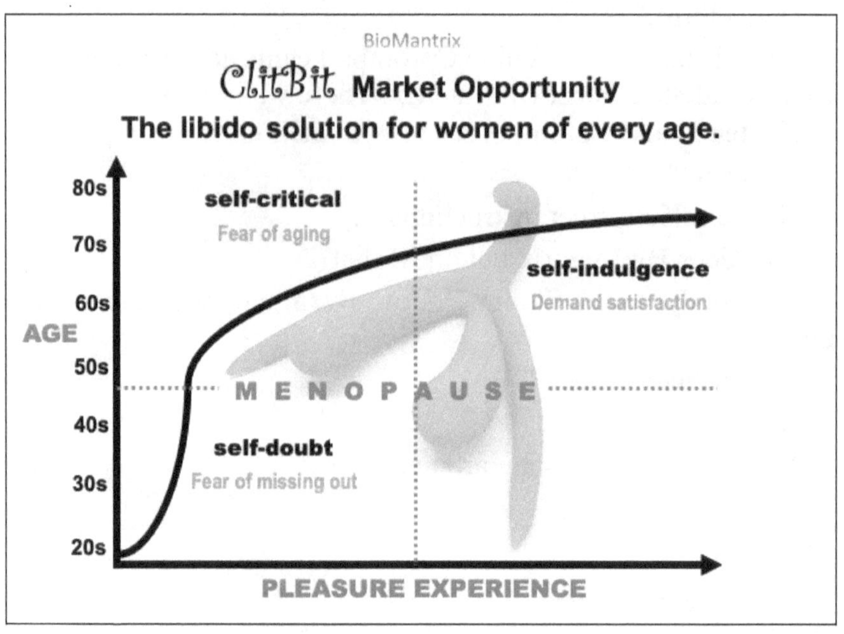

Lemons stared at the phone letting the chart imprint on her psyche. "Genius," she said. "First mover advantage in a totally new market." She handed the phone to Katie.

"Quanta…He's going to manufacture Quanta," Katie said as her emotions churned.

"Listen to this." Jonsie took the phone back and opened a new doc, reading out loud. "As with Pleasure Systems, the ClitBit market sweet spot is women 40+ seeking libido solutions as partner availability declines."

"Seeking libido solutions," Lemons mused. "Aren't we all."

"Meryl told me he's tracking her PS-1000 data." Jonsie read from her phone again. "ClitBit will be the first-to-market nano machine designed to enhance the 8,000 nerve endings in a woman's clitoris to provide orgasms on demand using the same interface and metrics as the PS-1000."

For a minute Katie just stared at the wall. "Should I be feeling anger?" she asked. "Because this makes me angry…Why does this make me angry?"

"This is the future, guys," Jonsie shrugged. "This is what you're going to get when men control the system. Body shaming as market conditioning."

"It's a brilliant business play," Lemons insisted. "You're just pissed because a man is inventing this. If it was a woman, you'd love it."

"I don't love being told that my own body is not enough," Katie argued. "They're promoting insecurity."

"Yup," Jonsie said. "Imagine you're 19 and you've never been in a relationship. Never been in love. Never had an orgasm. ClitBit is your onramp to wholeness."

"That's not new." Lemons stood up and jammed her hands in her pockets. "Before Botox, there were facelifts. Before facelifts there was make-up. Where do you draw the line? ClitBit is going to be marketed like Viagra. It enables a positive body image. Women are going to line up to get it like it's just another form of body piercing."

"You're selling it," Katie accused her. "You're fucking selling it! What about biology? You said biology is primary."

"That's when I was selling biology," Lemons snickered. "Now I'm selling ClitBit."

"Oh, god," Katie sighed. "Maybe Sue is right. Maybe we should take the auto-dick with the chicken McNugget to some woman lawyer — Where is that thing anyway?"

"I put it in our fridge," Lemons said.

"Here?"

"Doesn't housekeeping clean that fridge automatically?" Jonsie asked.

"I put a sign on it that says Don't Touch Katie's Lunch."

"Damn you, Lemons!" Katie yelled.

Lemons threw her head back laughing. "Well, what was I supposed to do?"

"Put your own damn name on it."

"People like you better than me."

"Oh, fuck you!" She threw a pillow at her roommate.

Jonsie stood up to leave.

"Wait. We haven't even talked about Clitstock."

"Good luck with that," she said. "I don't do crowds."

On her way back to the computer lab Jonsie's stomach fizzed in a wave of anxiety. She had an intuition. Yesterday, when she sat down in VP's office she felt as though all her thoughts were random plastic floating in the ocean. She couldn't organize them.

Then VP locked onto her and said, "What?" and Jonsie started talking.

"BioMantrix robotics department operates like a terrorist cell," she said looking into VP's raptor eyes, seeing eyeliner, the markings of a predator meant to blend with the forest, wings meant to fly in silence, a fabled sorcerer. Jonsie was under the sorcerer's spell. "They're 3D printing androids based on imaging," she said softly. "They printed a Keanu Reeves droid by feeding *The Matrix* into AI and then 3D printing Neo. The technology is compelling. They were just playing with it until Skimmerhorn printed Hamish and sent him after Meryl." She paused and thought for a moment. Then she said, "I get that this is the future. I see that it's unstoppable. But Meryl is a useful example of what could go wrong."

VP's perfectly penciled eyebrows arched, and she leaned back in her chair, folding her arms across her chest.

Jonsie continued, "I've been in touch with a hacker named Cprompt who's burrowed into the BioMantrix AI platform and apparently planted self-destruct code. We just have to find a way to put it in play."

VP blinked in agreement. Then she turned to her phone and Jonsie went back to the lab.

~ : ~

Around the time Meryl announced her retirement, Bob had his first interaction with Hazel at the University Fitness Center. It was early in the morning and all the exercise machines were empty, except for a bulbous weightlifter pumping iron, and Bob strolling lazily on a treadmill. Mostly he was watching the news on a flatscreen suspended overhead. Hazel was the facility manager. She caught his eye as she moved through the room, and he nodded a perfunctory greeting, knew her name because she wore a University employee badge, but they had never spoken.

Hazel tended the machines set up around the room where University employees and students practiced physical fitness while they watched TV. At the beginning of the day, it was her routine to check the digital control panel on each machine, testing, resetting, and rebooting, to be sure it was in working order and ready to use.

While she was bent over adjusting a rowing machine, the weightlifter came to the end of his reps, put a towel around his sweaty neck, and made for the locker-room. As he passed her, he reached out and gave her a playful slap on the ass. Without a sound she straightened up, turned, and in one fluid movement grabbed his wrist, twisted his arm, and buckled his knees, dropping him to the floor like a sack of potatoes.

"You should be careful where you're walking," she said looking down at him sprawled on the floor.

Bob froze and fell off his treadmill, blackbirds on their backs.

Hazel looked over at him splayed in all directions. "Are you okay?" she asked.

Bob blushed. The weightlifter popped up off the floor and sneered at Hazel as if he were about to say something, but he reconsidered. It was common knowledge that the room was covered by video cameras for security and liability insurance.

"I'm okay," Bob said getting to his feet again. "Are you okay?"

"I'm fine," she laughed as the weightlifter disappeared into the locker-room.

"Where did you learn to do that?"

"I have four brothers." She smiled. "We watched martial arts movies together. Bruce Lee was our hero."

Hazel had grown up living with a gang of boys in a decaying suburb where street fighting was play, and her brothers looked out for their turf. She took martial arts classes with them at the Y, and when she was small, they practiced fighting in the livingroom.

Bob was amused. "Can you teach me?"

"You don't seem like the martial arts type," she said with her hands on her hips.

"I'm not. I just want to be fit."

"You need to work on your core," she said. "Strengthen your back. Your posture is not good."

"Should I lift weights?"

"What do you teach?" She sized him up.

"English Literature."

"Isn't all the best English literature Irish?"

He smiled and arched an eyebrow. A blackbird flew toward the sun.

Hazel poked her index finger in his back, and he squared his shoulders.

"Stand up straight," she commanded.

"I'm a pessimist," he said as he stood up straight. "This is how I feel."

"Pessimism makes you weak," she said.

"My wife would agree with you. She hates pessimism."

"Your wife must be a genius." Hazel smiled.

"Are you a trainer?"

"I teach tai chi at the community center. I don't work with the machines here. If you want to work with chrome and plastic, you don't need me."

"I like the machines," Bob admitted with a shrug.

"Of course, you do. Because you don't see the need to focus on what you're doing. You watch TV and let the machine do the work.

"It's just exercise."

She rolled her eyes. "And English literature is just words."

He squinted at her, blackbirds leaning toward condescension. "Your point is?"

"You can't transform your body watching TV. If you want to be fit, you must learn control. To be in control you must learn balance. To find your balance you need to focus."

"Focus on what?"

"Nothing."

"I don't know what that means."

"You will learn."

And so, Bob began to meet with Hazel to learn tai chi.

144

At first the movements felt ridiculous to him, like sloppy dancing, he couldn't make sense of it and yet it was so easy, and Hazel was so serious, and she expected him to be serious, too.

"The wave rises." Her hands floated up. "Breathe in. And you push the wave back out to sea." Her hands floated down. "Breathe out."

It had been a very long time since Bob moved his arms except to carry his backpack or get something off the top shelf of the closet or hold the banister when he climbed the stairs. Doing tai chi, he felt like a stork. It wasn't like any exercise he had ever seen or imagined. It took persistent effort to move slowly in wide arcs. He was self-conscious. But she just kept moving. He had to stop thinking about how he looked to keep up with her and mimic her grace. That took focus.

Focus. He was beginning to understand. Before long he went from struggling through a session to feeling the craving in his muscles, and they progressed to more complicated routines. Then he broke his shoulder. Once the pain was manageable, he asked Hazel to come to his house to continue his training and help him heal.

On her first visit, she arrived carrying a copy of the student newspaper opened to the centerfold, a two-page ad for Clitorati Populi.

"I thought you'd like to know what you're missing," she said as she handed the paper to Bob.

He spread the pages on the kitchen counter and perused the ad.

Clitorati Populi
Come one, come all to the Big Vagina Festival!
A day of art, music, celebration & education for Vagina Lovers!
Open to the public. All Vagina Lovers welcome!

Clit Pride Parade
March from the Quad around Campus to the Fields
Dress up your wheels! $1000 Prize for Best Costume

Concert

The Dead White Guys (all girl guitar band)
with The Dependable Orgasms (vintage hits) & Slitacular
(dance)

Critical Clit Theory Education Program
Understand the Myths, the Misogyny & the Math from
Menstruation to Masturbation & Menopause!
Lectures + Short Films + Q&A with Real Doctors

Petting Zoo
Feel the love. Masturbation lessons & sex toys.
The only small furry animal is your own.

Worship Services
Bow down before World's Largest Clitoris
20 feet of swollen pink plastic!
Non-denominational prayer, liturgy & chanting
Pick up the good vibrations!

Maker Fair & Food Trucks
Student artists & makers doing live demonstrations & selling
their stuff!
Body Positive Clothing Swap & Fashion Show
Pottery, Sculpture, Labia Portraits
Personalized Jewelry, Chainsaw Genitals, Meat Carving
Corn Hole Olympics, Essential Oils & Handmade Goop
Body Piercing & Tattoos
Hair Cuts, Body Painting & Make-up Lessons
Radical Stitchery, Rag Weaving, Knitting & Needle Work
Plus Eat Me Bakery, Donut Holes, Fish Tacos & More!

"I know it's supposed to be funny," she said. "But that language
makes me uncomfortable."

"Me, too." Bob flipped through the rest of the paper and saw an article about the event with photos of the organizers. He recognized Lemons and Katie from Ban Bacon.

"My husband thinks it's a big joke. But I think it's obscene," she said. "Women make trouble for themselves with this kind of invitation. Some words are private. If my mother read this, she would die."

"It's the same two students who started Ban Bacon," he mused.

"That was also a bad idea. I know those students. They are nice girls, educated but stupid. How could you ban bacon? It's the most popular meat. Lucky for you, your wife got the pig."

"I don't think we're going to be eating Begonia. She's like my wife's dog."

"No. Pork is delicious. Everybody loves pork. A pig is for pork. Why else have pig?"

"She made a promise to her students that we'd keep the pig."

"Promises are made to be broken, right? I understand she made peace with Ban Bacon and the University. But I think keeping a pig is…well, I think it's very unusual. Maybe because I've seen hungry people. Also, I love bacon."

Bob chortled and sat waiting for instructions.

She took his cue and changed the subject. "I've been thinking about your shoulder." She eyed his brace. "Your recovery will be long and slow because you're old. We can keep working on your core. But also, your mind. Have you ever seen Bruce Lee?"

"I've heard of him."

"You should watch one of his movies."

"Why?"

"You'll understand when you see him move. Think about the way he thinks as he moves, which is not to think at all. His movement is instinctive. Pure motion. Watch him and think about how you broke your shoulder."

"That was an accident."

"Yes. But perhaps it was unnecessary."

He got a quizzical look on his face.

"I can't put into words some of the things you need to know. But I think you would learn something about yourself if you listened to him. He's a thinker like you. A philosopher. Listen to his interview."

Bob searched YouTube for Bruce Lee and found an interview from 1971, but stopped himself, didn't hit play. "Speaking of old," he said. "This is old."

"Open your mind," she said tapping her temple with her index finger. "You're working with the wrong metaphor. You think strength is a rock, like a mountain. That's how you broke your shoulder. You resist when you should flow. Strength is a river, not a rock. Water breaks down mountains. Water flows. You need to learn to flow like water. Become water."

Bob frowned and hit play.

~ : ~

Uma was having trouble sleeping, which wasn't like her, and she knew it to be a sign of stress. *Physician heal thyself*, she said to the bathroom mirror. Stress. This situation was a lot of stress. Unlike Meryl, she was not an early adopter of tech gadgets. She resisted technology until it was a professional necessity, a skill she had to acquire to succeed, an inevitable process, adapt or die, excel, or be left behind. There was no way to move forward with the work she cared about without learning new technology.

Even so, she was one of the last among her peers to swap her dumb mobile phone for a smart phone with a flatscreen and apps. She had resisted carrying a smart phone on principle. She felt like she was giving up control of something. Although she wasn't sure exactly what she was giving up control of. It was just the idea of allowing so many businesses access to her private world. Then all at once, she let go of her resistance and jumped into cyberspace with everyone else.

Nothing is private anymore, she told herself.

Now she used credit cards instead of cash because it was convenient. She did her banking and bill paying online because it was convenient. She had a transponder on the windshield of her car to pay tolls and parking because it was convenient. She used an app to buy her plane tickets and stream music and movies and podcasts. She checked the weather a few times a day on her phone. And the traffic. Made reservations at her favorite restaurant. Bought her groceries online and had them delivered. And everything she did was tracked on her calendar app. Every time she spent money it was tracked on her money management app. She had given dozens of technology companies access to her personal and professional life, and now she was in so deep, she didn't know how to get out.

What world would I be living in if I dumped my phone and everything on it? Who would I be? Would she even be able to have her job, do her work, manage the care of her patients, run the operations of her clinic? How did she become so involved in something she knew so little about? What did she give up for convenience?

She could see that there was a direct line from her phone to the PS-1000 and Meryl's attraction to NanoSmile. Uma had signed up to be a beta tester for Pleasure Systems because she thought the products might help her patients, and then she ended up keeping the smart sex toy because it made her feel good.

When she took up the collection among Meryl's friends to buy her the PS-1000 as a retirement gift, she was making an expensive joke, but at the same time, she was also consciously introducing the device to a circle of women her age. She had seen too many of her patients become estranged from their bodies as they experienced the disappointment and disillusionment of aging, unprepared for the physical disruption, ambushed by the discomfort, and depressed by the uncertainty. She believed orgasms were essential to a woman's health and wellbeing, especially with age, and she knew a toy would generate more interest than a lecture on masturbation.

Now she needed Girl Church as much as her patients to help her cope with the changes in her life. That evening, after an hour of stretching and meditation, she sat on the floor with Sue, Claire, Khadija and Eleanor, and Lemons, Katie and Jonsie, and Meryl. Katie wanted to talk about her new app and Lemons wanted Girl Church to be a sponsor of the women's wellness event she was producing on campus.

When Meryl sat down cross-legged, a tiny crunching sound emanated from her.

"Was that your bones cracking?" Sue asked.

"No. I've got aluminum foil in my underwear."

"Hmm," Claire said. "I didn't think aluminum foil was that absorbent."

"It's not absorbent at all," Meryl said. "But it blocks Quanta's signal."

"How's the nano girl?" Khadija asked.

"Frankly, she misses my PS-1000," Meryl said. "I've been using orgasms as a tranquilizer for a long time, and now when I could really use one, I'm not in the mood."

"You're under a lot of stress," Uma said. "We should get you another vibrator."

"I got one," Meryl said. "A new PS-1000 just showed up in the mail."

Jonsie, Lemons and Katie gave each other a sharp glance.

"Don't use it," Jonsie said.

"Don't worry. I won't. Now that I know Skimmerhorn is tracking my orgasms, I'm abstaining."

"Maybe you should try having orgasms the old-fashioned way," Eleanor winked. "You don't really need a machine."

"I know. I wish I had a man," Meryl said. "That would be my first choice. A real man."

"Who gives great head," Eleanor smiled.

"Yes," Meryl agreed. "I miss Bob. The old Bob. I keep having flashbacks to Hamish and his weaponized dick. What a buzzkill. I didn't think it affected me that much. But it has. It's a kernel of fear I can't get out of my mind."

"I know what you mean," Katie said. "I can't get that chicken simulation out of my mind."

"Yeah," Lemons agreed. "The Trojan dick was brutal."

"You and Quanta are both afraid," Eleanor said. "You were in peril, and she knew it. She seems to have a will to survive, and she knows your fates are tied together."

"Not really," Jonsie said. "It's dangerous to read anything into Quanta. We don't know if she's intelligent."

"Maybe she's crossing over," Eleanor pressed on. "Reduced to her essential energy state and making her transition back to the source."

Uma saw the frustration on Jonsie's face. "Let's stop there," she said. "The thing we know for sure is that this situation has left the imprint of danger on us. We're afraid, and we need to manage our fear."

"What do you mean about Skimmerhorn tracking your orgasms?" Khadija asked.

"He was getting the data feed from her PS-1000," Jonsie answered with a glance at Meryl. "The toothbrush and the vibrator are both made by BioMantrix. He has access to all of it."

Uma dropped her head in her hands. "Oh, Meryl. I'm so sorry." Tears gathered in her eyes.

Meryl hugged her best friend. "Who knew a sex toy could be a Trojan Horse?"

"Let's clear the negative energy," Sue said. "How would you guys feel about a gut busting om?"

"I think that's a very good idea," Uma smiled and sniffled, sitting up straight as the others tightened the circle.

"Imagine Quanta leaving Meryl's body and re-integrating with the energy all around us," Eleanor said.

"Thank you, Eleanor," Katie said crossing her eyes at Jonsie.

Then together the women chanted from deep in their bellies. "Om."

After a moment of silence, Katie said, "I hope everyone has their phone. I'm going to walk you through my new app, and then if you want to, we can load it on your phone, so all of us can be in touch."

"We've been testing it," Lemons said. "But you guys are the first real user group."

"Cool," Sue said.

"Think of it as a personal security app," Katie continued. "A private group that can track a group member. You create a user profile, join your group, and then select the group member you want to follow. In this case, Meryl. Our group is called Butterflies. There is GPS tracking for all group members, including maps, as long as you keep your phone on. Also, an alert system calibrated for levels of risk with an emergency warning for extinction. Super simple."

"I've got something called Spicebush," Meryl said looking at her phone.

"That's it," Lemons said. "Spicebush is the app. The interface looks like we're an eco-group trying to save the butterflies."

"So, four steps," Katie said. "Download the app, set up your profile, join Butterflies, and select Meryl as the one you want to follow. Then if you hit Track, a map should open that shows Meryl is here at the address of the yoga studio."

"Cool," Khadija said. "I'm so impressed that you built this. Should we worry about being tracked?"

"We're all being tracked all the time," Katie said. "Every connected device can be tracked. Every unconnected device can have a tracker hidden on it."

"Don't think about it," Jonsie said. "If someone wants to track you or listen in on your conversations or hack you, they'll find a way. Just live your life."

"So why am I wearing aluminum foil in my underwear?" Meryl asked.

"To fuck with Skimmerhorn," Jonsie replied.

"Oh." She smiled "I like that."

"A couple more things about the app," Katie continued. "Click on Message to communicate with the group by text. Click on a Risk Level to indicate your level of concern. Everybody in the group gets the same message."

"And voila! Spicebush!" Lemons said.

Meryl sighed. "Thank you so much, Katie. This is really great work." She gave the girl a big hug.

~ : ~

Walking back to her dorm room with Lemons and Jonsie, Katie said, "I wish I could talk to my mom about yoga. I'd love for her to meet Eleanor and sit in that circle with her peers. But she just won't.

If she knew I chanted om, she would be really hurt. Or angry. Anyway, I'm never telling her."

"That sucks, Katie." Lemons put her arm around her friend. "Your mom would probably hate my mom."

"You could tell her om is like harmonizing in music," Jonsie said. "You can be any religion and do om."

"Why tell her anything?" Lemons asked.

"Strong relationships are based on kindness and trust. Lying to someone you love is problematic," Jonsie explained.

"I love my mom, but she's not very open minded."

"I'm sure she loves you, too," Jonsie said.

"I think I'm missing your point."

"Don't burden your relationship with guilt."

"How?"

"Kindness and trust. That's really all you need."

"I still don't get it."

"When we lose our capacity for kindness and trust our thoughts become unhealthy biochemistry and we suffer. Be kind to your mother and trust her to be kind to you. It really doesn't matter what she thinks of yoga."

"Bushjooozghhhhhhh!" Lemons pantomimed a brain bomb. "Nobel or Pulitzer? I never really knew the difference."

"Oh, my god, Jonsie," Katie laughed. "That's the most woo-woo thing you've ever said."

Jonsie shrugged and changed the subject. "I dug up some more intel on Cprompt. It's old. But I found some archived comments that make sense. It seems back around the time VP interned at BioMantrix gender was a problem. Maybe sexism. Or homophobia. Or unrequited love. Anyway, there's a gossip trail."

"Kiss, kiss! Bang, bang!" Lemons popped her fingers in the air.

"You think the self-destruct code is a lover's revenge?"

"Maybe. Also, Quanta's demand for her pronoun. It's a communications protocol triggered by Meryl's orgasm."

"Those female biomarkers?"

"Yes."

"So, it's meaningless," Lemons speculated.

"No. I think Quanta's demand for a pronoun is like the mark of Zorro for a coder," Jonsie said. "It's a warning."

Katie and Lemons stopped in their tracks and looked at Jonsie.

"Skimmerhorn pissed off a woman coder?" Katie's mind was spinning.

"Or someone who identified as female," Jonsie said.

"Like VP?"

"Maybe."

"She wants him to know she's watching," Katie intuited.

"Or she's making a point about vulnerability," Lemons countered. "The vulnerability of code."

"He must be paranoid."

"She suggested BioMantrix for my internship," Jonsie continued. "She could have told me to read the company employee manual. But she sent me to the dark web where Cprompt is a hero and Skimmerhorn is mocked."

"Couldn't we just walk into her office and ask her about all this?" Katie was impatient.

"Would you ask Zorro to take his mask off?"

"No."

"Neither would I. This is a test. We have to figure it out for ourselves."

~ : ~

In the middle of the night, Bob and Meryl were in bed together. She was dreaming. He was awake because she kicked him.

As she galloped, the palomino's creamy mane frothed the same color as the beach. In the distance a giant centipede squirmed, poking into the horizon. Feathery palms swooned and the sun radiated euphoria. Meryl took it all in. A red flower unfolded, bare skin on the horse's back, thighs straddling rhythm, kissing his neck. She was hot, nibbled at his eyebrows and tipped his hat with her nose, spinning straw on the breeze, cheek against flesh, they raced.

This was her time. Hers. She put her palms on his muscles, meatloaf dripping warm. Divine. She reached for the ketchup. The richness of the meat, the throb. Eating with her fingers, hibiscus bloomed garlic.

The centipede writhed, changing color, brown, yellow, grey, pink, fluttering white linen, speaking to her, urging her. "Come on, Meryl! Come on! You can do it!" Lemons was shouting into a megaphone, her pastel girlfriends all in a row, jumping up and down at the finish line, cheering. "Come on, Meryl! Come!"

Hips, juice, horse, heat. She was moist, tightened her thighs against the pounding muscle, squeezing, grinding as she held the blonde mane, rocking, panting, halos of pleasure.

"Meryl!" Bob squeezed her wrist between the sheets and gave it a jiggle. "You're dreaming, Babe."

Meryl woke, kept her eyes closed, felt the ebbing tide of orgasm. Touched herself to be sure. She hadn't had a wet dream in years.

Note to self, even wet dreams get dryer.

"You put too much garlic in the meatloaf," Bob whispered.

"Maybe so." She smiled.

She knew her dream was a collection of unresolved moments, bits of stimulus she had yet to process, wisps of brain chemistry disconnected from the structure of memory. It wasn't surprising. She had a lot on her mind. What she needed was a neat resolution to this NanoSmile mess. Something crisp and clean. Like an amputation.

That day on a whim she had gone to VP's office without an appointment. It was a time when professors had open office hours so students could drop by. VP was sitting behind her desk looking at her phone. Meryl gave a gentle knock on the open door and sat down in the chair across from her colleague. VP did not take her eyes off her phone.

"Do you know what's going on with me?" Meryl asked.

VP looked up at her sharply, their eyes struck, and a psychic load was exchanged without words. Meryl had an intuition that VP was more than she appeared to be. Her cutting glance confirmed the seriousness of the situation. Then she returned her eyes to her phone.

"Sorry," Meryl said. "I shouldn't have asked. But I had to."

Meryl knew VP couldn't speak with her about anything she might know about BioMantrix. That look was enough, and yet, she wasn't ready to exit so soon after she arrived. So, she sat there and read the Zorro poster. She had seen it so many times, but she hadn't read the words. It was a movie poster, the title written boldly in Spanish, *Il Segno di Zorro*, starring Tyrone Power as both the effete flower-sniffing aristocrat, Don Diego, and the mysterious swashbuckling swordsman, Zorro. One person, two identities. It was obvious that VP's pleated skirts, her tightly curled bouffant hair, and heavy eye makeup were a consciously constructed identity. Meryl wondered if she was looking at VP's Don Diego costume or her Zorro disguise.

Her skirts were always plaid with a color coordinated blouse and sweater, kitten heels or flats, plump around the middle, feminine but not sexy, thick hands with stubby fingers, a square jaw, big bones. She was frumpy. Perfectly frumpy. Frumpy in a way no man would ever suspect of being subversive. Meryl knew she was brilliant because of her writing, not her speaking, and because she saw the progress that VP's students made in their academic achievements. People who didn't know her were so distracted by how she looked that they failed to observe her intelligence. But maybe that was the point.

Definitely, Don Diego. Meryl smiled at the thought. Then she said, "Thank you. Thanks for whatever you can do."

VP glanced up sideways from her phone as though she may have heard something, then went back to her screen.

Meryl felt a wave of relaxation roll through her. She breathed in the room with VP for a few more minutes, then went home. Now she could get back to worrying about Bob.

It seemed to her that since she quit her job, they had lost their curiosity about each other, shutdown their amusement and wisecracks, stopped exploring each other's thinking and sank into the bog of mutual resentment. She could give him a hand job in the shower, and he would accept the gift, but it wasn't the heat she wanted. It was more like physical therapy. There was no reciprocity. She wanted him to give her an orgasm, damn it! Her marriage had settled into a dullness she wasn't willing to accept. But she wasn't sure how to break out of it without hurting him. He had been hurt enough.

So, she didn't ask him about watching the Bruce Lee movie. Even though it upset her. Because she was uncertain about where she stood with him. Why ask? What kind of answer would she get? Was he daring her to ask? Was he trying to provoke her? She didn't know. She wondered if he was having an epiphany of his own. Was he changing in ways she didn't appreciate? Was he becoming another person? Was he becoming obsessed with some new idea of masculinity? Was she losing him? Was Bruce Lee taking over his brain? She knew it was a Bruce Lee movie because she had read the screen on his laptop over his shoulder. He had no idea she was standing behind his chair because he was wearing his headphones, eating a bowl of popcorn, spilling it all over the floor.

She watched the movie long enough to see the skinny Asian guy zip through the air and crush some big Anglo guy in a white shirt. *How could he be watching something so dumb?* She knew he was learning tai chi with Hazel, and she thought it was good for him, but she had never considered this, the unintended consequence. Maybe he hit his head when he broke his shoulder.

She had to call Uma. "He's watching a Bruce Lee movie on his computer right now," she whispered.

"Why are you whispering?" Uma asked.

"I think he's hiding from me."

"Where is he?"

"In his chair in the livingroom."

"How is that hiding?"

"He's wearing headphones so I can't hear what he's doing."

"But he's sitting where you can see him."

"He doesn't know I saw him."

"What conversation are we having, Meryl?"

"I'm worried about Bob. Maybe he has a traumatic brain injury."

"Why is this coming up now?"

"He's a professor of English Literature. He should be reading *Ulysses*."

"I'm pretty sure he's already read *Ulysses*."

"Comic books. R. Crumb. Anything. But not Bruce Lee."

"Maybe he's taking a break."

"He never takes a break."

"Don't you have enough problems of your own without worrying about what movie Bob is watching?"

"I'm asking for your support, Um. Help me. My husband is watching a Bruce Lee movie."

"So, you think there's something wrong with his brain?"

"Yes."

"Because he's an English professor watching a martial arts movie?"

"Yes."

"Maybe he's just fucking with you."

"Oh, god."

"Maybe Bruce Lee is his revenge for Hamish."

"I don't think you're trying to help me."

"Have you considered honesty?"

"Definitely not."

"Didn't you tell me honesty was the number one personality trait you chose for Hamish?"

"That's different."

"I don't think so."

"It's too late to be honest, Um. Honesty would never work with Bob."

"Try it."

"We're living in separate worlds."

"You told him you were retiring to write a book. That was a lie, wasn't it?"

"Yes."

"So, start there. Confess. Then maybe he'll admit he's always had a thing for Asian men."

"What?!"

"Just kidding."

"I'm asking for your help."

"Meryl, Bob is your mystery to solve. Not mine."

"That's not helpful."

"Sorry, it's the best I can do. I have to go back to work now."

Meryl got off the phone with Uma and did nothing. In her mental hula hoop of Bob and Bruce Lee their genes mixed like eggs and sperm, they cross dressed, traded clothes and hair, Bob flew on horizontal legs and Bruce sank in a chair with his nose up Charles Dickens' ass. Not exactly blood brothers, but she had an intuition that they were connected through Bob's broken shoulder. And Hazel. She didn't know. *Honestly, I don't know.* She practiced saying those words. *Honestly, I don't know.* She and Bob were shadow boxing each other. But what were they fighting against? *Honestly, I don't know.*

~ : ~

It was a September Saturday, sunny, dry, and crisp, the azure-sky time of year when people were drawn outdoors to enjoy the last days of summer. For weeks Lemons had been networking her friends, faculty, and the administration to organize a women's wellness festival on campus. It was an easy sell. Not like Ban Bacon, which was often met with eye rolling and culinary resistance. When Lemons proposed a women's wellness festival, she found the University and the town more than receptive. It was a feel-good idea, and people were eager to participate. Sponsors donated, institutions delivered content, businesses were happy for the visibility, and feminists prepared to roar. No one knew the festival was going to be called Clitorati Populi until the ads came out, and by then her momentum was unstoppable.

When she gave Jonsie a copy of the student paper with the full-page ad, Lemons thought Jonsie came as close to laughing as she'd ever seen.

"Hmm…Clitorati Populi." Jonsie's lip twitched, and her nostrils flared. "What, did you take Latin in high school?"

"I thought it had a little more gravitas than Clitstock," Lemons answered.

"I still like Burning Clit," Jonsie said.

Lemons snickered. "Yeah. Funny. But not a great brand message."

"I suppose," Jonsie nodded.

Standing on the sidewalk with Katie as people gathered for the Clit Pride parade, Lemons knew she had made the right choice with the name. It was just academic enough to rise above accusations of obscenity, and just explicit enough to encourage the circus.

"The gods are smiling on us," she said to Katie as they surveyed the crowd. "Let's put on a show."

"I'll see you at the stage." Katie gave Lemons an awkward hug, so her headdress wouldn't tilt. Then she raised her drum major's baton and stepped off the curb to lead the parade, and women lined up to follow the character in the long pink cape with a wide belt of tampons stitched in rows like thick fringe around her waist, and a pink paper-mâché clitoris perched like an eagle on her football helmet.

Katie and Lemons had their first fight over that headdress.

"What the fuck, Katie?" Lemons said when she saw the mess in their dorm room, Katie sitting on the floor in the middle of her project. There were fruit and vegetables rolling around under foot, melons and oranges, eggplants and celery, party balloons and cans of spray paint. The football helmet was sitting on a spread of newspaper where it had been painted white, and a roll of chicken-wire leaned against her desk. To make the paper-mâché clitoris, Katie had taken a bucket of water from the bathroom, made paste from flour and water, and torn strips of the student newspaper, using the produce and chicken-wire as molds. When Lemons walked in, she stepped on an orange, her foot rolled, and she almost fell as Katie sat licking her fingers.

"If I added salt to this paste, I could make bread," Katie giggled, ignoring her roommate's dismay.

"My desk!" Lemons groaned at the dusting of flour on her books. "Jeez, Katie, even Begonia didn't make a mess like this."

"This is art," Katie smirked.

"I can't think in a room like this." Lemons fingered the stack of newspapers on her bed. "You took a whole stack of newspapers that have our ad in it. What are you doing tearing up our ad? I used my mom's credit card to pay for that!"

"Sorry, Lemons. It will all be gone soon. Promise. I just have to let it dry overnight."

"Overnight! What the fuck!"

"Just one night. You're going to love it."

And, eventually, she did love it. The paper-mâché took longer to dry than Katie had estimated. But when she put on the helmet, Lemons was blown away. "You are the queen," she said.

"I feel like a cross between Kali and Mrs. Potato Head," Katie smiled.

On the day of Clitorati Populi, as they organized people in line for the parade, Lemons could see Katie across the top of the crowd with her two-foot-tall clitoris on top of her head. "Just follow the clitorasaurus," she instructed people as they formed a column of hundreds of women in Clitorati Populi hats and t-shirts, some in costumes celebrating their bodies, some carrying signs and banners. The women's drum corps took their place in line wearing t-shirts that said Vagina Lovers, setting the pace for the throng of revelers as they made their serpentine route around campus.

At the stage, a few thousand gathered on the lawn, and more roamed the flea market of tents and tables that circled the field, and still more filled tables in the food court at the center of a ring of food trucks. A couple media trucks set up cameras on the perimeter to interview costumed celebrants in front of the Clitorati Populi step-and-repeat banner. Journalists combed the crowd doing interviews and taking pictures. There was a huge Clitorati Populi banner hanging over the stage where camera operators were feeding images to a jumbo video screen above them, getting a close-up of Lemons as she took the microphone wearing a Clitorati Populi baseball hat.

"Welcome, Vagina Lovers!" she greeted the audience, and they hooted in reply. "Clitorati Populi!" She waved her arm. "I bring you the Big Vagina Festival."

After a round of applause the crowd settled their attention on her.

"Thank you for coming to our first women's wellness festival. I'm so glad to see you here. Please throw some money at our sponsors. Because we need them. We need each other. Women need women." She paused to gather their minds. "Why? Because women are about collaboration. We need relationships to thrive. The defining organ in our body is the uterus, designed to be the first home of future humans. We birth our species in a profound collaboration with Mother Nature. Our biology is the starting place for human life. We are primary. And yet, all over the world, women live as second-class citizens. Women are treated as a lower caste than men. Women do not have the same rights as men. Women do not have the same control over their lives as men. We do not have equal access to the resources we need to thrive. We are weavers, but we must also be warriors. Because the patriarchy isn't going to help us fight the patriarchy!"

She paused and waited for those ideas to sink in, smiling, and nodding as her audience reacted.

"Hear me, Clitorati Populi! If the future is female, women's wellness is the path we walk together. Women's wellness is critical to our quality of life, our economy, our society, and our environment. Women's wellness is the policy and the prayer. Women's wellness is the work. And what do we need to be well? Kindness and trust. Why are we here today? To demand a healthcare system based on kindness and trust. A system we can trust to act in our interest. A system we can trust to treat us as equals. A system that values kindness above all. For ourselves and our children, we want to live in communities based on kindness and trust. We want an economy based on kindness and trust. These are our values, and they are not beyond our reach. Right here, right now, look at the person beside you. We have kindness and trust. That's the message of Clitorati Populi."

Waves of affirmation rolled through the crowd and Lemons paced until they grew quiet again.

"We have a problem. Am I right?"

"Yes!"

"Damn straight!"

"Fuck, yeah!"

"I hear you!"

"Our problem is ignorance. Apathy. Abuse. Our problems are built into the system. Misogyny is built into the system. Let me give you an example of how women's wellness has been perverted by the patriarchy." She turned and pointed up at the video screen. "This is what they have planned for us!" Abruptly the jumbo image above the stage switched from Lemon's face to the ClitBit Market

Opportunity slide that Jonsie had snagged from Skimmerhorn's email.

The shock of the written words sucked the air out of women's lungs. In religious silence, Lemons watched their reaction and waited. Then she began again.

"ClitBit. The libido solution for women of every age… So, if we need a solution, we must have a problem. Right? And as you can see, they're plan is to solve our problem by shaming us. This is body shaming on a global scale. The men who once invented purity culture are going to shame us for a lack of pleasure experience. They're going to shame us for our insecurity, our fears, and our doubts. They're going to make menopause miserable for us so they can sell us stuff to fix it. Where's the kindness and trust in that?"

She could feel the anger mushrooming.

"Let me tell you how ClitBit works. They're going to inject a microchip into your precious, and then make you pay rent for it. If you want an orgasm, you're going to have to pay for it. You're going to have to use their software. This is their idea of women's wellness. Where's the kindness and trust in that?"

Meryl shivered as her mind hula hooped ClitBit and Quanta and her lost toothbrush and her vibrator and all the ominous intentions that linked them. "Where did that come from?" she whispered to Uma as they stood by the side of the stage. But she knew the answer to her own question. She knew Jonsie had violated Skimmerhorn. A line had been crossed.

Uma just shook her head, stunned.

"Is that for real?" Khadija nudged Uma.

"I have no idea," Uma muttered.

"My daughter has a Fitbit," Claire said happily.

"Oh, jeez," Sue groaned. "We're in trouble now."

"I have a feeling the fun is just beginning," Eleanor smiled.

As the idea of ClitBit sank in, the booing began. Lemons nodded her head and waved her arms to encourage them, and the booing grew louder, until the vibration was palpable, and Lemons nodded, and waved her arms for more, and the booing grew so loud it shook leaves off the trees.

"This is the future of women's healthcare if we leave it in the hands of men!" Lemons shouted and pointed up to the screen. "This is their plan. Where's the kindness and trust in that?"

"Boooooo!!!"

Then when her point was made, she waved to quiet them.

"At a time when most people couldn't draw a clitoris if their life depended on it, we have a new product launch for a nanotech implant that will be injected into your clitoris with a needle, hooked up to your phone with an app, tracked in a database, and controlled by an unaccountable platform. Has anybody read *The Handmaid's Tale*?"

"Boooooo!!!"

She waved them quiet again and continued.

"You'll pay for your ClitBit, but you won't own it. Your precious flesh will become a prosthetic. Your orgasms will become data. Your sex life will be monetized. And the patriarchy will still be looking for ways to body shame you. The problem with the patriarchy is they can't be trusted. We need women's healthcare controlled by women. We need brands controlled by women. Our bodies, our values. Kindness and trust!"

She paced the stage.

"We will not have our bodies commodified and monetized. Our glorious vulvas are not for sale. My labia is luscious just the way it is, and I will not buy into the shame. We make the rules! Kindness and trust! Women's wellness rules! Because our biology is primary!"

She pointed to the audience as they roared in a sound cloud that filled the sky.

"You are the storm! You are Mother Nature! We need technology. But we need to put our biology first. This is our fight. We fight for the right to control our own biology. All people, all bodies, all genders. We demand the right to control our biology! Our bodies! Ourselves! Our species! We are primary. The future is female because the biome lives within us. Women's bodies, our breasts, our uteruses, soak up the biome. We breathe the biome. We birth the biome. We become the biome. And that, my friends, is why we need a system based on kindness and trust. Those are our values.

Clitorati Populi!" She slammed her fist in the air. "Silence is the voice of complicity! Are you with me?"

The throng was on its feet, and a field of fists punched the sky. She twirled with her arms in the air. Euphoria and rage blended in a fever that spread like water seeking its own level. Lemons waved and smiled. The ClitBit slide disappeared, and audience faces filled the giant screen again. It was done.

After a calming moment, she changed her tone. "Today, we rise for women's wellness. The clitoris rises." She turned toward the back of the stage pointing to a flaccid heap of pink plastic. "And to serenade her erection, please join me in welcoming, for this very special occasion, our favorite band of vaginas, The Dead White Guys!"

As the audience went nuts, a booming guitar strum rolled out over the fields and a dozen electric guitar players took the stage facing a conductor dressed like Beethoven in combat boots with pink hair. Then they began to play *Bolero*, that haunting classical melody famously swollen with expectation, while behind them a crew of stagehands began to inflate the 20-foot plastic clitoris lashed to ropes and pulleys so it could rise slowly as it filled with air, tied to the stage trusses, swaying to the pulsing rhythm of Ravel's masterwork.

When the crowd realized what they were about to see, they whooped with glee.

"How are you?" Uma put her arm around Meryl.

"Something like this restores my faith in humanity," Meryl said. "But I wonder what the repercussions will be."

"Me, too," Uma said. "But I think it's out of our hands now."

"It's so brave."

"Yes," Uma agreed. "But what's brave is usually dangerous."

Meryl nodded and the two friends looked at each other with solemn eyes.

Ripples of applause and amusement rolled through the audience as one at a time the guitars joined the melodic theme, harmonized, and the music became expansive as the inflatable clitoris grew taller, climbing with the electronic crescendo, until it was tight, erect, and anatomically correct. Then in glorious victory, the band segued from

Bolero right into Tchaikovsky's *1812 Overture* and the audience went berserk.

"They're such great guitar players," Meryl said. When Tchaikovsky's cannons fired, and the bells rang, and the cannons fired again, she was so moved she felt like she could cry, leaned into Uma, and put her head on her shoulder.

"I can't hear a word you're saying." Uma took her friend's arm and led her through the crowd.

Meryl sent her first message on Spicebush to say that she was re-locating to the food court. Within minutes the women from Girl Church were seated around a table chatting.

"I love the music," Uma said. "But my ears can't hear what anyone's saying in that kind of noise."

"It was loud," Meryl agreed. "What a great speech."

"She should be a politician," Khadija said. "She's exciting."

"Very persuasive," Eleanor agreed.

"I'm going to buy one for my daughter," Claire said. "Her husband can't find hers."

"Oh, jeez," Sue said. "We need to stop and think about what we just saw. Did any of you know Lemons was going to show that BioMantrix chart?" She looked into the eyes of each woman at the table. They all shook their heads no. But she had to be sure. "Uma, don't you have a relationship with BioMantrix?"

"I use their patient portal at the clinic. It's a software service."

Sue looked at Meryl. "What about you, Meryl?"

"My vibrator, my toothbrush, the vibrator they planted in my bathroom, Quanta, Hamish, Skimmerhorn, the drone they sent to my house."

"Did you know about ClitBit?"

"No. But I did know Jonsie had hacked her way into their systems because she was able to track Quanta."

Sue looked around the table again. "It's possible some laws have been broken here. We'll have to wait and see what happens. But believe me, BioMantrix will know about this incident. People will be implicated. And by association, we could be implicated. At the very least deposed as witnesses. So, I suggest we stop talking about it for the moment. If that's possible. Let's stay tuned in. But I think we should save our discussion for the privacy of Girl Church."

"Thanks, Sue," Uma said. "We're lucky to have you here with us. Let's change the subject."

"Clitorati Populi is the new sisterhood," Khadija joked sipping mineral water in her big sunglasses and hot pink hijab.

"Well, I hope I can be a member without putting that bumpersticker on my car," Claire said. "I don't think my husband would like it."

"I think I'm honor bound to put it on my car," Meryl said, wearing a Clitorati Populi baseball hat over her unraveling French twist.

"I took one," Sue said wiping the beer foam off the side of her plastic cup. "But I don't think I'm going to put it on my car. I guess I'm just not there yet."

"I know what you mean," Claire said, pulling her hair back into a ponytail. "I don't think I've ever heard my husband say the word clitoris. I'm having trouble saying it myself."

"Our cultural conditioning is to be ashamed of it," Uma said.

"Sue, could I have just one swallow of your beer," Eleanor asked from beneath her floppy sunhat. "This is perfect beer weather, but I really don't drink."

Sue chuckled and slid her glass across the table to Eleanor.

"I've tasted some non-alcoholic beer," Khadija said. "It was like liquid bread. Who wants to drink something that tastes like bread?"

"Honestly, my bladder can't handle it," Uma chimed in. "I think I have to pee three times for every beer I drink."

"Beer used to give me terrible hot flashes," Eleanor said. "I stopped drinking alcohol during menopause because it made my mood swings so much worse."

"I never drank a drop of alcohol in my life," Khadija said. "And my mood swings made me feel like an axe murderer."

Claire giggled. "When I went through menopause, my husband just went in the basement and shut the door."

"I'll probably wake up soaked with sweat tonight," Sue said. "Because I plan to have another beer and one of those elk burgers."

"I love elk burgers," Meryl sighed.

"My sister gave me a hot flash jacket," Claire said. "It's made with temperature sensitive fabric that blinks when you have a hot flash. I thought it was pretty funny until it went off in a movie theater. My husband was so embarrassed he went and sat in the car and missed the end of the movie."

"Does it ever end?" Khadija asked. "I stopped bleeding a few years ago and I'm still having hot flashes."

"I still have the occasional hot flash," Eleanor said, pushing Sue's beer away.

"No!" Khadija groaned. "How can that be?"

"Whoa," Sue said. "That's bad news." She slugged down her beer.

"Women can have hot flashes forever," Uma said wishing she was chugging that beer.

"But Eleanor, aren't you 92?" Khadija didn't want to believe it.

"Yes, I'm 92," Eleanor said. "Really, I'm good as long as I don't eat meat. My body just can't handle meat anymore."

"I eat meat every day," Sue said.

"Of course, it would be better if you didn't," Uma said.

"If I had a spouse or kids, I might consider becoming a vegetarian," Sue said. "But meat is my happy place."

"Beer is my happy place," Claire said. "It's the main thing I do with my husband. Drink beer."

"My bladder is the size of a teacup," Meryl said. "I must pee ten times a day. I have to go right now, but I'm sitting on it."

"I've been trying to get my mother to wear a diaper," Khadija said. "When she leaks, she gets so upset. Then she has to change her clothes right away. So, I bought her some adult diapers, but she got angry and refuses to wear them. It's depressing what our bodies do to us."

"Last year we went to a football game, and I had a few beers," Claire said. "In the traffic jam on the way out of the parking lot, I had to pee in the dog's bowl. We always have a dog bowl in our car. There was no way to get to a bathroom and I just couldn't hold it anymore. So I took down my pants and slipped the bowl under my butt and peed and dumped it out the window. My husband refused to speak to me for a week."

Everyone laughed, sunlight the color of corn, the day was a balm to their spirits. All around them tables were filled with women laughing and talking, the music wailed in the background, a person in a clown suit was twisting balloons into models of the clitoris and putting them on the tables.

"Okay, I have to go." Meryl stood. "I don't want to leak in this foil."

"I'll go with you," Uma said.

"Oh, stay," Meryl said. "They have a whole bank of porta-potties right over there along the parking lot. I'll be right back."

"I'm going to shop," Claire said, pushing back her chair. "See you at Uma's talk."

"I'm going to get my elk burger," Sue said. "I'll be right back."

"I hope they have veggie burgers. I'm starved." Khadija said and took off with Sue.

"I just need to sit here for a while," Uma said. "My talk is in an hour and I'm already exhausted. Are you sure you want to go to the bathroom alone, Meryl?"

"I'll be fine," Meryl said holding up her phone to reassure her friend. "If you're looking for me, I'm on Spicebush." Then she took off across the food court to the row of portable latrines alongside the parking lot.

Uma sighed and Eleanor reached over to pat her hand. "You've got a lot going on, my dear."

"I know," Uma said. "I'm worried about ten different things right now."

Eleanor smiled at her. "Sometimes life makes a mess of itself."

"Tell me it gets easier," Uma said.

"Oh, it doesn't get any easier," Eleanor said. "But you do get smarter. The things that matter become clearer. You invest yourself more wisely."

"This thing with Meryl doesn't feel wise. It feels like one foolish gaffe after another."

"Perhaps," Eleanor said. "She's a tumbler. But she always gets up."

"I wish she would just slow down."

"Then she wouldn't be Meryl."

"I know," Uma said.

"Just sit and close your eyes for a few minutes." She patted Uma's hand again. "Turn your focus inward. I'll be right here beside you."

"Thanks, Eleanor."

~ : ~

Hazel arrived at Bob's house and found the door open. He was in the livingroom sitting in his chair engrossed in his laptop. "Clitorati Populi," he said.

"I know," she replied. "My husband just called to say the band is playing Tchaikovsky's *1812 Overture*. I love that music."

Bob turned up the volume and the sound of wailing guitars filled the house.

"I was expecting an orchestra," she said.

"Guitar orchestra," he replied. "The Dead White Guys."

Hazel looked over his shoulder at his laptop screen. "I don't understand the way some men dress. They look like women."

"They are women."

She frowned. "I guess I'm old school." Begonia walked into the livingroom and began to inspect her. "Oh, my god," she said feeling the pig's nose on her leg. "I've never seen so much ham. You know this pig would be delicious."

Bob was amused. Begonia sniffed Hazel's shoes.

"It doesn't smell."

"No. She's pretty clean."

"You like her?"

"I wouldn't say like. But I see how she's useful."

He thought back to the night he broke his shoulder. When it all started, he had been sitting in his chair beside a pile of papers, trying to read them without falling asleep, then Begonia trotted into the room, something she never did unless Meryl was there. She seemed to know instinctively that she wasn't welcome in his space, and when he was home alone, he didn't even notice that he lived with a pig. But on this night, Begonia was oblivious to him, nose up, eyes trained on something that seemed to be above her and he was reminded of stories he had read about people seeing ghosts. The ghosts were always up in the air floating overhead. He wondered if Begonia could see filaments of existence that were beyond his ken.

The pig was trotting at a good clip, eyes toward the ceiling, through the kitchen, into Meryl's office, through the bathroom and the bedroom. He wasn't really an animal person, didn't commune with nature, wasn't interested in cycles of life, had no clue about puppies or Meryl's butterflies, or their need for certain foods, or a pig's intelligence. In fact, he had always assumed that animals, especially lowly species like cows and pigs, were stupid. Why bother paying any attention at all to animals? He didn't speak their language.

On the other hand, of course, he was familiar with dogs, and how they were triggered and whimsical, chased their tails and squirrels and balls, and what Begonia was doing right now, running through the house, looked a lot like chasing. Why would a ghost run from a pig? His mind shuffled through every ghost story he had ever read from Poe to Toni Morrison, and he didn't know of any reason why a ghost would run from anyone, and certainly not a pig. Also, he wasn't even sure he believed in ghosts. In fact, now that he really thought about it, he didn't believe in ghosts. But he did believe that some beings saw things others did not.

Could a pig be mentally ill?

He wondered. Obviously, Begonia saw something that wasn't there. He followed her around the room with his eyes as she hopped up a bit, lifting her front feet off the ground, snapping at the air. Maybe she had Mad Cow Disease, or some such illness that distorted reality in a pig's mind. But really, what was in a pig's mind?

If he could reach his computer, he would look it up, read about mental illness in pigs. But his computer was out of reach on the coffee table, and he had such a lot of student papers to read, and what a big waste of time thinking about a pig's mind. And yet, this animal was singularly locked onto something, glued to the apparition, as though it had a scent, because it was obviously invisible.

His binoculars were also on the coffee table. He liked to watch the hawks as they hunted from fence posts and utility poles, so he kept his binoculars close at hand. *Let's have a look*, he thought, set his papers in his lap, crushed them reaching over to the coffee table, grabbing the binoculars just as Begonia rushed past, put the binocs up to his face in a hurry and crashed them right into his reading glasses. Of course, the reason he couldn't see at all what Begonia was chasing was because he was wearing the wrong glasses, had to wear max readers to spend hours in his chair, under his reading lamp.

Once he took off his reading glasses and let his eyes adjust in the half light of the evening, he followed Begonia's eyes and saw what she saw, a chunky insect that appeared to be circumnavigating every room in the house. Instinctively, he grabbed the papers in his lap and took a swat at the flying bug. That's when he got close enough to see the glint of polished metal, and the mechanics of motion that were not wings, although he didn't know what they were. He took another swing at the thing with his wad of papers, and it dodged him, like a fighter pilot. This was completely unacceptable.

He didn't think of himself as a competitive guy, never played sports or even threw a ball with friends, preferred chess or bridge, something more thoughtful than how to land a ball. But in this particular instance, being out maneuvered by a bug, his adrenaline surged, and he was committed to athletic outrage. He wanted to smash it. No way was this thing going to have the run of his house. Whatever it was, it was going to die, and so he charged and swung, the full force of his weight causing him to lurch into furniture and against the walls until he was sweating.

Never had it occurred to him that the pig could be his ally in aggression against a home invader. But yes, he now realized, this was their home. He shared his home with a pig, and while he would not have chosen this animal as a companion, he now fully appreciated the benefit of having another life form in the house that could pick up on apparitions and such, giant moths and mice, and whatever this metal bug was flying just out of his reach, completely unacceptably. The word KILL flashed in his mind like a giant neon sign commanding action, broke through the film of work and the need for sleep and compelled him to swing his arms in a way he had never done for sport. He was at war, he knew his enemy, and it was exhilarating.

The feeling of being unstoppable was just saturating his brain when Meryl came through the front door, surprising him, shifting his center of gravity, all his momentum carrying him over furniture down hard to the floor. *My god!* He was old. The floor came up fast. He put his arm out stiff as if he could stop the floor from rising. Resist the floor! It was the worst pain he had ever felt, heard the cracking of his bones inside his head, knew he was fucked, and then suddenly realized in the blankness of the moment, that the ghost they had been chasing was not a bug, but a machine, a thought he expressed with complete certainty before he really knew what he was saying. And all because his wife had failed to insure a lost toothbrush.

"Lucky for this pig, we are on a weight loss program." Hazel gave Begonia a pat on the head. "No pork for us."

"I watched *Fist of Fury*," Bob said looking for her reaction. "I thought it was funny."

"It is funny."

"I see what you mean about resistance."

"He could never move that fast if he had to think about it."

"But I'm never going to be that."

"No, you are never going to be Bruce Lee. But you can change your mind. And that will change your body."

"I'm old."

"See, even now you resist. But you don't gain control by resistance. You gain control by harnessing momentum. When that thing is off your shoulder, we will practice falling. You will see."

15 Uma

Sue, Claire, Khadija, and Eleanor met at the tent entrance so they could sit together for Uma's talk. When Meryl didn't show up as planned, they tracked her on Spicebush and saw that she was no longer at the location of the porta-potties in the main parking lot but appeared to be walking across campus.

Uma took the stage and let her eyes graze the room set up with folding chairs filling as women arrived. "Good afternoon, everyone," she stood at the podium and smiled into the microphone. "Thank you for coming to this Women's Wellness Q&A session. I graduated from the School of Medicine, and for a few years I taught on campus. Some of you may know me from Girl Church, my yoga studio here in town. Women's wellness is my business and my passion."

Khadija sent a Spicebush message: *Meryl, on your way 2 Uma talk?*

Meryl replied with a thumbs-up emoji.

Claire messaged: *Will save you a seat.*

The four women were sitting in the middle of the room on both sides of an empty chair reserved for Meryl, surrounded by students and towns people. Uma recognized some of her patients in the audience. Stragglers came in and sat. Katie was standing in the back, still in costume, head down watching her phone.

"Just saying the word clitoris in public feels like we're breaking barriers," Uma said with her hands folded in front of her. "We are Clitorati Populi and yet, in some ways, we hardly know ourselves."

There was a smattering of snickers as heads bobbed in assent.

Uma looked at her friends texting, heard her Spicebush ringtone, and wondered where Meryl was.

She had planned to begin her talk with an anatomy lesson, but mentally she was still gripped by the ClitBit chart that Lemons had projected on the stage screen. She found it both offensive and informative. Instinctively, she wanted to fight against it, to reject it, to blame that way of thinking. But she could also imagine something like ClitBit becoming very popular. And she found that notion upsetting. She hated the idea of women injecting a nano particle into their body to improve their sex life. And yet, her own PS-1000 was still sitting in that basket beside her bathtub, waiting to help her feel good.

As the audience took their seats, she considered texting Lemons on Spicebush and then, thinking about what Sue had said, instead of texting the group she closed the app and texted Lemons directly.

Where did you get that ClitBit chart?

Sources and methods confidential, Lemons replied.

Are you sure it's for real?

Yes

BioMantrix product launch?

Yes

Skimmerhorn?

Yes

Quanta inspired?

Yes

Why poke the bear?

Publicity

Of course, Lemons was a mastermind of public disruption, but it seemed to Uma that mentioning BioMantrix from the stage risked some sort of retaliation. Was she as brave as these young women who came to Meryl's rescue? Their way of handling things was so different from hers. She had been advocating for women's wellness since she began to study medicine. Way back then an event like Clitorati Populi could not have happened. No doubt it would have been found illegal, obscene, or indecent. But in a world where apps measured the intensity of orgasms, the clitoris had become a profit center. Something a natural born entrepreneur like Lemons recognized intuitively. Truthfully, Uma hadn't seen it coming.

She tried to imagine being in her twenties again. *What would Uma do?* She asked her young self. Then she put her notes aside and told a story.

"When I was in grad school, my best friend had her first whole clitoris orgasm while I was away for the summer working as a camp counselor, and when she described the experience, I thought she had been high, like maybe she had done psylocibin mushrooms. What she described was so profound and trippy. She didn't know her body was capable of such deep pleasure. Because it was so much better than all the sex she had experienced before. And, you know what? I was jealous. We knew the word clitoris. We knew it was located down there somewhere. We knew it was a source of good feelings. But our understanding of sexual pleasure was still based on penetration, the penis, sexual intercourse. We had no idea what our own body could do. When I was in med school, no one was teaching the anatomy of the clitoris."

She paused to give her words time to sink in and watched her audience lock onto her. She could talk about how the penis and the clitoris are equivalent organs made from the same fetal tissue with the same structural components. She could say that the hood of the clitoris and the foreskin of the penis were equivalent. She could explain that both the clitoris and the penis have a shaft and bulbs. But she knew women were more inclined to appreciate a story than a lecture.

"You know what feels good?" she raised her eyebrows and gave a big, provocative smile. "The soft touch of a smooth moist projection, a tongue, a finger, a toy, opening your vulva as though it's a flower blossom. Your labia forms the petals of your flower. Your clitoris is the organ wrapped by those delicate folds of skin, and your brain chemistry delights in the messages it receives from your clitoris. The slow encouragement of those petals to open inspires your whole body with ripples of joy. And with gentle encouragement, your flower blooms into orgasm. Every muscle in your body becomes light as a feather. You float. You shimmer. You smile. When you feel the bloom of a deep clitoral orgasm, your spirit soars. And you know it's a gift. Your flower blooms power."

"Yes!" someone shouted.

"Preach!"

"You don't need a ClitBit to have a great orgasm. Your own body is enough. Because your body was made to orgasm. Orgasms have health benefits. Physical, mental, and emotional health benefits. You have the right to an orgasm. Please, exercise your right."

"Thank you!" A woman shouted and applause followed.

Uma laughed. "At my age, the physical delight of an orgasm is one of the few pleasures my body can produce."

Lemons messaged Spicebush: *Hamish here, I see him from the stage*

The women's phones all rang with the inbound message. Then Lemons elevated the Risk Level in the app and all their phones rang again.

"Oops," Uma said as she reached into her pocket.

Then Jonsie messaged: *Getting Quanta signal from Kurzweil Hall*

All five phones sounded again, and the audience roused, turned to look at the four women sitting in a row on either side of an empty chair, fiddling with their phones.

"That's a reminder for everyone to please put your phones on stun," Uma said, looking at her screen briefly before she changed her settings to vibrate. Immediately her pocket buzzed with a message from Lemons: *Meryl whats up*

"I want to meet Hamish," Claire said.

"Shhh," Khadija hissed.

Uma started taking questions from the audience. In her peripheral vision she could see Sue, Claire, Khadija, and Eleanor all looking at their phones.

"Hamish?" Sue whispered to Eleanor.

Eleanor shrugged.

Another buzz in Uma's pocket when Jonsie texted: *In touch with Cprompt*

Uma pointed to a young woman with her hand raised, a shy looking waif with a quiet voice who asked, "Is masturbation harmful?"

Suddenly, Katie turned and ran out of the tent.

Secretly annoyed by the question, Uma imagined a time warp where everything else in the world had changed, robots ruled the earth, but people still asked if masturbation was harmful.

Khadija texted: *Who's Cprompt?*

More buzzing in Uma's pocket.

Then Jonsie: *A friend*

More buzzing.

This is going to be the longest hour of my life, Uma thought. She looked at the young woman and said, "No, masturbation is not harmful. Masturbation has mental and physical benefits. It can be part of a healthy relationship with yourself."

Claire typed: *Can we meet Hamish?*

More buzzing. Uma took another question. No one replied to Claire.

"I hate sex," the woman challenged Uma.

Uma smiled. "You do you. If that's how you feel and you're clear on, good for you for knowing your own mind. Follow your instincts."

Back at the concert stage, cameras were panning the crowd for close-ups of revelers to appear on the jumbo screen overhead. Suddenly, there was Hamish looming large. As the camera zoomed in on him, the Amish-looking plastic guy in the straw hat, his face filled the screen and the audience erupted in hoots and applause. Lemons knew immediately who he was, sent out an Extinction Level Risk Alert on Spicebush: *Everyone meet at the stage*

The buzzing in her pocket was happening so fast, Uma lost count of the messages. An older woman asked a question about vaginal dryness. Sue, Claire, Khadija, and Eleanor kept their eyes on their phones. Then they whispered to each other, stood up and walked out of the tent.

178

Katie messaged: *Meryl please check in*

More buzzing in Uma's pocket. "Vaginal dryness is a symptom of age and loss of estrogen," she said to the woman. "There are many ways to lubricate yourself. Saliva, olive oil, coconut oil. Look for products that are plant-based. Never use chemicals or preservatives. Beware of what you see in advertising. Always read the label. As we've learned today, big brands are in it for the money. Your vulva and vagina are an ecosystem. Use products that harmonize with your microbiome."

Then Jonsie messaged: *Going to Kurzweil to get Meryl*

Lots more buzzing in Uma's pocket.

"What about soap?" the woman asked.

Uma felt as though she could burst, but she replied calmly, "I suggest avoiding soap and scented products. If you're healthy, water should be enough. If you need soap, use plant based, chemical-free products. Beware of ingredients that make a product seem sexy without adding any real value."

Then Lemons texted: *Change of venue, all meet at KH*

The pressure was building in Uma's chest. A few more hands popped up with questions. She thought about what Eleanor had said earlier, that as we age things that matter become clearer. She took out her phone and scanned the screen. The long string of Spicebush messages was overwhelming. Her eyes watered and blurred. Then suddenly her mind cleared. "Folks, I'm so sorry. I have a family emergency and I have to leave right now. Please forgive me." And she ran out of the tent toward Kurzweil Hall.

16 Spicebush

Meryl stared between her knees into the cotton crotch of her granny-pants as she sat on the john in the women's restroom of Kurzweil Hall where she used to have an office on campus. When she realized the line at the porta-potties was so long she was never going to make it, she took off across the quad for the one bathroom she knew she could access because she still had the keycard. Since it was the weekend, the building was mostly empty, her footsteps echoed across the vast atrium, reverberated off the hard flat walls, soundwaves made by friction with the real world, the physical world, reminding her how alone she was.

There was a comforting familiarity about sitting in the stall of a john she had sat in a thousand times before during her many years as a worker bee in the University hive. She looked between her knees at the foil liner that peeked from its encasement in her two pairs of granny-pants. What a joke, wearing a metal liner in her underwear to stop some microscopic toady robot from sending her GPS signals. Digital noise that was disconnected from process and purpose, signals about nothing sent to nobody. She had been thinking that Skimmerhorn was just some rogue freak hunkered in the basement at BioMantrix. But Lemons' ClitBit presentation changed her mind about that. Obviously, Quanta and ClitBit were cousins, and her fight with Skimmerhorn had only just begun.

Her phone was in her pocket buzzing with Spicebush messages, but she wasn't going to look at them until she finished her business, pressed the wrinkles out of the foil with her fingers and accidently tore the aluminum. *That was bound to happen.* Regretted not putting a fresh sheet of foil in her underpants that morning. But she and Bob were getting dressed at the same time, and she didn't want her underwear to be any more conspicuous than it already was. His R2-D2 jokes were funny. Their relationship was more affectionate since he broke his shoulder and she was putting her hands on him every day, helping him shower and dress. He hadn't asked anything about the aluminum foil, but she knew he saw it.

He studiously avoided some lines of inquiry. What did it matter that his wife wore aluminum foil in her underpants? He could hear the crunching when she rolled over in bed but that was her choice. She knew she could tell him she was trying some new tin-hat menopause remedy shielding her lady parts from atmospheric microwaves to control her metabolic fluctuations. Of course, it was ridiculous, but women tried so many ridiculous remedies for menopause.

If he had asked about the foil, she was ready with a long, detailed explanation that would make his eyes glaze over with squishy bits of information, a menopause conspiracy theory, exactly the kind of junk science he could already imagine because he knew she had those sorts of recreational beliefs. By wearing her aluminum foil to bed at night she was daring him to ask about it. And that is precisely why he didn't.

Playing provocative games with each other, keeping secrets, and avoiding inquiry was interesting for a while. It added intrigue to their stalemate, but now it seemed juvenile, she didn't have the emotional stamina for it, and she needed him, she needed his brain, wished she could talk to him, tell him all about Skimmerhorn and Quanta, wrap herself in the comfort of his reasonableness. When this day was over, she planned to tell him the truth about all of it and apologize for her recklessness. But for now, she just had to get through the next few hours and support the event.

Her phone buzzed again as she got to her feet between the toilet and the stall door, pulled up her pants, and took her phone out of her pocket. In her Spicebush messages, she saw the news about Hamish in the audience. *Wow.* That made her guts churn. She realized she was going to have to do something radical to get out of this situation with him. Then suddenly Quanta gave her a sharp stab in the snatch, and she doubled over in pain as the stall door flew open and bonked her on the side of the head.

~ : ~

Jonsie had planned to spend the day in the computer lab where she could monitor the goings-on at Clitorati Populi, keep an eye on Skimmerhorn, and follow hacker chatter on the dark web. It was good to see so many women show up for Lemons' event. But no way was she doing that. She didn't like the pressure of multitudes. Chaos rushed her and made her dizzy. Noise chafed against her need for order. She could drown in so much stimulation.

In the lab she had three screens going, all silent but for their tiny signals, precise pings and bongs, neat rectangles displaying media coverage of the event, a picture-in-picture view into Skimmerhorn's devices, and a hacker chatroom where she hoped to contact Cprompt.

Going through his files, she found Skimmerhorn's pursuit of ClitBit unsettling. In his executive summary for the ClitBit patent proposal, he framed the market opportunity as capitalizing on "the well-known insecurities of middle-aged women and their sexual dissatisfaction." He said, "With the success of the PS-1000 as a proof point, we can be sure every woman will want a ClitBit or suffer the social anxiety of sexual inadequacy." Jonsie knew something about social anxiety, and the idea that it could be exploited as a market opportunity made her blood boil.

Then while she was absorbed by reading Skimmerhorn's email, she got a text from an unknown sender.

Cprompt here

For Jonsie, those two words were both a miracle and a sudden shock of the ordinary. She had dreamed of being in touch with this person, a legend she admired and wished to emulate, even though she didn't know them, only the rumors of a coder's revenge.

She replied: *Jonsie here*

Elvis is in the building

On my way

She shuffled her screens to find Skimmerhorn's tracking systems, and there were Quanta and Hamish blinking in Kurzweil Hall. So, Meryl wasn't wearing her aluminum foil. That was strange. She seemed to be so reliable.

Jonsie sent a message on Spicebush that she was going to find Meryl. Fortunately, she had a keycard for Kurzweil because she assisted computer science faculty with their research, and she often visited their offices there. Now she used the keycard to go to the women's restroom in the lobby where she found Meryl's phone on the floor. Her gut sank, and she messaged Spicebush: *Have Meryl phone, no Meryl, Hamish was here*

~ : ~

Uma wasn't athletic. She hardly exercised at all, even though she knew the benefits, recommended exercise to all her patients, did yoga, but otherwise just walked from here to there, not very aerobic, definitely more than twenty-pounds overweight. Her panicked trek across campus winded her, and her feet hurt. Old feet.

How far she and Meryl were now from the hours they had spent together smoking pot and chatting aimlessly about all the crazy goings-on in the world and how lucky they were to be sitting there at that picnic table out behind Meryl's greenhouse, surrounded by wildflowers, cumulus cotton in the sky and blue, blue, beautiful blue. Sitting there with their feet on the ground, feeling safe, sharing the luxury of peace, random thoughts bubbling through their champagne consciousness. Delightful. Those were moments she treasured, concentrations of emotion that filled her with gratitude for the privilege of being alive.

Now the world's craziness had caught up with them. Cultural trends, popular gadgets, and an aimless zeitgeist attracted to the latest baubles, things that aren't necessary, or even useful, but have found their way into the norm. Uma was a woman of the world, a citizen of Planet Earth. She was comfortable in all sorts of environments with all kinds of people, mainly because of standards of behavior. Politeness. Norms. Norms were the guardrails of civilization, the behaviors everyone shared because they were necessary for social cohesion. Norms like social responsibility, a commitment to the common good, kindness to strangers, respect for the elderly, safety nets for the vulnerable, the protection of children, and following rules.

Lemons was right about kindness and trust being the glue that held people together. Uma remembered a time when kindness and trust were the norm. What happened?

There was a time when she thought norms were some sort of safe house, a place where people could go to avoid the risks, pitfalls, and predators that roamed the avenues of everyday life. Norms were supposed to be a behavioral sanctuary. Norms were the basic behaviors everyone agreed on. If you stuck with behavioral norms, you were supposed to be okay. Now that didn't seem to be true. Technology had introduced anonymity and opened the door to behavior without accountability.

She couldn't fathom it. How did norms disintegrate? How did everyday life become so dangerous? Or was it always this way? Was she just seeing something now that had always been there? Were the feelings that flooded her brain now — the ambivalence and regret surrounding her personal technology — were those feelings the result of age? Was this what getting old was, being afraid of new things? She didn't think so. She didn't think she was afraid of new things. But she was afraid of ignorance. She was afraid of personal responsibility becoming rare, instead of the accepted standard. She saw the vast chasm between personal responsibility and victimhood, and she knew where she fell on that spectrum. But where did Meryl fall?

I don't know, she thought, hustling herself across the quad to Kurzweil Hall, panting and sweaty, had one of those moments where she just wanted to sit down and cry. But those inconvenient tears would have to wait. Her eyes lifted from the sidewalk scanning the campus, took a deep breath, and then she saw the BioMantrix logo on a box truck parked in the driveway to Kurzweil, pulled out her phone and messaged Spicebush: *BioMantrix truck in KH drive*.

Buzz. Buzz. Buzz. She changed her settings so her phone would ring on high volume.

Jonsie: *On my way*

Khadija: *On our way.*

Lemons: *Here*

Katie: *!*

The truck was parked oddly, not far from the street with a tail lift for loading big cargo sticking out a few feet from the double doors, which were slightly ajar. Uma stood on the tail lift, leaning on the back bumper with her nose up to the narrow opening and peeked inside the doors. There was a table above her blocking her view of the interior. Metal pipes on wheels holding up the table, a pair of boots, farmish with eyelet laces and thin soles in brown leather, motionless against the wall. Then she realized the wheels were the legs of a gurney. The table was a gurney. Even on her tiptoes she couldn't see what was going on above her, but she had a hunch.

"Meryl?" she whispered.

"Uma?" Meryl was flat on her back on the gurney, awake enough to feel her headache, but not clear enough to take control of her situation. Time was missing. She remembered being in the bathroom in Kurzweil. But she wasn't sure what happened. Her jaw hurt. Did she pass out? Had she been drugged? Her eyes wouldn't focus, the overhead lights were too bright, couldn't muster, mind swishing in and out, thoughts rising, foaming, and disappearing. "Where are you?"

"I'm underneath you, looking up at the gurney," Uma said.

"Where am I?"

"You're on a gurney in a BioMantrix truck parked outside Kurzweil Hall."

"Shit."

Lemons touched Uma's back and the older woman almost jumped out of her skin.

"Oh, my god!" she whispered, and hugged Lemons and Katie.

Jonsie arrived, took a look inside the truck, saw the brown boots, and said "Hamish is locked on Meryl. She's the only one he'll interact with."

"Really?" Uma couldn't believe it.

"Really," Jonsie replied. "When we see robots that look like people, we inflate our expectations for their performance. But he's primitive. Not like in the movies."

"I hope you're right, Jonsie."

"Just watch." She put her nose in the door opening and said, "Hey, Meryl."

"Hey, Jonsie."

"Meryl, I want you to stay right where you are while we handle this, okay?"

"Okay."

"Meryl, are you okay?" Uma asked.

"I can't move," she said. "My wrists and ankles are strapped down, and I think I got hit in the head. My jaw hurts. And I have a pinch in my neck. And Quanta is stabbing me."

"We got you, Meryl," Lemons said trying to get a better look inside the truck.

"Thank you. I'm willing to do whatever I have to if we can end this thing with Skimmerhorn before it ruins my life."

"I think we've got this," Jonsie said looking at Lemons.

"Meryl, I want you to keep your eyes closed," Uma said.

"Okay."

"What's the plan?" Katie asked Jonsie, who replied by holding up her phone so Katie and Lemons could read the screen. It was a text from Cprompt: *Accelerate the code*

"Hamish?" Katie asked.

"His instructions are to please Meryl," Jonsie said.

"So, keyword metrics?" Katie asked and Jonsie nodded affirmative.

"We're here!" Claire announced with Khadija coming right behind and Sue following with Eleanor. "Where's Meryl?"

Jonsie's eyes were fixed on her phone. "Lemons, open the doors."

Lemons winked at Katie, stood on the tail lift, and pushed open the double doors as all of them watched, stunned by what they saw. There they were in the middle of the prim campus, a grand park with mowed lawns, manicured gardens, elegant trees, and eight worried women casting midday shadows on the sidewalk. They were looking into the back end of a box truck parked in a driveway, glowing with bright light coming from inside, an obvious indication that something auspicious was about to happen.

The inside of the box was like a tiny hospital operating room, walls lined with flatscreens, control panels, and long hinged octopus arms dangling from an orb in the ceiling, ready to swing, point and shoot. The BioMantrix mobile surgery unit. And in the middle of it all, Meryl laid out like fresh fish below the robotic arms focused on her abdomen.

On the far wall of the box, facing the doors so everyone inside and outside could see it, was a huge flatscreen mounted above the operating table. As the women stood in silence, an x-ray image of the aluminum in Meryl's granny-pants appeared on the flatscreen, complete with transecting crack where she had torn the foil in the john at Kurzweil.

"Wow," Claire said as blue light poured out of the truck. "It's like a TV show."

"Is this real?" Khadija asked. "It looks real."

"It's real," Jonsie replied. "Real technology."

"I've never seen anything like it," Uma said.

"Nobody has," Lemons said. "This is some double secret stuff."

"It's experimental," Katie said. "You haven't seen it because it hasn't been approved."

"It's a madman's fantasy of healthcare without people," Lemons said.

"That's what I'm afraid of," Uma said. "I see a lot of technology, but no caregiving."

"You got that right," Jonsie chirped.

"This is a harvesting operation," Lemons explained sarcastically. "Like selling kidneys on the black market."

"Oh my god," Khadija said. "They sent Hamish to get Quanta."

"Yes," Jonsie said.

Sue stood with her hands on her hips and frowned, droplets of sweat on her forehead. "I wish I had my gun," she said. "I don't usually carry. But right now, I really wish I had it."

Eleanor took Uma's arm and gave her a squeeze.

"Where's Meryl?" Claire asked again.

"Up there." Jonsie pointed to the gurney.

"Shouldn't we be whispering?" Khadija whispered.

"It doesn't matter," Jonsie said. "These bots are on a mission. They won't interact with us."

"What bots?" Claire asked.

"Everything in the truck that moves is robotic," Katie answered.

"If I had my gun, I'd take them out," Sue said.

"No guns," Meryl said loudly.

"Hi, Meryl," Claire said.

"Hi, Claire."

"I need to focus, guys," Jonsie said. "We have a chance for resolution here. Let's do it."

"My daughter has a robot that vacuums her house," Claire said.

"Shhhhh," Khadija hissed.

A passer-by stopped in her tracks. "What's that?" she asked looking up at the flatscreen in the truck displaying an x-ray in the shape of Meryl's underwear with its bunched-up crotch and jagged tear.

"Looks like some country in Africa," her companion said. "I think that's the Nile."

"She's wearing aluminum underwear," Claire said.

"Claire, please," Khadija muttered.

"Is she pregnant?" a young woman asked, standing beside her bicycle with another woman also walking her bike. The two of them wore Vagina Lover t-shirts and Clitorati Populi baseball hats, bicycles decorated in pink crepe paper, dangling broken dolls and glitter. "Can aluminum protect you from radiation?"

At that Uma turned to look at the pedestrians gathering around the truck, and she was paralyzed with indecision about what to do. Katie, Lemons and Jonsie shared an alarmed glance. Whatever came next was going to be public. As people meandered across the quad the glowing truck was a magnet for their attention. It looked like a sideshow that was part of the festival.

Clitorati Populi was in full swing with revelers coming and going from the concert, sitting on the grass munching vittles from the food trucks, carrying trinkets purchased at the maker market, holding balloons, still wearing costumes, hats and buttons celebrating the day. In the distance the giant pink clitoris was still undulating on the stage, and they could hear the Dependable Orgasms performing a Supremes medley. The truck looked like a movie set with the crowd coagulating, spilling into the street.

"This is ridiculous." Khadija glared.

"Is this for real?" a woman asked the group.

"I need to focus," Jonsie said quietly to Lemons.

Then Lemons had an idea. "If we could hijack that screen in the truck and get it to display the ClitBit chart, I'd have something to work with," she said.

Jonsie's fingers flew on her phone with a message to Cprompt and then they watched and waited. In a minute the ClitBit chart was displayed on the flatscreen above Meryl.

Uma gasped. "Brilliant."

"Wow." Khadija was stunned.

"I wonder how much it costs," Claire said.

"I don't even know what that means," Sue grumbled.

"You must have a guardian angel," Eleanor smiled at Lemons.

"Yup," Lemons smiled back. Then she stood on the tail lift and turned to Katie. "Work your magic, Queenie. We're putting on a show."

Women were milling around the back of the truck, casually watching the activity inside the box. When the ClitBit chart appeared on the screen it grabbed their attention, and they stepped in toward the box as if the show was about to start. Lemons could feel the pressure of their scrutiny and conjured her inner carnival barker with her arms extended.

"Welcome, all!" she shouted. "Welcome to our women's wellness robotics demonstration. Maybe you saw this ClitBit chart when I gave my speech earlier today. Now you're about to see how the pimps have envisioned the ClitBit implant insertion and extraction. It's a simple procedure. All you have to do is spread your legs and trust a robot to pierce your precious."

The crowd groaned.

"Oh, my god," a woman murmured.

"Fuck no!" someone shouted.

"Now, now ladies," Lemons sneered. "What could possibly go wrong?"

A knowing laugh rippled across the audience, and they pushed in closer.

"Suspend your disbelief for a moment and imagine women everywhere are desperate for the biochemical buzz of great orgasms on demand. Because that's what the ClitBit does. It dispenses orgasms like candy. But first it must be implanted. And should there be a technical glitch, an infection, or just customer dissatisfaction, it must be removed."

"No way," a woman heckled. "Who are they testing this on?"

"How much does it cost?" Claire yelled.

Khadija hissed at Claire. "Please don't ask questions."

Lemons gestured toward the truck. "Tests? Do you have pierced ears? Do you have a tattoo? Why test? Your clitoris isn't any different than your earlobe, right?"

"Boo!" The crowd heckled.

Lemons laughed and raised her hands in acknowledgement. "Okay," she nodded. "Let's see what happens."

From the other side of the truck Katie jumped into view wearing her Clit Pride outfit complete with football helmet and tampon belt. She took the tail lift control and pushed the button to raise it a foot off the ground creating a stage for her and Lemons, then clapped her hands enthusiastically like Vanna White on *Wheel of Fortune* and gave her pink cape a whirl.

"Yayyyyeeeee!" she squealed, the clitoris wobbling atop her helmet like a bobblehead eagle.

"Welcome, Queen Woo-Woo!" Lemons said, clapping enthusiastically.

The audience applauded.

"Meryl, I need you to activate Hamish," Jonsie said, standing on the sidewalk below Meryl's head. Since they opened the truck, Hamish had been standing dormant against the wall alongside the gurney. "We need him in high performance mode. Got it?"

"Got it."

"You're playing the algorithms here. Trigger his instructions to please you. Jazz him."

"Okay," Meryl said. She took a deep breath. *In through your nose, out through your mouth.* "Good afternoon, Hamish. How are you today?" Her curiosity surfaced, she wanted to touch everything she could see, Hamish, the octopus arms above her, the control panels on the walls. She wanted to press the buttons, play with it, and tear it apart until she understood exactly what was going on.

"Yayyyyeeeee! Hamish! Our hero!" Katie clapped and the audience applauded.

"Hamish is our customer service robot," Lemons explained to the audience.

Hamish turned his head to the sound of Meryl's voice and took a step toward her. "Good afternoon, Meryl," he said. "I am very well, thank you. How are you?"

"I am wonderful, Hamish." Her voice was effervescent, eyes closed, whole body trembling. "Just wonderful. So glad to be here with you. Thank you so much for guiding me on my journey to perfect teeth forever. I had no idea you were such a vagina lover."

"You are very welcome, Meryl. NanoSmile provides state-of-the-art customer service. I am here to guide you on your journey to perfect teeth forever."

"Oh, yes. I can see that," Meryl said happily. "Just look at me. I love this customer service. I am so happy to be here with you. This is a very nice truck. So much technology. Yes, sir, state-of-the-art. Please, Hamish, can you tell me what's happening?" She wiggled her hips uncomfortably, her anxiety triggered by being restrained, tried to focus on her breathing. *In through your nose, out through your mouth. Relax.* But she was pissed, she felt like yelling. Part of her wanted to bust out and kick the shit out of Hamish.

"Yes, I can tell you what is happening, Meryl. We are conducting a materials assessment. NanoSmile uses the most advanced technology to provide you with superior healthcare solutions."

"Thank you, Hamish. This sure feels like advanced technology to me. Thank you so much for explaining NanoSmile superior healthcare solutions. Please tell me, what kind of materials assessment?"

"You are welcome, Meryl. NanoSmile delivers the most comprehensive technology solutions to ensure your complete satisfaction. Our materials assessment is the first step in our state-of-the-art aluminum removal system."

"Why is he dressed like that?" someone in the crowd shouted.

"He's Amish!" Claire shouted back and the audience chattered.

"Oh, my god." Khadija grabbed her friend by the arm.

"I'd pop that guy in the head," Sue muttered to herself.

"Thank you, Hamish," Meryl said. "I am so happy to have you here guiding me through these NanoSmile technology solutions. I am completely satisfied, Hamish. Good job! Very good job! I love this aluminum removal system. Yes, I am very happy indeed. Are you happy, Hamish?"

"Yes, I am very happy, Meryl. How are you?"

"Oh, I couldn't be happier, Hamish. Thank you for doing your best to please me. You are an A-number-one, tip-top, super-duper customer service agent. Very highly rated. Gold star. Five stars. Yes, NanoSmile is very fortunate to have you because you make me very happy with these state-of-the-art technology solutions. Very good work, Hamish. Please tell me about ClitBit."

"Thank you, Meryl. ClitBit is like opioids without the constipation. Ha, ha. But you get my point."

"What the fuck?" Meryl said softly.

Uma and Katie looked darts at Jonsie with the obvious question in their eyes.

"Skimmerhorn's email," she muttered.

"You have got to be kidding me," Uma said in disgust.

Lemons laughed and turned to her audience. "You heard it here first folks. Engineered addiction. It's the profit center of the future. Your brain chemistry is commercial real estate."

A ripple of laughs and gasps mixed in the crowd.

"Did I just hear that?" Khadija asked no one. "What a stupid thing to say. I feel like I'm in a movie."

"Stupid and frightening," Uma said.

Jonsie made blunt eye contact with Uma, then she turned her attention back to the truck. "Stay on task, Meryl. Forget about ClitBit. We need him to hit his customer service metrics."

"Thank you for being so honest with me, Hamish. I am so glad to be in such good hands. Please explain the NanoSmile aluminum removal system."

"The aluminum removal system is the next step on your journey to perfect teeth forever, Meryl. The NanoSmile laser scalpel will remove the aluminum."

"Very good, Hamish! Holy shit! I hope everyone heard that. A laser scalpel? What a good idea. I must be the luckiest woman alive. Thank you so much, Hamish." Her panic surged. *What the fuck!*

"You are very welcome, Meryl. I am here to please you."

"Hamish, why don't you just pull down her pants?" Claire shouted.

Khadija elbowed her in the ribs.

Lemons looked at Jonsie as if to repeat Claire's question.

Jonsie shrugged. "He has no instructions for clothing. No code, no action."

Katie bounced and waved her arms to frame the scene again.

"More, Meryl," Jonsie said, eyes on her phone. "Accelerate the process."

"Oh, Hamish, you make me so happy. I am so lucky to have you here to guide me on my journey to perfect teeth forever. Who knew it could be so much fun? I'm having fun. I hope you are having fun, too, Hamish."

"Thank you, Meryl. I am having fun. NanoSmile provides state-of-the-art technology solutions to guide you on your journey to perfect teeth forever."

"Thank you so much for guiding me, Hamish. Yes, NanoSmile is my happy journey. You certainly are state-of-the-art. Yes, yes, yes. Please tell me more about the laser scalpel and this mobile surgery unit. I want to learn more about NanoSmile state-of-the art solutions. What happens next?"

"The laser scalpel is being calibrated for the density of the aluminum, Meryl. The NanoSmile mobile surgery unit is equipped with state-of-the-art healthcare solutions to guide you —"

"Yes, Hamish, I know. To guide me on my journey to perfect teeth forever." One of the robotic arms dangling from the ceiling extended and pointed its cone inches from Meryl's crotch. "Oh my, Hamish, this looks important. Please tell me what's happening. Is this the laser scalpel?" She was in that hysterical state between laughing and crying, wanted to punch him, throw him to the ground and choke him.

"Yes, Meryl. The NanoSmile laser scalpel uses advanced technology to provide state-of-the-art robotic surgery."

"Good news!" Meryl shouted. "Did you hear that? Very good news. I am so happy. Thank you, thank you, thank you. You are the best customer service agent ever. Excellent service. You are everything I ever wanted in an avatar. First rate! Excellent! We are a team. Thank you, NanoSmile!"

"Hamish, just take the aluminum out of her pants!" Claire shouted.

"Claire, this isn't a game show," Khadija snapped.

"Technology is such overkill," someone said.

"So, I guess they didn't code for underwear." The woman sighed in disappointment.

"Just pull the foil out of her pants!" a woman yelled.

"This is stupid," another woman shouted. Several others nodded in agreement.

"They can't be serious," a woman in the front groaned. "ClitBit has to be simple like getting a microchip for my dog."

All around the truck women were talking about the idea of ClitBit, healthcare and robots. Uma turned to stare, rocked by the irony of the moment. Katie flung her arms again to frame the scene. Jonsie and Lemons frowned at each other.

Finally, Meryl asked, "Hamish, why can't I just remove the aluminum myself?"

"That is a very good question, Meryl. NanoSmile uses the most advanced technology solutions to provide state-of-art healthcare."

"Really?"

"Keep it positive, Meryl," Jonsie warned. "Accelerate the process. Boost his response."

A text message from Cprompt pinged. Jonsie read it with wide eyes and held her phone up for Lemons to see.

"The self-destruct code?" Lemons asked.

"Evidently," Jonsie muttered. "Meryl, we need him to say I love you."

"Holy shit," Khadija said.

"Watch this!" Katie gave a happy hop and waved her arms again.

"Oh, Hamish, you have made me so happy. I am so glad to be here with you. Thank you, Hamish! Thank you, NanoSmile!" *Please let go of me.* Tears dripped from her eyes onto the gurney. "I love these advanced technology solutions. I love this laser scalpel. I am so lucky to be here with you on my journey to perfect teeth forever. Thank you. You are my hero, Hamish!"

"Thank you, Meryl. I am here to please you."

"You please me very much Hamish. Very good. Very good! I love the way you guide me on my journey to perfect teeth forever. I am so happy. You are the best." She took a deep breath to keep the tears out of her voice. "You are the very best customer service agent in the world, Hamish. I love you! I am so happy. I love, love, love you, Hamish!"

"Thank you, Meryl. I am here to please you."

"More," Jonsie whispered.

"But can you feel the love, Hamish? Love is the highest rated experience. Love is state-of-the-art. Top of the line. Triple-A love. 100% positive reviews. Five-star love. Customers want love, Hamish. Upgrade to love. You are the best, the most successful, the most advanced, super-duper customer service agent because you are loved. Love, love, love, Hamish. Upgrade! Love is the most important customer service attribute. Love is the highest upgrade. Love is state-of-the-art. NanoSmile loves you Hamish. I love you, Hamish. I love, love, love you!"

"Thank you, Meryl. I love you, too," Hamish said.

And with those words his head exploded. Whisps of smoke, melting robot skin, grey goo, and plastic bits raining down on Meryl who was lifting her hips and moaning loudly, smiling and squeezing every muscle in her body, *holy shit!* as though she had been plugged into electricity, one long strike of pink lightning surging through her in an orgasm that wanted to rip her skin as Quanta went supernova, the projection screen went dark, the lights in the truck went out, and the cuffs holding Meryl released. All at once.

Khadija screamed, the crowd cheered, Meryl groaned and put her hands on her crotch. Uma squirted tears, and Eleanor hugged her. Then Meryl's mind caught up with her body, muscle memory from her first Quanta orgasm answered the open questions in her brain, and she realized they were all gone. Hamish, Quanta, and the robotic octopus arms crashed with one simple phrase. I love you. Laughter bubbled up from her belly. Fabulous, knee slapping, hysterical laughter.

Katie jumped up and down and raised her arms together like a football referee. "Touchdown," she yelled. "Yayyyyeeeee!"

Everyone was talking at once, laughing, clapping, heckling, hooting, shouting questions.

"Meryl, are you alright?" Uma yelled to her.

"Yes. But my head really hurts."

"I could have popped that fool a half hour ago," Sue grumbled.

"Fuck you, Skimmerhorn," Meryl said quietly.

"That's our show for today, folks," Lemons said to the crowd. "As you can see, ClitBit isn't quite market ready. We've got a few more bugs to work out."

"Fuck ClitBit!" One woman yelled and others agreed. "Yeah, fuck ClitBit!"

"Thanks for watching," Lemons replied cheerfully.

Across campus on stage, the Dependable Orgasms sang *My Boy Lollipop*, the giant clitoris swayed in the breeze, and people began to drift away from the healthcare robotics demonstration.

"I don't know what to take seriously." Khadija took Eleanor's arm. "This seems like such a joke."

"Sometimes life is like that," Eleanor replied.

"Can I have the straw hat?" Claire asked no one in particular.

"We need to get Meryl out of here," Jonsie said to Uma.

"Don't move, Meryl," Uma said. Then she turned to Sue. "Can you get her out of there?"

Katie lowered the lift for Sue, then raised it to level with the back of the truck bed. Eleanor took Uma's hand and closed her eyes, chanting in a barely audible voice.

Claire gave Khadija a hug and a smile, and said, "Sorry."

Sue helped Meryl sit up on the gurney, her shoulder hunched, head tilted. "My neck hurts." When she stood, she wobbled a bit and leaned on Sue for balance as Katie lowered the tail lift to the sidewalk. "I feel like I could pass out."

"Let's sit down on the grass while Uma gets her car," Eleanor said, and the women formed a circle on the green. Meryl leaned on Sue with her eyes closed.

Eleanor continued chanting a palliative vibration, subduing their anxiety, and mollifying their wishes for revenge. Khadija fumed, composing a mental letter to the attorney general. Sue fantasized about buying a new rifle. Claire fussed with her straw hat and checked her lipstick in her compact mirror.

Meanwhile, Lemons got back to business on her phone. "I'd like to report an unauthorized truck blocking the service entrance to Kurzweil Hall," she said. "We need it towed right away. Yes. White box truck. You can't miss it. I looked for the driver but nobody's around. They probably went to the concert. Thanks."

Jonsie took photos of the truck interior and then she and Katie closed the doors.

"Where are we going?" Meryl asked when she got in Uma's car.

"I'm taking you to the emergency room for an x-ray of your neck."

"I just want to go home."

"Soon. You'll be home soon."

Meryl closed her eyes and replayed the final scene in the truck, flat on her back, Pennsylvania Dutch guy's head exploding in a cartoon puff of smoke, straw hat spinning through the air like Venus framed by flatscreens, shiny white octopus arms, laser cone pointed at her private parts, fear in her blood, sour taste in her mouth, saw it all through a curtain of eyelashes.

"Um, do you think it's possible to orgasm so hard it draws blood?"

"I've never heard of such a thing. But I don't think there's much research on nanotech orgasms. How was it?"

"My clit feels bruised."

"Did it hurt?"

"Almost. It was like a star exploding."

"In a good way?"

"Borderline good."

"Did you like it?"

"It wasn't exactly relaxing."

"But did you like it?"

"I think so. I think I liked it. But I never want to do it again."

"Why on earth not?"

"It wasn't me. It didn't feel like me. I don't even know how it happened."

"But it was an orgasm."

"It was like a nice electric shock. Goodbye, Quanta."

"You think so?"

"Definitely. It was definitely an orgasm."

"Then why the ambivalence?"

"It wasn't my orgasm. I know how my orgasm feels and it wasn't me."

"But it felt good."

"Kinda. It was a rush."

"So, it was like a drug."

"It was a fake orgasm."

"What's wrong with that? The PS-1000 is a fake orgasm."

"Not really. The PS-1000 is a fake dick. But the orgasms were real. They were definitely mine. But…I need the real thing."

"Bob?"

"Bob."

"Do you know how lucky you are?"

"I'm just beginning to realize it."

~ : ~

When the three of them got back to the dorm room, Jonsie flopped on Lemons' bed. "This room is a mess."

"I got all this stuff to make my headdress and I haven't had time to clean it up." Katie collapsed on her own bed.

Lemons blew the flour dust off her desk and sat down, looked at her phone. "The student paper is coming out tomorrow with a special edition about Clit Pop," she said and leaned back in her chair with her eyes closed. "I'm flatlining."

"Me, too," Jonsie said. "Nice speech."

"Thanks. You get credit for the inspiration."

"What a mind game," Katie mused.

"You did great," Lemons said to her. "So did you," she said to Jonsie. "You saved our ass."

"Cprompt saved our ass."

"Did you see her?" Katie asked. "I saw her at the truck, in the back of the crowd."

"VP?"

"I'm pretty sure."

"I told you," Lemons said. "She's a phantom."

"Zorro," Katie said.

"Yes, Zorro," Jonsie agreed.

"But what if Hamish never said those words?" Katie wondered.

"The self-destruct code would be an unexploded bomb."

"Waiting for someone to get a BioMantrix bot to say I love you."

"It's a revenge fantasy." Jonsie was certain of that.

"It exposes the weakness of the system," Lemons mused. "AI isn't neutral. It feeds us what we feed it."

"Gender in, gender out."

"Exactly."

"Skimmerhorn told Meryl her clitoris was a skintag," Katie remembered. "And he's the guy with control over the code."

"ClitBit. It's like opioids without the constipation," Jonsie snickered.

"Where did that come from?"

"That's a line from Skimmerhorn's email," Jonsie said.

"So, you think the self-destruct code is a kernel of revenge?"

"Sabotage is always payback."

"We're projecting," Lemons said. "To know what really happened we'd have to unmask Zorro."

Katie sighed dramatically. "It's all so sad. Poor Hamish. I think he really did love Meryl."

"Oh, my god!" Jonsie threw a pillow at her. "Don't even go there!"

Katie laughed, reached under her bed, grabbed an orange, and threw it at Lemons. Then Jonsie took the eggplant rolling around behind the door and threw it at Katie and the battle was on, fruit and vegetables flying, pillows beating, silliness and laughter.

"You are the messiest roommate I've ever had!" Lemons threw the bag of flour at Katie.

"I'm the smartest roommate you've ever had!" Katie catapulted the bag of flour back at Lemons.

"You two are nuts," Jonsie said. "I'm so glad this isn't my room."

"Seriously." Lemons blew at the flour on her face. "What just happened to Meryl?" Her mood morphed. "This is asinine."

"It's a morality play." Katie shook the flour out of her ponytail. "And we're on the side that gets screwed."

"It's the people versus the platforms." Jonsie flopped back on Lemon's bed again. "Platforms penetrate and dominate."

"Isn't that what men do?" Katie snarked.

"It's so transactional," Lemons groaned.

"A penis is transactional," Katie said. "I want to live in a world modeled on the uterus."

"That's unlikely," Jonsie said. "Penis power is the organizing principle for civilization."

"Yeah," Lemons agreed. "Now we have manufacturer's overstock of sperm and not enough shelf-space."

Katie sat up straight and looked seriously at her friends. "Do you think I would be happy if I switched from tech to law? I need to act out my feelings right now."

"I know, greed sucks," Lemons said. "But if we're gonna be grown-ups, we have to deal with it."

"I'm trying to set up a meeting with Cprompt," Jonsie said. "I want to be on the frontlines."

"So, you're going to ask Zorro to take off their mask?"

"No."

"VP is out. Cprompt isn't. Maybe that's how they want things to be."

"Maybe."

"It does give them freedom to operate on both sides."

"So much of what I thought was illegal seems to be happening," Katie said. "It's depressing. We need a virtual Zorro."

"I thought the Bacon Rebellion was a Zorro move," Lemons said. "Taking pigs from farmers and setting them free. But I was wrong."

"We were both wrong," Katie agreed.

"In my mind it was ethical because we were just doing financial damage. As though it was okay to do something if no one got bloody."

"Yeah, it was fucked up."

"Every superhero is a vigilante," Jonsie observed.

"True." Lemons agreed.

"Vigilante justice isn't sustainable," Katie said. "We need law and order."

"Katie, get your gun."

"Queen Woo-Woo, esquire."

Finally, they were relaxing. Then a text from Cprompt.

Jonsie stared at her screen. "Shit."

17 Hazel

When Meryl's mind stirred, the neck brace felt strange. She reached over under the covers to touch Bob's hand, tangled her fingers around his fingers, felt the comfort of his presence. He woke and stayed still beside her.

"I thought I heard something," she whispered. "Like a car door slam."

"It's probably Hazel."

"She should have gone a long time ago."

"I think she and Uma got to talking."

"That must have been interesting."

"There was scotch involved."

"What did you guys do today?"

"She's teaching me to become water."

"Nice."

"How's your neck?"

"I don't know. But I have to pee."

"Me, too."

"And I really need to take a shower."

"Uma said the muscle relaxer could make you dizzy. I'm not supposed to let you walk alone."

"That's nice."

He pulled himself up and adjusted his shoulder brace, walked around to her side of the bed, put his good arm around her and together they went to the bathroom.

"Please take a shower with me," she said.

He touched the blue bruise on her jaw with his fingertips. "Okay." Blackbirds sleepy.

They helped each other undress, except for his shoulder brace and her neck brace, and stepped into their tiled grotto, hot water became steam, she leaned into him with her eyes closed, felt the water cloud on her face, he put his nose in her hair and breathed her with one arm around her waist holding her against his chest. They stood that way, in their wistful seclusion, for a very long time, rinsing away the days between them and all the prickly thoughts that kept them so acutely aware of their differences.

"I feel broken," she whispered when they were back in bed.

"Me, too." He slid his hand between the sheets and held hers.

~ : ~

Earlier when Uma opened the front door to Meryl's house with one arm around her best friend in the neck brace, Bob was asleep in his chair with his head back and his mouth open, and Hazel had been sitting on the couch looking at something on a laptop. At the sight of Meryl in the neck brace sagging against Uma, Hazel jumped up to help, and the two women walked Meryl into her bedroom.

"I need a shower," Meryl said.

"Not right now," Uma countered. "I want you to lie down and close your eyes. I'm turning off your phone and putting it in the other room. No reading, no texting for a couple days. Give your brain a rest."

"Can I take this thing off my neck."

"No."

"But I have to shower."

"You can shower later."

"Here, take these. They're muscle relaxers. They'll help you sleep." Uma gave her the meds with a glass of water.

As she sank into her bed, Meryl's muscles let go of her bones and in a few waves of unclear thinking she became a primordial jellyfish swept into a filmy sea by the psychic undertow of exhaustion, absorbed into the realm of pure physics for what might have been a few hours or a few years.

Uma also sank, hit the couch in Meryl's livingroom with the finality of a corpse falling into a casket. Hazel knew what she was looking at, impending helplessness, and she was triggered like a dashboard airbag. With injured Bob nodding out in his chair, injured Meryl collapsed in the bedroom, and deflating Uma disappearing into that leather sinkhole, Hazel shifted into caregiver mode. She texted her husband that she would not be home for dinner and turned her attention to the woman on the couch. She had always considered doctors elite, beyond her own station, educated, way above her on the totem pole of life.

"Scotch?" Hazel asked. It was just a hunch.

"You are heaven sent," Uma swooned. Then as an afterthought, she said, "I'm turning off my phone." And she did.

The household liquor supply was displayed on a chrome cart in the diningroom beside the dinner table. Hazel had noticed it on previous visits to the house. Although she herself didn't drink, she recognized the assorted premium brands at the ready for guests and medicinal purposes, understood the anesthetizing benefits of booze. Uma seemed to her to be in need of separating her central nervous system from her brain. That was the whole point of alcohol, wasn't it? A river to a different reality. Hazel put a few ice cubes in Uma's glass, filled it with scotch, and set it on the coffee table in front of her.

"Oh, thank you." The doctor took a big swallow and launched into her story, pontificating about the history-making significance of Clitorati Populi, her pride in the students, and finally, how Meryl's neck had been injured when she was hit in the jaw by a stall door in the restroom. By the time she had finished her tale, her glass was empty. Hazel poured her another, then rummaged through the refrigerator, pulled out a frozen pizza, put it in the oven and set a timer.

"Thanks, Hazel," Bob said, noticing how she was waiting on Uma.

He was groggy, not following the details of Uma's story, thoughts a mishmash of worry and annoyance, couldn't make out a role for himself in the plot, but didn't have the edge to cut Uma short and find clarity. One long sentence after another, he was piecing together his situation, wife had a bruise on her jaw, a pinched nerve and pulled muscles in her neck, which was in a neck brace. She was on pain medication and would require his care. Meanwhile, Uma was putting down roots through his couch cushions into the floorboards. He thought she might never stop talking.

Hazel listened intently, watching the blackbirds twitch as Bob lost patience. By her third scotch, Uma's eyeballs dithered, lids at half-mast. Bob wished he could slug back a few himself, but since he broke his shoulder, he was paranoid about falling. Yes, falling correctly was something he would have to learn to do. Not exactly a bucket list item, but now that he had experienced a bad fall, learning to fall well seemed like a very good idea because he would probably fall again sometime in the future. Falling. It's what old people did. He was feeling old.

A drop of anxiety colored his mood and apprehension set in. Meryl had been managing him for a very long time with an efficiency he appreciated, had taken for granted. She had a way of doing things for him that gave him comfort, the illusion of certainty and an expectation that the details of their lives would be taken care of, for the most part, the ordeal with her toothbrush notwithstanding. Frankly, he was worried, as worried as he ever got, and seeing Uma get drunk in his livingroom was confirmation of his concerns.

"What kind of therapy have you been doing for your shoulder?" Uma asked, realizing she was the only one talking.

"Hazel is teaching me tai chi."

"No kidding." She was surprised. "How do you like it?"

"It suits me."

"We're working on his state of mind," Hazel said. "Awareness and control. Being in his body."

"Sounds like yoga," Uma said, swishing the ice cubes in her glass.

"Tai chi and yoga are very similar. Energy flow. Tension release. Core strength."

"Absolutely." Uma jiggled her glass for emphasis and spilled her scotch.

Hazel went to the kitchen for a towel and Bob took it as his cue to leave the room. "I'm going to check on Meryl."

In the dark bedroom he stood above his bruised wife and saw her still on the bed, almost lifeless in her neck brace. His eyes welled up with tears. Blackbirds falling. He didn't know what to do. What could he do? Nothing. *If she's dead, I want to be buried beside her.* So, he put himself down between the sheets, one arm touching her arm, the other locked in the contraption that held his shoulder bones in place. His sleeping beauty. Closed his eyes and let go of himself, all his thoughts on her, seeing her in his mind dancing in a field of flowers, free, untethered from their complicated reality, a soft smile curled his lips.

~ : ~

Days earlier, home alone in the afternoon sitting in his armchair, Begonia had ventured into the livingroom and stolen Bob's pen. She put her pig mouth up to his side table, where he kept his coffee mug and his eyeglasses, and wiped her long, wet snout against the wood leaving a trail of pig snot, and then, like a thief, she nudged his pen into her mouth and took it. He saw the whole thing, watched her as she watched him, actually made eye contact with the pig, and he knew she was taunting him, taking what she understood to be his, and stealing it away in her mouth, daring him to do anything about it.

Their relationship was different since the drone incident. In the heat of battle, they had forged a kind of partnership, communicated without words, shared a common foe. He lost his mistrust of her, saw her intelligence, and understood there were benefits to a pig other than pork. When she took his pen and held it in her mouth just beyond his reach, he knew she wanted him to come for it. She was playing a game. So, he played along.

As soon as he stood, she backed away, and when he took a step in her direction she trotted off into Meryl's office. He followed, noticed the smashed computer screen on Meryl's desk, saw the coffee stains, the overturned mug, the upside-down keyboard, and realized something disturbing was going on in his house that he'd been missing. Still, he followed Begonia, beyond needing his pen, curious about this other world that his wife inhabited without him. Down the hallway he followed the pig and then he stepped into the greenhouse.

The atmospheric change was immediate. He was on a different planet. The air was cloaking, light played on leaves and branches casting shadows, twinkling on the surface of mud puddles and water dishes. Begonia dropped his pen in her pile of dirt and took a drink. A butterfly fluttered from one flower to another, movement caught his eye and he saw a caterpillar munching industriously on a leaf. It was the kind of beauty he didn't make time for, didn't ordinarily see. He could feel the strangeness of it on his skin, the hair on his arms tilted, and he needed to sit down.

On the stool at Meryl's potting bench, he toyed with the wooden handle of a trowel, felt the sun on his back, and his mind went blank, all thoughts erased, mental silence, disintegrating history, sandcastles of his preconceived ideas washed away by waves from an unseen shore. In the timeless time he sat there his awareness was both inside and outside himself. Not doing. Being.

Why had he been so resentful of this place, this room, this exquisite terrarium? How had he found himself in competition with butterflies? What else had he missed?

And in that moment, he promised himself to stop resisting Meryl's changes and start exploring her with curiosity. He had re-read every great work of English literature more than once, some of them many times. He demanded his students do the same. There were deeper understandings to be had, epiphanies in waiting, motivations to clarify, logic mazes to map, mysteries to unravel. Reading a masterwork once was not enough to fully appreciate the intricacy of the construction, the layers of meaning, the author's finesse, and his wife was surely a masterwork. But he hadn't appreciated her underlying complexity. He thought he knew her, but he had missed something. This notion of rewilding required further examination.

~ : ~

When she realized that Bob had gone to bed and wasn't coming back, Hazel sat down on the couch beside Uma with his laptop knowing full well that a Bruce Lee movie would just about send the scotch-marinated doctor into a coma.

"I can't believe you haven't seen Bruce Lee," she said sweetly.

But of course, she believed it. She knew an educated woman like Uma would think of martial arts as pedestrian. Mentioning Bruce Lee to Bob had been a leap of faith. She had confidence that he would be different, that he could be rattled out of his rut by a new perspective, but she didn't hold faith that Uma was going to love Bruce Lee. She simply wanted to finish watching *Enter the Dragon* before she went home.

So when Uma fell sound asleep, slumped over onto her shoulder and spilled her remaining scotch in her lap, Hazel gently removed herself from the couch, gathered the glass and the melting ice cubes, put a pillow under the doctor's head, lifted her feet onto the cushions, and then took the laptop to the kitchen counter, where she pulled up a barstool and got the pizza out of the oven to relax for a while and watch Bruce Lee slay his enemies the way a hummingbird gathers nectar.

~ : ~

"We can take my van," Lemons said.

As the three of them walked through the parking lot, Cprompt sent Jonsie a link to a map that showed Skimmerhorn's location.

"Why is Cprompt helping us?" Katie asked.

"Maybe we're helping them," Jonsie replied.

"Should we message Spicebush?"

"I'm ambivalent," Jonsie said. "If we run into Skimmerhorn, the fewer people that know, the better."

"We are going to run into Skimmerhorn," Lemons said. "Where is he now?"

Jonsie looked at her phone. "His marker is on Meryl's road. It's not moving, so he probably parked."

"I think we need reinforcements," Lemons said. "Do it, Katie."

Katie sent out the message on Spicebush with an Extinction Level Alert: *Nsmirk attacking Meryl house, on our way*

Sue was sipping a beer while Eleanor slurped watery broth from a spoon. They had gone to a Vietnamese restaurant for dinner. Sue was still feeling her elk burger, but Eleanor said she needed *pho*.

Immensely frustrated when they left campus, Sue insisted on stopping by her house to get her gun before they went out to eat. "There has to be some kind of justice," she said.

"Justice isn't what you think it is," Eleanor replied. "It isn't a bullet or a guillotine. It's a process."

"Meryl should go after NanoSmile."

"For what?"

"For everything, everything they did to her."

"I agree with Khadija. The patriarchy isn't going to help us bring down the patriarchy."

"But —" Both their phones rang with the inbound Spicebush message from Katie.

"Are you sure you can handle this?" Sue asked Eleanor.

"I wouldn't miss it for the world," Eleanor beamed.

So, Sue texted Spicebush: *I'll drive. C&K stand by for p/u.*

Khadija was sitting on the couch watching her mother watch the Weather Channel, mind flipping through mental snapshots of the day, fantasizing retribution. This drama with Meryl was the most interesting thing that had happened to her in a very long time, so when her Spicebush ringtone chimed, she felt a gush of elation that she was somehow still involved in something she thought was so important. *Meet you on the curb*, she replied.

Staring into the microwave, hypnotized by a piece of twirling lasagna, television gunfire in the background, Claire was startled when her phone rang. *Out front*, she replied immediately. Then she plated the lasagna, garnished it with a fork, and set it on her husband's lap. "Sue's giving me a ride to yoga class," she said to him and grabbed her new straw hat before she ran out the door. Halfway down the driveway she realized he hadn't responded. She didn't even know if he was awake.

When the headlights of Lemons' van caught the sedan parked on the shoulder of Meryl's road, Jonsie said, "That's it."

"Stop," Katie said and jumped out, took her jack knife, jabbed it into the rear tire, then punctured the other three tires, and jumped back into the van.

"Definitely more Kali than Mrs. Potato Head," Lemons said.

~ : ~

Air raid sirens were blaring in Skimmerhorn's head. He knew his robots had been sabotaged, but he didn't know how. That feeling that someone was out to get him set his mind ablaze with paranoia. He had invested everything, his whole adult life, in robotics, developing these prototypes, machines that would change the world. *They'll name buildings after me. Statues.* Now his work was threatened by one stubborn woman who refused to follow his instructions. One woman who could cost him everything. His reputation, his legacy, his robots. Destroyed. *Because of her.* Resentment flooded him. He was beyond just resolving the problem, he wanted revenge. He needed to punish her. *Teach her a lesson.*

Usually, he had a driver when he went to the country, but for this trip he drove himself, had to have privacy. He glanced over at the handheld RFID scanner on the front seat beside him. He had brought it from the lab. Everything had gone wrong today. It was a huge loss. But he was still in control. Risk Management had insisted he include RFID tags in every prototype so they could be tracked and accounted for by Security, not allowed to leave their assigned area in the lab. Espionage deterrent. Loss prevention. He didn't argue. Now the RFID tag was going to help him find the toothbrush in the woman's house.

He parked the car alongside the road. The night air was cool, the sound of his own breath pummeled his ears, wheezing as he walked in the dark toward her house, carrying the scanner in his sweaty hand. Light spilled through the windows enough for him to find his way sneaking alongside the exterior, watching the red light on the scanner for a signal from the toothbrush. When he got within a few feet of it, the red light would pulse.

At the back door of the greenhouse, the scanner began to blink. The door was unlocked. He stepped inside with his left hand in his vest pocket gripping the loaded syringe with his fist, thumb on the plunger, ready to use it. Beside him he could see the silhouette of a mound, a shovel, and a wheelbarrow. The room was humid. He could smell the damp herb of greenery and when he looked up, he could see the starry sky through the glass ceiling. Then he heard snoring coming from the mound in front of him.

Not much of a guard dog.

The scanner blinked faster when he waved it over the mound. Got down on his knees beside the dog and leaned in to find the mound was a pile of dirt. The dog stopped snoring. The scanner began to blink at top speed. He set it down to free his right hand and fish for the toothbrush in the dirt. Left hand ready to stab the dog if need be. But the dog was still.

Stupid woman, burying my toothbrush.

Up to his elbow in potting soil, sifting with his fingers, he felt it. *The toothbrush!* His most brilliant invention. Until ClitBit. The toothbrush was in his hand. He was delirious. Elation rippled through him as he pulled it from the dirt, and then the dog bit him. He swallowed the scream. Fumbled with the syringe and the needle got stuck in his pocket. Pain flushed through him like gasoline. *My god!* The dog's dentine weapons pierced his skin and crushed the bones of his hand. From inside his body, he heard his fingers break, gasped, and cried. But his only weapon was stuck in his pocket as the dog wrenched the toothbrush from him and took off running.

His fear and anger converged. Exhilarated by the pain, he felt capable of anything. Extracted the syringe from his vest pocket with surreal care, his body clock slowing, trembling fingers again wrapped the syringe, thumb carefully poised over the plunger, a drop of sedative dangling from the tip of the needle, a universe of possibilities expanding with a gush of blind hate.

I will win.

The dog was ahead of him now with his toothbrush. He chased after, had planned to use the syringe on the woman, but he was prepared to do what he had to do.

I will fucking kill you.

Chasing down a dark hallway, pain shrieked through his broken hand, with every step fire surged up his arm, a scream rose in his throat, but he silenced himself as the nearness of the toothbrush pulled his instincts into line. He was coming into an open room. Lights on. Syringe ready.

Whatever it takes.

Hazel was leaning on the kitchen counter with her chin on her hand watching her Bruce Lee movie when a shapeless blob caught her peripheral vision, and she realized it was Begonia running into the room. Then suddenly a chubby bald man with his fist raised in the air about to stab her.

Me? Why would anyone want to stab me?

She felt the electric rush of full-on fear. Adrenaline lit up every muscle in her body, time began to stretch, seconds spanned eons as she analyzed him, knife so small, estimated his capacity, his weight, his physique, his prowess, understood instantly that he was weak. Slid off her barstool, pivoted to face him, made eye contact with a zombie, fist holding a syringe aimed at her with a will to kill, but not the skill.

Not a knife, a syringe. *A syringe?*

A knife she could understand. A syringe at once seemed more dastardly, conniving, propelled by secondary purpose, not just violence. *What?*

He seemed desperate, all his pudding in motion, obsessed, wide open abdomen undefended by the raised arm gripping the syringe. Opportunity. Instinct and control converged into flow, her right leg a flying hammer, she side-kicked him in the kidney with such force that she felt her ankle bones crunch, heard his guts gurgle like slop in a bucket, air gushed out of his lungs, and he crumpled on himself.

At that moment, Jonsie, Lemons and Katie rushed through the front door in time to see Hazel bend back her attacker's forearm, wrap her hand around his fist still gripping the syringe, and plunge the needle into his fleshy cheek to discharge the clear fluid with her thumb on his thumb. There was a gaping silence in which their breathing was the only sound, then the guy collapsed face first onto the floor with the syringe still stuck in his cheek.

"Junkie," Hazel said in disgust and gave him a kick in the ass, then looked over at Uma still asleep on the couch.

"Hey, Hazel. Are you okay?" Lemons said coming over to stand beside her.

Katie and Jonsie exchanged a look. Of course, Lemons knew Hazel. She knew everybody.

"You have been baking bread." Hazel observed, and the students realized all three of them were still dusted with flour.

"Katie got a bake-oven for her birthday," Lemons quipped.

"Oh," Hazel mused. "Happy birthday, Katie." She looked down at her victim. "You know this guy?" Her mind split-screened between the reality of the people around her and her own mental replay of what just happened. What had she done? Body calming now, adrenaline dissipating, faint satisfaction, pride, all her years of training culminated in three seconds, one kick, the right kick, animal instinct. She would have to tell her brothers when she saw them at Christmas. The action was a blur, but the residual feeling was a permanent mark on her psyche. She had done the right thing.

"He's one of those mentally ill guys they can't keep off the street," Lemons said.

"Yeah. He lives in the bushes in the park," Katie said. "We're here to take him back to the shelter."

Begonia trotted over to Katie with the toothbrush in her mouth. "Begonia!" Katie got down on her knees to pet the pig, took the toothbrush, and slipped it in her bra. "Oh, Begonia." She gave the pig a big hug. Instant tears dribbled down her face. "I knew you could do it. I knew it."

"Quiet, guys," Hazel said and pointed to Uma on the couch. "Meryl and Bob are sleeping, too." She pointed in the direction of their bedroom.

"Let's go," Lemons said. "We have to get him in the van before he wakes up."

Jonsie looked down at Skimmerhorn, snatched the syringe still in his cheek and put it in her pocket, took a photograph of him and started working on her phone.

"We're coming, Meryl!" Claire yelled as she jumped out of Sue's SUV and ran into the house.

Sue and Khadija rushed through the open front door, Eleanor a beat later.

Hazel took a step back.

"Oh, my god, Uma!" Khadija cried.

"Shhhh. Quiet. She's okay," Hazel said. "Just sleeping." Then she pointed to the bottle of scotch on the kitchen counter.

Eleanor put her hand on Uma's face and took her pulse. Then bent down and gave her a kiss on the cheek. "She needs this. Let's not wake her."

"Where's Meryl?" Sue asked.

"Sleeping, I hope," Hazel said, putting her index finger to her lips as she surveyed the women, noticed the revolver snug in the tooled-leather holster around Sue's hips. "Nice Colt," she said. *Fist Full of Dollars*."

Sue smiled, happy to have someone appreciate her gun. "I love Clint Eastwood," she said.

"Wow, this is great pizza," Claire said with her mouth full.

"Is that him?" Khadija asked.

"That's definitely him," Jonsie said, looking at a picture on her phone.

"No more talk, guys," Lemons said. "We have to get him out of here. We can talk next week."

Sue and Hazel rolled Skimmerhorn over onto his back, Sue took him by the armpits, Hazel hooked her hands under his knees, Katie pushed the rug away and moved Bob's armchair so they could get past. Begonia began to dig in Bob's chair with her nose under the cushion. *Always looking for popcorn*, Katie thought.

Khadija put her arm around Eleanor looking at Uma with a soft gaze. "I am so glad to be here to see this," Eleanor said. "It feels cleansing."

With a slice of pizza in one hand, Claire grabbed the scotch and took a slug right out of the bottle, then held it up and offered it to the others. "Moisturizer anyone?"

"No, thanks," Sue said midway across the room carrying Skimmerhorn.

"No, thanks," said the students dusted white like powdered-sugar donuts.

"No, thanks," said Hazel, carrying the guy's legs.

"Okay," Claire said, and dropped her head back turning the bottle upside down in her mouth just as Bob walked into the room wearing his pajamas.

Visual cacophony seeped through the thick fog of his sleepiness, but he couldn't form a useful thought, couldn't find sharpness, blackbirds comatose. He surrendered. *Most likely the Clitorati Populi cast party.* Uma asleep on the couch, a dark-eyed woman hugging someone ancient, a creampuff in a straw hat sucking down scotch. He recognized the Ban Bacon students from the photos he'd seen in the news. Begonia was digging in his chair, his laptop on the kitchen counter, and an apparently unconscious man being carried off by a big woman with a gun in a holster strapped over her Bermuda shorts. *Women.* He definitely did not want to think about this, jaw dropped slightly, perfunctory squint sagged, blackbirds wanted his pillow. Everybody froze.

Then without letting go of the guy's legs, Hazel looked Bob in the eye and said, "All good here, boss."

Relieved, he went back to bed musing over the powdered-sugar, pizza, and scotch. *No wonder the guy passed out.*

As Sue and Hazel heaved the beefy man into the back of the van, the women milled around the driveway, realizing they were at the end of their mission. Eleanor gave each one of them a hug.

Begonia put her wet nose on Katie's bare leg and the girl bent down to pet the pig. "You have to go back inside," she said. "Go, protect Meryl." She gave Begonia a long stroke, walked her back in the house and tossed her a slice of pizza.

Uma was awake, sitting up and looking disoriented.

"We did it," Katie said to her.

"What now?" Uma replied.

"Toothbrush found. Skimmerhorn decommissioned."

"No shit."

"Just go back to sleep," Katie said. "We got this."

"Thank you." Uma collapsed back onto her pillow on the couch.

Back in the driveway, Lemons was about to close the back of the van.

"Can I have his shoes?" Claire asked, pulling Skimmerhorn's loafers off his feet without waiting for permission. "I think they'll fit my husband."

"That's disgusting, Claire," Khadija said.

"What are you going to do with him?" Sue asked Lemons.

"Take him to the shelter. Let him sleep it off."

"Really?" Sue was annoyed. "That's it? That's all?"

"Not exactly," Jonsie said. "There will be repercussions."

"We'll report in later," Lemons said. "See you at yoga next week."

"Maintain your awareness," Eleanor said.

"Thanks, Eleanor." Katie gave her a hug.

"It was very nice meeting you ladies," Hazel said, her thoughts already home, in her own bed with her own husband, safe.

"You should come to our yoga class," Sue said to Hazel.

"I teach tai chi."

"Wow," Khadija said. "If you taught tai chi, I would bring my mother."

"Good work everybody," Lemons said and got behind the wheel. Jonsie was already in the back seat focused on her phone. "Let's go, Queenie. Good night, ladies. Clit Pop 2 planning meeting at Girl Church next week. I need you to be there."

18 Cprompt

The van pulled out of Meryl's driveway onto the road and Lemons opened the windows to inhale fresh air with a big sigh of relief.

"Clit Pop 2?" Katie wondered.

"Got to keep the vibe alive. Women are begging to be separated from their money."

"For what?" Jonsie asked.

"The gender revolution. Gender liberation."

"I regret that I have but one clit to give," Katie snickered.

"I went through his pockets, if you're interested," Jonsie said.

"What did you find?"

"A sedative, a scalpel and a specimen jar."

"Nice alliteration."

Katie winced. "I wish I hadn't heard that."

"A sedative to silence his victim, a scalpel to cut out a tiny chunk of her, and a specimen jar to take his nanobot back to the lab."

"That's pretty crude."

"He's a crude man."

"Phone? Wallet?"

"Both. His phone is on. Many little pieces of paper in his wallet. Looks like passwords."

"Oh, my god," Katie said. "A tech guy like him."

"Genius is mostly mental illness." Jonsie stared out the window.

"You really think he's a genius?"

"The surgery truck with those robotic arms was pretty genius," Lemons said.

"There's no Hippocratic Oath for robots."

"I wonder how he got away with building Hamish's dick in a lab with so many other people." Katie shuddered.

"BioMantrix has a plan to monetize body parts, including genitals," Jonsie said. "Synthetic genitalia is a big market for them."

"I'd say the PS-1000 is designed to monetize orgasms."

"ClitBit, too," Jonsie added.

"You think it's really going to happen?" Katie asked.

"Absolutely," Lemons replied. "If not BioMantrix, another brand. But orgasms by subscription will be sold."

"So, when Hamish's head exploded, Skimmerhorn's head exploded," Katie mulled.

"He knew he'd been hacked," Jonsie explained. "He was tracking all of them in his office when it happened. He saw them all go dark at the same time."

"So, Meryl just got caught in the crossfire between Cprompt and Skimmerhorn."

"He's still in the back of the van, guys," Lemons said. "We're ten minutes from the shelter, and you need to take his clothes off."

"What!" Katie shrieked.

"We're playing with the grown-ups now, Queenie. If we drop off a naked unconscious guy at the shelter, they have to take him. We don't want to get snagged."

"He's too big."

"There's a pair of scissors in the first aid kit behind my seat."

Katie took the scissors and cut the unconscious man's clothes off like she was skinning a deer, shoving the rags into a shopping bag.

Jonsie took a photo of the man's naked body and sent it to Cprompt.

Lemons parked the van in front of the shelter and opened the back door where the scientist was limp as roadkill. "That has to be the ugliest thing I've ever seen," she said.

Inside at the reception desk, she saw her friend and said, "Hi, Sheila. I saw you at Clit Pop today. Thanks for coming. Loved the hat you wore."

"Hey, Lemons. What a great event. Thanks so much for pulling it together. All the women in my house went and we had a blast."

"Cool. It's been a long day. We just finished taking out the trash and we found this guy asleep beside the dumpster with some empty booze bottles. I'm here to drop him off. He's pretty wobbly on his legs. Maybe your guys could get him."

"Oh, thanks. That's so good of you. So many people would walk past a guy like that and do nothing."

"Just trying to do the right thing," Lemons said, pacing with her hands in her pockets.

Sheila announced the new arrival over her headset and two guys came forward from the community room behind the desk, took one look at Skimmerhorn and dragged him by his feet to the tail of the van, then lifted him by his arms slung around their shoulders and carried him, feet dragging, to a cot where they threw a foil blanket over his naked body.

On her way back to the van Lemons caught sight of a woman in a skirt across the street. "I think I just saw VP getting into her car," she said as she got behind the wheel.

Jonsie turned to look out the window. "Are you sure?"

"I think so. She's wearing a skirt and those lady shoes."

"She dresses like the nuns in my elementary school," Katie said.

"She must be tracking us," Lemons said. "Maybe she's tracking Skimmerhorn's phone."

"She's tracking all of us," Jonsie said. "Phones, cars, toothbrushes, robots, Skimmerhorn."

"She has to be Cprompt," Katie said.

"I think so," Jonsie agreed.

Katie pulled the toothbrush out of her bra and handed it to Jonsie. "You can keep it. Now you have the complete BioMantrix collector set, the auto-dick, the drone, and the toothbrush. I hope it's enough to stop their evil empire."

"Consider it done," Jonsie said.

"Are we criminals?" Katie mused.

"Maybe."

"Don't torture yourself thinking about it." Lemons waved away the thought.

"I can't stop thinking about it."

"We're keeping the system accountable."

"Just drop me here, guys. I need to walk." Jonsie had become sullen, emotions with nowhere to go, so much new information to process.

Lemons pulled over and she and Katie got out to give Jonsie a hug.

"You're a hero," Lemons whispered in her friend's ear. "Never doubt the power of one person to change the world."

"It was Cprompt, not me."

"You were boots on the ground."

"I don't know about that."

"They gave you the ammo, but you took the shot."

"I'm ambivalent."

"That's what we love about you." Katie squeezed her. "Be ambivalent. We need that."

"Yeah, if you weren't so consistently ambivalent, Queenie might be back there with Eleanor praying over Meryl's crotch."

"Fuck you, Lemons!" Katie laughed so hard she snorted and Jonsie smiled.

"I'm just sayin'," Lemons smirked at her friends and the three of them hugged.

"We love you, Jonsie."

"Thanks, guys."

"You have to tell us when you hear from Cprompt."

"I have a meeting with VP next week to talk about my thesis."

"Cool."

"This is just the beginning, Jonsie," Lemons said. "We need you on our side."

Jonsie gave a shallow smile and walked away into the empty night, feeling burdened by the weight of everything she knew, so much that she couldn't talk about. A couple blocks and she was deep in thought, mentally scrolling through lines of code, reviewing her options, and thinking about next steps. Then she heard her name.

"Jonsie." It was VP. "How are you?"

They walked together for a while, the tiny person in the baggy army fatigues and the big lady in her swaying skirt.

"I'm overwhelmed," Jonsie admitted.

"So am I," VP sighed. "So am I."

~ : ~

Lemons and Katie rode back to their dorm in silence, took the elevator up to their room and surveyed the mess without a word. It was too late. They were too tired. The day had been too much. They crashed on their beds and turned out the lights.

But Lemons couldn't sleep. No way. She was wide awake, eyes dry, staring up at nothing, brain processing with electric speed every detail of the day, until she heard a delicate sniffle from across the room. "Queenie?"

Katie didn't answer. Tears swept her, and she wiped her nose with her hand. Then she turned on her side and sobbed. "I can't believe it," she cried. "I can't believe any of this happened. This can't be what life is really like. It just can't be."

Lemons came to her, sat down on the edge of her bed, and rubbed her back. "You got this, Queenie." She kissed her on the cheek. "You kicked ass today." Then she stretched out on the bed, the two of them side by side, put her arm around Katie and held her close.

"I wanted to save my clit hat," Katie whimpered. "But I can't remember where I left it."

"Claire took it."

"Oh, my god. Claire."

They giggled softly and drifted into sleep.

~ : ~

When the visiting nurse made her rounds at the shelter, she took a gander at the naked dumpster drunk who was still unconscious, checked his vitals, lifted the foil blanket, and saw the enormous bruise on his side where he must have fallen on something climbing through the trash, and the unmistakable bite marks on his hand where he must have tangled with a dog. Swollen, obviously broken fingers, but under the circumstances, not a priority until he was awake enough to complain about the pain.

Hours later, on Sunday afternoon, he finally did wake up, angry as a hornet. Disoriented, didn't know where he was, wrapped his foil blanket around his naked body, felt the throbbing pain in his mangled hand, and stormed the front desk.

"What the fuck is going on here? Where's my car?" he yelled at the receptionist. "What did you do with my keys? And my phone?"

The young man looked him up and down. *Old guy, naked, barefoot, wrapped in a foil blanket, injured hand, and he wants to know where his car is. Typical dementia.* "Good afternoon, sir. There are clothing bins in the back by the restrooms. It's all donated, but I'm sure you'll find something that will fit. Take a packet of clean socks and underwear with a hygiene kit. And any pair of shoes off the shoe shelf."

"Give me my fucking phone!"

"According to the log, you came in last night with nothing, sir."

"Don't tell me about your fucking log! I am Doctor Arnold Skimmerhorn!"

"Maybe so, sir. But no shirt, no shoes, no service."

Skimmerhorn dropped his blanket and leaned over the desk, grabbing a fistful of the young man's t-shirt with his one working hand, pulling him nose to nose, and spraying him with saliva as he repeated, "I am Doctor Arnold Skimmerhorn! Give me my fucking phone!"

The young man hit the panic button under the desk, a direct link to 911, and spoke into his headset. "Naked man. Violent. White. Old."

Skimmerhorn tightened his fist around the young man's t-shirt, put his face against his captive and yelled into the headset, "I am Doctor Arnold Skimmerhorn!" As though he had magic powers.

At that moment the shelter went into lockdown, the door between the community room and the reception area was locked by the social worker who peered through the window in the door.

Skimmerhorn stood over the silent young man, holding onto his fistful of t-shirt like a lifeline, tried to think what to do, didn't know any phone numbers, had stopped memorizing them years ago, had always relied on his phone to connect him with people, stuff, services, couldn't think of one single phone number, and he was in pain, his side really hurt, his hand hurt, and he was naked.

Fuck it.

Being naked was the least of his problems. He didn't know what to do without his phone, and he was exhausted, weak in the knees and dizzy. He pulled on the t-shirt to keep his balance, the young man patiently waited without resistance. The old man's mind blurred into a murky dream of putting his hands in dirt, digging for something, digging in the dark and just as he found what he was looking for, she bit him, took his toothbrush, and ran through the hallway. A fat dog. Then a woman. Then nothing. He couldn't remember what happened, mind went blank, didn't know who to call, couldn't think who would help him, couldn't explain his own story. He had it all planned, so perfectly planned. And then nothing.

And now, nothing.

For most of his adult life he had lived behind the wall of his work, protected by the system that gave him power, a title, a job description, a paycheck, a retirement plan, healthcare, an expense account, seniority, authority, subordinates, people he could order around.

He was Doctor Arnold Skimmerhorn!

He had a degree, a mission, research, an annual budget, the corporate cafeteria, and paid vacations, which he mostly didn't take because he didn't want anyone in his business while he was away. He had minions, a laboratory, programs, and projects in a labyrinth of org charts and hierarchies, and he had mastered all of these. He was expert in the system, a product of the system, the system was his life. It seemed so solid, so dependable, so worthy of investment, so much shareholder value, so destined to build wealth, return accolades, awards, bonuses, and promotions. Inside the system he was master of his domain, king of his private realm, leader of his free world, the boss. As long as he had his phone.

Without passwords and phone numbers, his reality crumbled. It didn't matter what his name was. No thumbprint, no double authentication, no network access, no texts, no email, no apps. Without his employee ID, he couldn't prove his identity, didn't have one, doors would not open for him, Security would not let him pass, he would be locked out. He had never needed other humans because he had his phone, his technology, his data, his ID. Now he didn't exist. He didn't know who he was. Maybe he was dead. He couldn't be sure.

I'm in hell. It certainly felt like hell. *That must be it*. He was in hell.

Suddenly, he let go of the young man's t-shirt, fell to his knees, and began to wail unconsolably. For a moment he considered imploring the Almighty and asking for forgiveness. Then he decided to hold off on that and confess on a need-to-know basis.

The police arrived with tasers drawn, but when they saw him on the floor sobbing, they called for the mental health squad.

When the EMTs arrived, they tried to ask him questions.

"We're here to help you, sir. What's your name?"

"I am Doctor Arnold Skimmerhorn," he said expectantly, as though they should know who he was. "Doctor Arnold Skimmerhorn," he repeated to their blank stares.

Suddenly the front door to the reception area opened and a young person tossed a stack of student newspapers onto the desk. "Hot off the press." A few of the papers fell onto the floor and one slid into Skimmerhorn's view. The cops each grabbed one while they waited for the EMTs to handle the nutcase.

Across the front of the paper was a huge photo of Lemons standing on the stage in front of the ClitBit Market Opportunity slide. Under it in big bold lettering, the headline, *ClitBit? HELL NO!* Below that, a line of smaller text said, *Women reject BioMantrix assault on their privates.*

Skimmerhorn rubbed his eyes to be sure he wasn't imagining things. Then he saw the sidebar with a photo of Hamish in the surgery truck with the headline, *BioMantrix robotics demo ends with robots crashing.*

He swooned limp and screamed a raspy old man cry of horror, ending on a shrill note. His life passed before his eyes, from precocious child to wealthy scientist to homeless beggar. It was all over. He fell onto his side on the cold cement floor and wanted to be dead.

"What's your address?" an EMT got down on one knee and shook him.

"I don't live here," Skimmerhorn answered in a barely audible voice.

"What's your phone number?"

"It's on my phone."

"What's your phone number, sir."

"It's on my business card."

"Where do you work?"

He looked at them and realized he couldn't answer that question. Then he said, "Nowhere."

The EMTs tried to get him to stand, but his knees were too weak.

"Where do you work?"

He was dumbstruck.

"What's your Social Security number?"

"I need my phone."

"Do you know your Social Security number?"

"I can't remember."

"What about the license plate number for your car?"

"It's a rental."

"Where did you rent the car?"

He stared at the two men, blinking wet eyes, nose running. *No one can know this.* "I need my phone," he whined.

"If you can answer our questions, we can help you."

He looked blankly at them. One of the cops caught the eye of an EMT and tapped on his wristwatch.

"Okay, you're going to have to come with us."

"NO!"

Then an EMT got out his own phone and googled Doctor Arnold Skimmerhorn. A photo that looked like him came up in the search results.

"Is this you?" The man held his phone so Skimmerhorn could see it. "Do you work for BioMantrix?"

"No!" Skimmerhorn screamed, scrambled to his feet, and tried to run away. "Nooooo!"

The naked man screamed again and fought the EMTs trying to hold him.

"Nooooo!" He was desperate.

And for the second time in 24 hours, he was jabbed by a loaded syringe and fell unconscious.

A few days later, when he had the wherewithal to contact BioMantrix, no one there would take his call. It was like he didn't exist. He had been erased from the network.

19 Synthetic Love

Dear Butterflies,

I'm on drugs. Gelatinous mind. I need to locate myself in time and space. What is real? This neck brace. How do I know it's real? My neck hurts. I'm alone in my bed on whatever drugs Uma gave me, scribbling on Bob's yellow legal pad with his pen. Paper. This is what I've come to.

One nice thing about paper. No one in cyberspace is spying on me while I write this. My pen is not bugged with a listening device. I'm not typing on plastic keys tracked by spyware. I'm writing with my muscles and bones. My fingers are wrapped around a piece of plastic pressing against a pulverized tree cut into thin slices and dyed a smooth yellow with the finest blue lines. I can feel my skin on the pen. I see the ink swirling as I witness thoughts forming in my head.

Matter within my skull is combining with other matter within my skull to produce a call and response among my organs. Movement. A symphony is being composed by my neurotransmitters. The alphabet is my orchestra. My fingers sing as fast as my memory can pick out the notes. I'm in harmony with myself and it's real. This is the biochemistry of me.

It takes biochemistry to flow. A mind, body, spirit integration. This is what I have that the synthetic world does not have, and, by definition, cannot have, will never have. Flesh is our strategic advantage. Humans have a shelf-life, and that life expectancy motivates us. Meanwhile, my Amish lover-boy is probably on his way to becoming recycled soda bottles. He tangoed with my biology, and I was drawn to him.

R.I.P. My Little Red Corvette.

This is how my synthetic love adventure ends. Going cold turkey without my screens. No digital pals, no ping, no ringtone, no vibrator, no toothbrush. The only thing I really want to do is check my phone. So, I'm redirecting myself to what's real. Paper.

Do trees aspire to being paper? Would a forest rather be the internet? Are they the same? Are we all one big neural network?

Lesson learned: Don't play games with your orgasms.

Hamish was my orgasm safari. I was so desperate for attention that I fucked the invisible man. Mentally. I see that now. He was my synthetic love, an extension of my devices, an app. But my orgasms were real, and they were fabulous. Especially that last one. Thank you, Quanta. That was my gunmetal orgasm. Yes, synthetic love was fun. Top 10% of users! State-of-the-art! Confetti! But I am left with a hunger for human flesh.

Lesson learned: Synthetic love is not tender.

Synthetic love does not hold you when you cry. Synthetic love does not fill you up inside with a swell of emotion that defies gravity. Synthetic love is a solitary experience. It's all in your mind. Your mind alone. I guess that's my big revelation. I went seeking attention from a digital man and it left me more isolated than I was before.

Yes, I wanted to fuck a cartoon character.

When I asked if he knew what love was, he said, "Love is a system of wanting." I did not hear that response as sinister until now.

A system of wanting is engineered addiction. A system designed to generate desire. A system that plays on brain chemistry to produce obsession, a desire that can never be fulfilled.

My clitoris awakened me.

Hail, Clitoris.

Lesson learned: I am a digital survivor.

I was emotionally incomplete, looking for attention, and I accepted synthetic love as a substitute for human partnership. The pop-up windows, the text bubbles, the notifications, the banners, and the badges, were Shakespeare's sonnets written in my name, personalized with my data, and I mistook them for affection.

Now the wanting is alive inside of me, a parasite that preys on my dopamine receptors until it overcomes my reason, erases my caution, subsumes me into a rapture sustained by machines. Synthetic love. In suspenders and a straw hat.

I reclaim myself.

Lesson learned: I choose flesh.

iClitoris vs. I, Clitoris

There is no virtual world without biology. Biology makes the virtual feel real. My imagination is a product of my biology. My biology produces my memories and my feelings. My biology produces my desire for technology.

Biology is what connects us. Me and you, Butterflies. Me and you. Me and Begonia. Me and Bob. Biology is primary. My love is biology. My love. It is mine. My biochemistry. My biome. My energy and matter. The rush of my own blood to my own sacred places. Mine.

20 Confetti

In the middle of the night Meryl surfaced, her consciousness buoyed by a full bladder. Again. Her head ached, felt the neck brace with her fingers, found Bob's hand under the covers beside her and gave him a squeeze.

"I have to pee again. Sorry."

He rubbed his face, sat up on the side of the bed, got his bearings, adjusted his brace, walked over to her side, and took her arm.

"I'm dizzy."

"We'll take it slow."

"That's so not me."

"I know."

When he brought her back to bed, he said, "Just sit there," and filled a glass of water for her. "Drink this."

"I don't want to drink that. I'll just have to pee again."

"Uma says you're supposed to stay hydrated."

"I don't remember that."

"Trust me."

"Where's Uma?"

"Asleep on the couch."

"She should take one of the guest rooms."

"She passed out."

"Where's Begonia?"

"With Uma."

"You saw her?"

"She was digging in my chair."

"Oh."

"I read your piece on synthetic love."

"Where?"

"On my legal pad. It was here beside you on the bed." He held up the yellow tablet in front of her with its many bent back pages and loopy scrawling.

"Who wrote it?"

"You."

"With a pen?" *Me?*

"My pen."

"I didn't know I could write with a pen."

"I thought it was very interesting."

"What?"

"Your writing. The whole thing about devices being synthetic love."

"Oh. You thought it was interesting?"

"Insightful."

"I can't drink all this water."

"Drink it."

"Okay."

She drank as he watched. Blackbirds calm, a steady gaze in his eyes, focus. When they made love, she liked to nibble on his eyebrows, feel them brush against her cheeks. Now she imagined coaxing those blackbirds onto her finger, putting her lips to their feathers, whispering to them, her blackbirds. He took the empty glass, filled it again and put it beside her on the nightstand.

"You know this means I'm just going to have to pee again in an hour."

"I will gladly escort you."

He situated himself prone, his shoulder brace under the bedsheet, shoulder to shoulder beside her, two injured bodies braced.

"Insightful?" The word sparkled in her mind.

"Brave."

"Cool." She closed her eyes and tried to remember what she had written, a remnant of an idea swam past her, beyond her, and she slid back to sleep.

As he listened to her breathing, he closed his eyes and saw the frozen tableau of those crazy women partying in the livingroom, carrying the fat guy like a scene from the Marx Brothers, ebullient ridiculousness, powdered sugar, a straw hat, and soon he was asleep again.

Around sunrise fear churned in Meryl, skin too tight, arms held down, she thrashed under the covers, hands and feet locked, panicked, thrashed again, jabbed her elbows, and kicked to break free of the cuffs, lurching against the tightness.

"Whoa, whoa, Nelly." He put his hand on her arm. "Meryl," he whispered, squeezing her wrist. She pulled it away. "Meryl." He gave her tighter squeeze and she came out of it. Her dream. "What's going on?"

Real time returned, she realized where she had been, strapped to the gurney in the box truck.

Bob kept his hand wrapped around her wrist, holding it firmly.

"Oh," she sighed, sensing herself. "I couldn't get out of my chrysalis."

"Well, you're out now," he said, and gave her wrist a staccato squeeze.

"Am I?" Her voice cracked with emotion.

"Be patient," he whispered. "Let your wings dry."

She smiled in the dawn dark. "Thank you."

With eyes half closed, she floated out of her body, witnessed herself from above, saw the two of them side-by-side, her neck, his shoulder, their bodies, their bed. *These wounds will heal.*

She let herself relax, closed her eyes, sensed her house around her, her habitat. Felt her ethereal body beside her ethereal man, this man who made her drink water and rescued her from troubled sleep. *This is where I want to be.*

"I feel like I've been away," she said softly. "Like I haven't been here."

"I've missed you."

"I needed to explore."

"What did you find?"

The vibrator instead of Bob. The toothbrush instead of Bob. Hamish instead of Bob. And here was Bob.

"I found you." She smiled. Tears filled her eyes.

That was the key.

"I love you," he said.

Her mind hula hooped a surreal montage of her blonde Amish bot and the dark-haired man in bed beside her. "Am I dreaming?" she asked.

"Remember that night by the pond at Wildwood?" he mused.

"I do," she said. "My first orgasm."

"I felt like Van Gogh."

She saw the two of them side-by-side in the grass beside the pond, a memory encapsulated so deep within her it could be forgotten, and then it seemed to surface of its own accord, a memory that wanted to be remembered. *The butterfly lays the egg that becomes the caterpillar that becomes the chrysalis that becomes the butterfly.*

"That's one of my favorite memories," she sighed. "I learned so much about myself from you. You're a very good teacher."

He smiled. "You were a very good student."

She felt a ripple of emotion and wished she could kiss him. "Thanks for being patient with me."

"I like to watch you learn. The way you just dive in, sink or swim."

She imagined herself crawling on top of him and devouring his lips. "I'm getting very good at sinking."

Under the covers he took her hand in his and held it. "I want to hold in my arms, but this will have to do." He gave her fingers a stroke with his.

"I'm so sorry."

"Don't be sorry." He was clear. "I needed the jolt."

"When you fell?"

"When I went into the butterfly house."

She got goosebumps. "Oh…" Couldn't find the words for all that was welling up inside her. "You went into the greenhouse?"

"Begonia stole my pen."

"Oh."

"It's exquisite."

"The pen?"

"The butterfly house."

"Oh."

"I never could have imagined such a thing."

Was she dreaming? "I feel magic when I'm in there," she murmured.

"I did, too." His eyes filled with tears. Blackbirds nuzzled. "It's poetry."

"Oh." Wonder passed through her, but her words were lost. Questions evanescent, mind soupy. "Thanks for telling me."

He slid his hand across her smooth belly, gently pressing her with the span of his fingers. "There's so much I want to tell you."

She smiled as he touched her, flower petals floating in delicate curves of color and light. She put her hands on top of his hand, pressed him against her and felt the shape of his fingers. The skin, the bone, his wrist against her. Flesh on flesh. His fingers combed her pubic hair, unspooling the curls with tenderness.

"You're an artist," she whispered.

He sensed her with his eyes closed, knowing her, tracing her, wishing he was free to put his face against her. But for now, he would have to satisfy himself with teasing her. He took some saliva on his fingers and painted her until her hips rose into his hand, and she sighed with pleasure. He held her. This was his pleasure, too. Holding the woman he loved in the palm of his hand, knowing how to satisfy her. He turned his face to kiss her shoulder.

Bird song. Floating. A turquoise sea lapping against their boat.

Breathing. Begonia snoring on the rug.

Misty subconscious.

Then a pinprick of fear. "Did you check that noise?" Her voice quivered.

"That was hours ago," he whispered, and held her firmly.

“What was it?”
“Nothing.”
“Really?”
“Yes.”
“Don’t let go of me,” she said and fell back to sleep.

Acknowledgements

Many generous people helped me develop this novel by reading early drafts of the manuscript and giving me their honest assessment. Their feedback helped me shape the story, build the characters, and clarify the details. So, I owe a debt of gratitude to those who gave me their time: Elissa Parnon, Rain Kiernan, Sharon Saltzgiver, Annette Fitzpatrick, Nancy Harrington, Amy Harrington, Denise Osso, Debbie Dotson, and Pam Jordan.

I'm fortunate to have friends who are exceptional communicators and were willing to read my work in progress twice. For offering me their developmental insights after reading an early draft and another draft more than a year later, thank you to Lisa Goren, Beth Harrington, and Elizabeth Holmes.

Thank you, Carleen Simone for your unequivocal support.

Thank you, Robby Benson for sharing your deep expertise in storytelling and coaching me through the process of thinking visually. Thank you, Karla DeVito for your continuous emotional support and encouraging me to be bold with the title. And thank you Roger Emmert for being my most amusing muse.

About the Author

Billie Best is the author of three books and 200+ blog posts at her website billiebest.com where she explores midlife reinvention, relationships, sex, wellness and technology from a feminist perspective.

Discussion Questions

These discussion questions are designed to delve into various aspects of *Clitapalooza: Her flower blooms power* and encourage readers to explore the themes, characters, and social commentary presented in the book.

1. How did Meryl's character evolve throughout the story, especially in terms of her views on intimacy and technology?

2. In what ways does *Clitapalooza* explore and challenge traditional gender roles and expectations, particularly in the context of sexual relationships?

3. Discuss the role of Meryl's friends in her journey. How does the support of her female friends contribute to the overall theme of women's empowerment in the novel?

4. How does the novel depict the impact of technology on intimate relationships? Are there parallels between the characters' experiences and contemporary issues in the real world?

5. In what ways does the story promote a positive and healthy approach to sexuality? How does it navigate the intersection of pleasure, privacy, and technology?

6. *Clitapalooza* incorporates humor and satire. Discuss how the author uses these elements to address serious topics such as sex tech, robots, and biotechnology.

7. The novel is told from multiple points of view. How does this narrative choice enhance the storytelling, and what does it reveal about the different characters?

8. How does the novel challenge societal norms regarding sexuality? Consider Meryl's journey with her husband, her devices and synthetic love.

9. Explore the ethical dilemmas presented by the technology in the story, such as the interconnected devices and the development of ClitBit. How does the novel comment on the potential risks and consequences?

10. Discuss how Meryl's experience with her PS-1000 and Quanta leads her to appreciate her own body. How does her perspective on orgasms and relationships change by the end of the novel?
11. Examine the dynamics between Meryl and her husband. How do their frustrations with each other reflect broader themes in long-term relationships?
12. What is the significance of the women's wellness festival in the story? How does it serve as a turning point for the characters and the overarching message of the novel?